EVERY

9

SECONDS

CARROLL SILVERA

EVERY 9 SECONDS

TATE PUBLISHING
AND ENTERPRISES, LLC

Published by Tate Publishing & Enterprises, LLC
127 E. Trade Center Terrace | Mustang, Oklahoma 73064 USA
1.888.361.9473 | www.tatepublishing.com

Tate Publishing is committed to excellence in the publishing industry. The company reflects the philosophy established by the founders, based on Psalm 68:11,

"The Lord gave the word and great was the company of those who published it."

Book design copyright © 2015 by Tate Publishing, LLC. All rights reserved.
Cover design by Joseph Emnace
Interior design by Manolito Bastasa

Published in the United States of America

ISBN: 978-1-63449-927-9
1. Family & Relationships / Abuse / Domestic Partner Abuse
2. Fiction / Family Life
15.01.29

With all the love in my heart,
for my daughters.

ACKNOWLEDGMENTS

To my daughter, who throughout her life has always encouraged and supported me and, more importantly, loved me always.

To my parents, you have taught me so much in life.

To my readers, Sally Silvera, Carol Bradley, and Darlene Watts, my appreciation is beyond words.

To Ruvie Pogoy, who edited this book.

To Gavin de Becker, whose wonderful book *The Gift of Fear*, made it a necessity for me to write this book, as well as yet another.

To all the characters within these pages, you have profoundly enriched my life.

And last but not least, to Gregory, who instills within me the need for my fingers to fly across the keyboard.

Thank you.

Silver Threads

The Threads of our Lives
Are They Silver or Gold
Does the Lord Have a Hand
In All that You Hold
Is the Truth in Your Heart
Do You Hold It in Hand
Has the Decision Been Made
In an Intricate Web
Of Joys and of Sorrows
To Strengthen Our Hold
Or is it to Spin Silver to Gold
(Carroll Silvera)

He will sit as a refiner and purifier of silver.

—Mal 3:3

1

The room shimmers in the light of the crystal chandelier over the tub, casting the room in a soft, golden light. The steam rises from the enormous bathtub, and I suddenly feel exhausted. How much longer can this go on. I can't think; I simply seem to be on auto-pilot. Taking a deep breath, I think, *I should do yoga, I'd feel better.* But then, you have to feel better to do yoga. Isn't that the way with everything in life? I shed my clothes and slide down in the wonderful, hot, sudsy water. Nothing has ever felt so good. What is that poem I wrote the other night? It seemed to explain it all...

The fragrance of Paul's Himalayan Musk drifts into the room, and I feel the tension slowly vanish.

With each passing year, for the last ten years, they have both in turn become more ill, either physically or mentally, and I am worn out. Physically and emotionally. Always thinking that this will be the last time, always wanting them to be who they used to be, I rally 'round each incident.

Mother has been in and out of the convalescent hospital for weeks now. With each new stroke, she seems to recover a little less of her physical abilities and her mental acuity. The strokes seem so severe. I ask her if she is in any pain, and her reply is "Only my ego..." After the first "incarceration," as she termed it, I would go in the evening and visit her, and she would cry and tell me how lonesome she was.

"Oh, Mother, I am so sorry," I would say. "You will get better, and you will be able to come home."

"I hope so," she would reply. But she had a hard time doing the physical exercises, so progress was, to say the least, slow. Then one afternoon, as I sat visiting with her, I asked her, "Are you lonesome, Mother?"

"Whatever gave you that idea? I've never been lonesome in my life."

Such a lady! So she is going to recover.

Mothers,… as I write this, I pray continuously for guidance. I cannot think of a more complex subject or state of being.

My mother, too, is old now, grown feeble of body and of mind, unable to do the things she once did. She is dependent upon the graciousness of others and, to her credit, continues to find that graciousness.

She was brought up with grace and manners that are usually extended only to the well-to-do; she has taught us those things as well. Being the only daughter and granddaughter, she was more than likely doted on by all. She possesses a lilting laughter, and a charming smile that somehow looks shy, feminine, as if she has some special secret. She has sharp, expressive eyes that smile with laughter, blaze with anger, and have that piercing look of great intelligence. A fine patrician nose, with skin of porcelain beauty. As a young woman, she was blessed with beautiful hair that was thick and the color of deep rich mahogany. Of average height and a stocky build, she would seldom, if ever, be satisfied with her weight or the way she looked.

I doubt she had any aspirations of greatness, or felt able or worthy to aspire to any. In part, this stems from the era in which she was born, but more than anything, "who she was," as there have been great women throughout the ages.

Never being one to adorn herself, as a young woman, she seldom wore makeup, or dressed up. But when she did, she was striking.

When asked about her life, her reply is always "I gave birth to, and raised four children in six years."

I have never wanted anyone to love me more than I wished for this woman, my mother, to love me. I would seek that for most of my adult life. In the men I married (there were to be many) and the relationships with those I cared about, this would be my quest, my obsession.

Mothers are thought to be an extension of God. Well, that may be true, as He is said to be jealous, loving, and merciful. "Vengeance is mine," saith the Lord. And Mother! At least mine. I truly am who I am, because of my mother. Her quest for perfection was, and continues to be, unlimited. Everything she ever wished for herself she wished for us, and her by extension—without considering what we ourselves wished for. She was unable to see us as anything but an extension of herself. And in herself, she found only fear, and lack, and anger, coupled with great intelligence and a quick wit, but with such a sharp, critical tongue. I can't remember a time that I pleased my mother for more than that one instant, for more than that one performance. Any display of adoration, of homage, must be repeated constantly and with consistent depth, for her to believe she is loved and adored. She must always be right and will argue until you give up; it is most certainly in your best interest to do so. Her mottoes to us as children were many and profound. "*Can't* never did anything," so of course, you succeeded, or you didn't try. "Do unto others, before they do unto you." Now that's a good character builder. "Do as I say, not as I do." Another profound statement.

Having learned at the feet of a tyrant, and at times she was that, I, too, told my poor children some, but not all, of these things. What a great disservice we do to our children by continuing a poor example of love and understanding.

We must consider, however, the time in which I was raised. These things were thought to be good, even loving. The world is a harsh and unpredictable place, and you must be prepared to "do battle." To this day, my father refers to her as *The Queen*. And he continues to do her bidding, as there is no wrath so great as those scorned.

If you should be so unlucky as to have displeasured her, you could and would be subjected to screaming that so terrified you, you were unable to distinguish the words issuing forth from her mouth, leaving you cowering in the small recesses of your mind, if not in fact in a corner of the room. On some occasions, the silent treatment would seem more to her liking, and I really couldn't decide which was the lesser of the two.

She no longer screams at me, nor gives me the silent treatment, but she dismisses me as if I am no more important than a fly on the wall.

I have fallen on my knees as an adult woman in anguish, stripped to the very core of my being, expressing my profound love for this woman, my most obsequious desire for that love to be requited. Pleading with her to acknowledge a love for me and an appreciation of that love, as well as an acknowledgment of my accomplishments to make her proud of me, to be worthy in her eyes, only to look up at her, seated in her chair, with hands folded, fingers laced across her bosom, peering down through eyes slit in anger and confusion, as if to say, "How dare you speak to me in this manner!"

I truly believe that prior to our entrance on this earth, we have predetermined our lessons in life and who we are going to interact with to learn those lessons.

It is with humility and laughter that I think back to a time prior to my entrance on this plane called earth, and must have said, "I can do that, and yes, that too."

I can only assume I had been on the "other side" so long that I no longer had a realistic idea of life on this side. How harsh are the physical manifestations of lessons here.

How disconnected we are from our loving Father in heaven. So unrelentingly real are all physical manifestations of pain and suffering offered up by our fellow human partners. Most often, I find it supremely difficult to keep in perspective the positive idea that time is so fleeting and precious—that the trials and tribulations of life are only an illusion at best, and that the only tangible reward is that we perfect our souls in this journey called life.

I took her home and made things as comfortable as possible. By November, she was back in the emergency room, unable to speak or move her left side.

Throughout the winter, this repeated itself in varying degrees of severity, but each time, after a couple of weeks, back home she comes.

I've tried to talk them into going into a retirement community, to sell the house, to try and enjoy life with people their own age and in similar circumstances; but they will have none of it, and Daddy is worn out. I am worn out…

Why do I do this?

I can't seem to relax even when I have the freedom to do so. I have this whole evening, or what is left of it, as it is nine o'clock. The water is hot and steaming as I slide further down in the tub.

Thank you, Lord, for the "little things."

The telephone jolts me out of my trance. I better answer it; it could be Daddy or Samantha.

"Hello," I say into the phone.

"Cara, you have to come down here now! Your mother had another stroke, and I resuscitated her because she doesn't have a 'no code,' she is screaming and hollering, throwing things and so mad, she told me to call you right now."

"She isn't mad, she's scared," I say to the nurse on the other end of the line. "I'll be there in thirty minutes." Realization dawns on me that "the hospital administrator" in me has corrected the nurse.

The drive there is long and desolate, as I live in the woods with the deer, bears, cougars, and raccoons. It is so hard, I think, as I speed toward yet another skilled nursing facility.

Going in the back entrance, as Mom's room is the first on the right as you walk in.

There lies my mother in the bed, sobbing as if her heart will break. Broken dishes litter the floor, with water from the carafe dripping down the front of the nightstand. The bedpan having been flung across the room, the stench of urine and feces fill the room.

"Oh, Mother… I am so sorry. Can you tell me what's the matter?"

My heart is breaking. She looks so small and somehow fragile, although she still weighs 180 pounds, even though she hasn't eaten for weeks now.

"They said I had another stoke," she cries. "I didn't. I didn't. She"—as she points to the nurse who has materialized out of nowhere—"was pushing on my chest and spitting in my mouth."

"Oh, Mama, she was just doing her job. You have a "full code", and she has to do that." I bend over and hold her in my arms, tears running down my face, as she, too, sobs in my arms. "Are you in any pain?" I ask.

"No," she sobs into my shoulder. "But I miss your daddy. I want to be with your daddy. I am so alone without your daddy here. I need to go home now, please take me home now. I can't stay here anymore…" My heart feels as though it will break as I rock her back and forth in my arms. Lord, please help my mother. She is just a little girl and is so frightened, silently I pray as I tell Mama, "Shush, shush, it's going to be all right."

"Daddy's so tired, Mama—he's been down here all day, and he had to go home just to rest for a while."

"No! No!" Screaming, she flails her arms and throws herself from me. "No one comes to see me. You've just left me here. And they are mean to me."

I look at my mother and the black and blue of her arms, the large bruise that covers most of her left leg, and her blackened eye, knowing how they got there.

"No, Mama, they're not mean to you. We're here all day, and you keep falling. You have to learn not to climb out of bed until you are stronger."

For the first time I am aware that the nurse is still in the room.

"Can you give her something for the anxiety?" I ask the nurse.

"She has no order. I'll have to call the doctor," she says.

"Fine. I'll wait here until you get an order."

"I hate her!" my mother yells. "Keep her away from me."

"Mother, Mother, it's all right."

"Don't leave me, please don't leave me…I don't want to die," her words pleading as she sobs in utter terror, clinging to me with a tenacity I had never before experienced.

"Shush, shush, oh, Mama, it's going to be okay, I won't leave you," as I cradle her in my arms, brushing the hair away from her face and rubbing her back. "Mama, it's going to be all right."

"Why do you keep calling me that?" she asks, suddenly looking at me as though she has never seen me in her life.

"Call you what?" I ask, pulling back from her so I can see her face.

"Mama. Why do you keep calling me that? I am not your mama."

The sobs are rising in my throat; I feel panic. Sadness envelops me, and my world is shattered.

Lord, help me to help this woman who I have so longed to love me.

I swallow hard, and with the tears streaming down my face, I say, "Yes, you are my mama, and I am here for you, and everything is going to be all right. I will stay, and you can rest. Can you do that?"

"If you say so, but I don't think that's right," her voice childlike.

Ah, the elusive nurse returns with drugs. Mother takes them willingly. And I wet a washcloth with warm water and wash her face and hands and brush her hair and tell her over and over that everything is going to be all right.

Who will tell me that? I wonder. My personality wishing it to be Samantha, the *mother* in me, praying she never has to experience this pain, this sense of pervading helplessness.

Please, Lord, take me in the wee, small hours of the night. Or in the garden.

It's 2:00 AM, and she lies sleeping. I go to the nurses' station to tell them I'm going home, that I would like to speak with the doctor tomorrow and if they will move her closer to the nurses' station.

They can. But they ask that I get her to sign a "no code."

"I have to talk to my father," I tell them, "but…yes, I will take care of it."

I climb in the car and turn the seat warmers on. Someone as stressed out as me invented them, I am sure. I can feel the warmth as it climbs up my back. And I let out a little sigh. What am I going to do? My father is eighty-five and overwhelmed, and my mother is eighty-two, and a frightened child.

Was she always so frightened? Possibly. That would certainly explain her actions all these years—the anger, the cruelty.

It is as if I had never seen her before tonight. Or, is it simply all the illnesses that have invaded her body over the years? But that brings me full circle, doesn't it?

I've always believed that it is our minds that cause our bodies to be ill. You know, "dis-ease."

I've spent a lifetime reading metaphysical books explaining the unexplainable, and believing it. I truly believe that you can manifest anything, that there is nothing so powerful as your mind. What you think is pretty much what, and who, you are. And if you are confused about those things, you are confused about life. *Know thyself…*

That we asked the Lord to allow us to become manifest so that we could pay witness to the wonders of the world. To see and feel the beauty of the earth. To virtually "smell" the roses. That in the beginning, being only energy, we could be the rose, be the trees, a natural part and parcel of them, but could not witness them.

So, does it not stand to reason that we have not only responsibility for our lives and thoughts, but control as well, control over what we do, and how it affects us?

Over the years—many, many years—I have shared these thoughts with my parents, and they have truly listened, listened with interest. But, how difficult it is to understand something that is so simplistic as to be beyond comprehension. That our lives are in our hands, and that by asking, we can receive. That is so simple, that it is truly unbelievable, and that is the difficult part. You must believe with not one doubt that it is true. True that you are saved by the grace of God.

Such a tiny little sentence that can make your life change forever.

But Mother only thought it was an interesting concept, and although she gave it much thought, she could not believe anything so simple could really work.

And in all honesty, I, too, fail daily in my total acceptance of this miracle. But I am daily reminded of the truth in it.

The Jaguar speeds over the dark, lonely country road, shadowed by giant evergreens and maples, the moon lighting my way. At three in the morning, no one is on these roads. People have to get up and milk cows and tend to their families.

I click the garage door opener, then slide the Jaguar into the space beside the tractor and the truck.

I have gone from stiletto heels and a suit, to jeans and a flannel shirt. From a desk and a briefcase, to a chainsaw and a wheelbarrow.

In the last ten years of my life, I have carved out a place in this wilderness.

I have been overwhelmed by the enormity of the task. By the necessity to learn to drive a cat. To use a choke chain on a log, and the real life pain of hearing a beautiful two-hundred-foot tall tree fall.

To stand laughing hysterically, with a shovel in my hand, as after days of heavy rain, the earth would bubble up and flow like lava to the beach below me. As if a small woman and a shovel would have any effect.

How awed I have felt in the presence of this beauty and grandeur our God has given us.

The house is elegant and friendly as it rests with dignity in this open space in the forest of our maker. As I knelt on the earth… what is that poem…

White, with deep hunter green shutters at the windows and lofty columns with Corinthian caps, roses trail over the impressive front porch. The imposing "Kramer Lions" sit at each side of the front steps, as if *en garde*, the house having been "scaled down" considerably when I got the divorce from Skip. There was no money, only myself and Daisie, my tiny, little dog, and I long ago gave up such lofty ambition. It is impressive by local standards and is still a formal, yet comfortably elegant, old-fashioned sort of house. It is "home."

The moonlight flickers invitingly through the faint, foggy mist of night, and I lean on the steering wheel of the car and sob.

Remember what a difference a day makes, I tell myself, as I gather my things and trudge into the dark, welcoming house. Daisie greets me lovingly, stretching her little body and arching her back, not unlike a cat, releasing a small whimper, as if to say, "Where have you been, Mommy?" I bend to collect her in my arms and ascend the staircase to bed, *yet again.*

Here, all is safe, all is blessed by the light. I will be renewed and strengthened.

I will rest.

The summer passes, and my gardens are neglected, and my life has become one of travel and heart-wrenching sadness. A life in which I have no control. Just response. Response to the needs of my parents. I am surprised that I find joy in helping them. Certainly this has not always been the case. Resentment is something I have nurtured for years, concerning my mother in particular. Nothing I did, said, or gave was ever enough, and if it was enough, it certainly wasn't right.

I watch daily as her health improves within the confines of the skilled nursing facility and her appetite returns, as the doctor finds medications that control her psychosis and her depression.

What wonderful miracles drugs can accomplish. As my cousin said, "*I think it should be in the water.*"

She is once more getting dressed and has her hair done and seems to be happy and quite pleased with herself.

She has befriended a small, precocious lady, Irene whom others would surely assess as "crazy," but they are sharing the same room, and she has made the first overture to my mother.

She was an English literature teacher and that was of great interest to Mom.

Beneath the dementia of her mind lie profound thoughts, and they carry on long conversations, as my mother waits patiently for Irene to find the speech patterns locked in her damaged mind.

Something profound in itself. Mother would have found this repugnant at an earlier time in her life.

Lessons to learn, one way or the other.

Mother now experiences the frustrations and the reality of knowing, without the ability of expression, of having others judge you by how you speak and your ability to perform the most simplistic of tasks.

Irene is unable to control her bowels and bladder, she is often soiled and smells. But Mother rings for a nurse, and she and Irene laugh about it.

Mom goes to speech classes, physical therapy, and walks with a walker and a nurse as long a distance as she is able.

Often, as I come into the facility, I hear this voice I recognize saying, "There, that's my daughter." I look and find a woman, bent over a walker, with a nasal cannula and oxygen bottle being pulled behind her, in a robe and slippers, shuffling with the aid of a nurse. Her face is pallid, the flesh loose and hanging.

Shocked, always shocked, to see she is talking about me. I am her daughter. This old and disabled woman, who is so happy to see me, her eyes sparkle.

The sobs mount in my throat as I momentarily look away and fight for control.

"Mother. You look wonderful! Look how far you've come today."
The nurse says, "Yes, and tomorrow we will go further."

Lord, bless this kind person, these persons who so selflessly give of themselves daily.

I run daily from the nursing home to the home of my parents, with groceries, food, and laundry. Watching as my father deteriorates beyond what I thought to be a sustainable life, but always, still, at my mother's beck and call.

Daddy is old and stooped now, frail, this once giant of a man I have had the great pleasure of calling Daddy. His once jet-black hair has turned to silver, and the green eyes flecked with brown, weep easily now at life's great and small injustices. His "movie star" looks have faded over the years, but the essence of the man who once told me "The best thing a man can do for his children is to love their mother" has not been diminished by life. He is at once kind, considerate, and gentle, with a great capacity to love and nurture. Quite a feat for a man raised in a family of mostly men. He, too, has visions and an unwavering belief in our Heavenly Father. He has survived World War II, hard work, and the hardships of the Great Depression. He's farmed and has been a white-collar worker, but more than anything, he has given his life to his family.

With a need to be busy and always looking for a "deal," he has found and sold scrap and built his own houses. Born in an era when education was not always possible for the common man, he never graduated from high school, nor had a college education.

Still this gentle, strong man, this gentleman would be the man by which I would measure all the men in my life.

I am worried he is lonesome. And I try to convince him to come and stay with me. But he says, "He is too tired to be lonesome." And so throughout the summer, he visits Mother, and sleeps—setting the alarm so he can see her in the morning and choose her clothing for her, to help her dress. Returning home to sleep, once more setting the alarm so as to spend the evening with her so she is not lonesome. And he sleeps. He and I are both rail-thin, and exhausted.

Mother is, well, angry. And demands to go home.

She screams at me that, "I just want her to die in there." She screams at Daddy that he "just wants to throw her away, not to ever let her go home again."

She cries and sobs, and turns her face away from me when I try to console her.

2

Peter is tall and dark, with the worries of the world hanging on his rounding shoulders. Tired from self-exposure to the pressures brought on by his need to excel, to feel secure. Seeking a world of order, certainty and power. Sensitive, and uncomfortable in that sensitivity, he appears to be uncomfortable in his own skin. Age coming on him without the comforts it brings of knowing *who you really are.*

Ever needing to be proper and right, never allowing for improprieties, he has sacrificed pleasures and lessons in this life, he has accepted these sacrifices in resigned defeat. Always measuring his self-worth by society and the accumulation of security, i.e., money. He is only late in life acknowledging, albeit with some trepidation, his real worth and his profound achievements.

A gentleman, with no offending behaviors. Never given to the outward expressions of vulgarity. Never indulging in drink or profanity, he finds it offensive in others, often even shocking. I am certain he finds me shocking.

I think in some other life, he must have been a monk in a monastery, having taken a vow of silence. The spoken word being of profound importance to him in this lifetime. But only from others. He is not inclined to share his feelings with anyone, if in fact he himself acknowledges he has feelings.

As a young man, he professed an agnostic bent. But of late, he is more likely to listen to the argument for a Supreme Being, although he still wants "proof."

Loyal to those he deems worthy, as most of those born under the sign of Leo, he tries to be dependable, exuding a grace that few men possess.

Success has been his touchstone, and he, to his credit, has achieved that, even in his mind.

Critical and unrelenting in his quest for understanding and the tangible, he can be harsh and unfair, when your explanation is not something he can grasp, for he cannot be in error.

Leaving most people to their own lives, he is, however, always observing and making his own judgments as to how they, or he, would best deal with their problems. Slow to anger, his anger is so intense as to leave him with frustrations he has learned to master and mask. Is not that anger, nothing more than fear manifesting itself? Fear of failure, of judgment, of disappointing those that love you, and are dependent on you.

For much was expected of him. He has slain his dragons, at least temporarily on any given day. In this life, they were many and mighty, the pain, at times, profound.

A yearning for beauty and elegance he has manifested in his dress, speech, and his carriage. Born and raised by a woman of great intelligence with a demanding and often vindictive need to control, he is determined to not have that happen in his life, and so he, himself, has become the "controller."

He has come this morning, on his way to visit our parents. I have fixed him breakfast, and we have gone outside. The day is clear and mild as we wander about the grounds of my "estate," as he refers to it.

As always, our conversations become ones of philosophical beliefs, and we are in our element as our discussion gathers momentum.

"I have always tried to learn from others' mistakes," he boasts to me, wanting fiercely to believe he could escape the pain and suffering he saw around him, not wishing to follow in those tortured footsteps.

"Ah, but is that not like having someone tell you what 'love' is like, or to try and explain the fragrance of a rose?" I ask him. "I don't believe you can attain wisdom without experience and intelligence."

There is no response, only a clearing of the throat, as he searches desperately for a retort.

I absolutely cannot be right.

He reiterates the story of the one hundredth monkey, which by and of itself is interesting, to say the least.

It is the theory of clinicians and scientists that "one monkey learns to do something of importance to its evolution, within its own environment. It then teaches the monkeys within its own group how to perform this action. When one hundred monkeys are doing this, every monkey in the world will automatically know how to perform this act at birth."

"So, you think that you will learn how to 'be' by osmosis. Is that a correct understanding?" I ask.

"Well, I try not to get involved," his speech, slow and succinct. "And, I didn't end up getting some girl pregnant when I was fourteen."

"That was the *best* thing that has ever happened to me," I tell him, quite matter of fact, for it is very much the truth. Disregarding his intent of insult to me.

"Really?" he says. "How so? Seems to me it pretty much ruined your life."

"Ruined my life? Without those children, my life would not be worth living, and I have never had any more children, and I have never done anything to prevent that."

"Really, ummh, interesting way to look at it, I guess."

We are quiet for a time, and finally, that "quiet" disturbs him, and with a flip of his hand, he says, "So continue."

"Okay," I say.

"And what about God, do you now believe in God?" I ask.

"Well..." he begins slowing, searching for the perfect words, "I believe in 'grace,' as I understand it."

"And have you accepted that 'grace'?" I ask, knowing the ground is becoming shaky, but an interesting conversation I can't pass up.

"What do you mean by acceptance?" he asks, looking at me as if I were a foreign entity.

"I think you have to accept it into your heart and soul, or 'grace' is simply a word."

"So tell me what you think 'life' is about, you know…the purpose of our lives," he says it with genuine interest, yet wanting desperately to change the subject at hand.

"Oh, it would take too long." I laugh.

"I have all day," he says. Sitting down at the picnic table, stretching his legs out, resting his elbows on the table, his Prada sneakers extending out into the Irish moss.

"Okay…now you understand that this is not in any order, I have not prepared to give an oratory."

He laughs. "I'm sure you'll manage."

Somehow his sarcasm is never offending to me, as it rushes off like water on a duck's back, too, I have been conditioned by my mother from birth and I, too, am starved for someone to talk to about things of this nature. Happily, I get on with the conversation.

"I believe that the growth of the soul is all that matters. That to hear the musings of your soul is lyrical. That we are all a part of a *godhead*, so to speak, that as we evolve, those around us evolve, much like your hundredth monkey theory. That our personality, or ego, is what seeks fame and fortune. That, that same ego, or personality, is who fears, and is angered. That the soul is incapable of those emotions, as it knows the truth of our being, which in fact would remove the necessity for emotion at all. That only by acceptance can we be quiet, and paradoxically, only by being quiet can we find that which will produce acceptance. That acceptance leads to humility. A profound humility.

"That we are here together to witness each other's lives. To give strength and courage on the road to that acceptance and humility. I believe, as little children, say before the age of seven or even twelve, you remember what it was you came here to learn, to experience. Unless, of course, your childhood is fraught with horrific events."

"Why twelve?" he asks.

"Well… maybe not specifically twelve, but before you are introduced to peer pressure. To the pressures of the world: to be, to perform, to excel. A child's soul remembers and responds to its strengths. You know, haven't you had times in your life when you have made decisions and you could literally feel that shift taking place in your life? A nearly imperceptible feeling, certainly, but…a shift nonetheless."

"You are being too abstract." He watches to see what effect, if any, this comment has on me.

"It is a very abstract thought, thing, how can I not be abstract? But…" I say, "you know, physic phenomenon is as old as man. Okay, let me see, I don't believe we are judged per se, only that we are held accountable for what we know in our soul. I do, however, believe that once you do know, once you have felt the hand of God on you, you are responsible and are most certainly held accountable."

"By who?"

"By the rest of your soul group. You don't think it is an accident that we all are playing this little game of life together, do you? To me, that would be bizarre. I don't think there are any accidents. I think everything has a purpose. God is very orderly, the universe is very orderly. It is not so much what happens to us, but our response to it, that counts. In totality, love is a verb."

"So…let me understand this—you think everything is planned, predestination, so to speak. There is no devil, no evil in the world. Am I understanding you?"

"Well, certainly, there are things that happen that are evil. But as far as the devil, isn't he called Lucifer, that means light. So that would mean to me 'that to light things' means knowledge, and God created everything, so why would the devil have so much power? Perhaps Satan was let run amok to help us to learn. He did give us free will after all. There is only one power. And that power is God, or at the very least, a divine universal intelligence. I think He gives you gifts, talents, whatever. And you have a grave responsibility to execute those gifts generously, using whatever avenue He affords you."

"So you don't believe that sickness and disease is of the devil? And what about insanity?"

"Oh, Peter, you know I think dis-ease is a physical manifestation of your thinking, your fears really, and as far as insanity goes, well, there is a fine line between insanity and genius. Didn't they think Einstein to have been insane at one time? The same goes for love and hate."

"And just how do you know what the 'truth' is?"

"I think it registers in your heart as peace, it's that simple."

"So, my sister is a very complex person."

"I think your sister is only complexly simple." I laugh.

"But you are judgmental."

A statement not a question, I think to myself. Certainly out of context. Have I offended him?

"Maybe, but then, too, advice and judgment may just sound the same to people. I am after all, *very experienced*, I have had a very diverse life, to say the least." I chide him. He does hate me to comment on his affairs, even when I have been asked, or included in the conversation.

Rubbing his hands together, as if he was washing them, he says, "Let's get some lunch."

I knew this wouldn't last long.

Talk about complexly simple…this man is an enigma to me.

3

The doctor says Mother can go home.

Oh, Lord, now what? We have been through this before. They simply can't take care of themselves. With neither of them well, it is an impossible situation. They won't leave their home, and they will not come home with me. They fire everyone I hire or rescind every order I give. So in the end, I clean their house, do their laundry and shopping, bathe them, and feed them. It is easier than arguing with them. And Mother knows that will work.

"Come home with me," I say, my heart not in my words. It is the right thing to do.

But they will hear not a word of it.

July and August are warm and sunny, the summer days drifting by in a haze of small triumphs and bitter defeats, as I travel to and from my parents' home. The housekeeper and the twenty-four-hour care once more, have gone by the wayside. I diligently seek new help, paying them with my own money, until such a time as I am able to arrange for reimbursement.

"No need," my mother admonishes. *Who do I think I am,* she asks, angry at her own incompetence and wishing I would quit meddling. Peter says if it weren't for me, they would have long ago succumbed to their own inadequacies. Is that what he wants? Is that what the rest of them want? For me to just let them die? Unbelievable, if true.

I arrange their medication in the little daily dose containers and find the hired nurses aides still get them mixed up, or don't give them.

Mother complains about the food on a nonstop basis and still cannot get up to cook. But she is able to tell you step by step what to do.

The mind is an amazing thing, I think, as I watch her try to coordinate her efforts, unable to follow her own commands. My father, not doing what she told him. The phone not working like she thought it would, and it is because Daddy has "messed with everything." For my mother cannot be wrong. She does not watch television, because she can't remember how to turn it on or off. I watch as she holds the telephone in her hand as if it were a foreign object.

Visits with friends and family are stilted and rehearsed as she struggles for words to entertain them, and they struggle with words and action to prove all is as it was.

She will no longer dress or bathe, and I really can't discern how long it has been since she has let me help her brush her teeth.

I still did not know and could not comprehend the outcome.

"They leave the laundry room door open," she would shout in her frustration. "The food is awful." Her speech slurred and often incomprehensible, the result of the many strokes.

Anger a common bond between us; I don't notice the new anguish and torment pulsing behind it.

After one horrendous day of fighting for control, of both myself and them, I arrive home, exhausted and sobbing. Frustration and sadness infiltrating my very soul, too tired to any longer cope with any more of *this*. I call Peter, and sobbing, tell him how dreadfully difficult it is.

He does come over, but infrequently, and he doesn't stay long enough to see the enormity of the problem. After nearly ten minutes of me sobbing and trying to tell him what is wrong, he says, "I think I need to speak to someone rational about this. Then maybe I can help you."

"Someone rational?" I nearly shout at him. "And just *whom* do you think that might be?"

"Maybe Pops," he says.

"Didn't you listen to me? They do not know what is going on. Mother's mind is damaged beyond repair, and Daddy is exhausted, incoherent most of the time."

"They seemed fine to me," he says.

"Fine," I say. "How nice for you." I hang up. *Asshole.*

Peter sits across the breakfast table from me, as we eat omelets, fluffy and delicious with little green onions, diced ham, and red peppers. The biscuits, light and fluffy; the homemade raspberry jelly, from my garden, delectably perfect.

I guess he thought about what I said, who knows. He called at seven this morning and said he was "on the ferry." I cannot fathom why he can't let you know in advance what his plans are.

However, I am happy to see him, and happy to know he will go to visit our parents, if only briefly. Their condition a frustrating experience to him, with only obligation and guilt bringing him to their home—and me yelling at him.

There is trite conversation over breakfast, and I wonder what he has on his mind, as he is anything but trite.

"So," he begins, clearing his throat, his fingers laced loosely, his elbows resting on the white tablecloth. "So," he begins again, "I would like to get to know you better, and I feel that if I knew about your money, your finances, so to speak, I would in fact know you better, you know, how you view the world, what you think is important."

I am laughing so hard, that the biscuit in my mouth is in danger of spewing across the table.

Truly perplexed by my lack of restraint, he says, "Why do you find that so humorous?"

"Peter," I say, still laughing, however, I can clearly see he is serious. "How are you going to know me any better than you already do? I've always told you what I think, how I feel about everything, isn't that what drives you crazy about me? And, too,

I've been your sister all your life. Who would know me better than you?"

"Well, yes, but…" He is clearing his throat again.

I wonder silently how in the world he has risen to such a high position of authority when he is so tentative in his speech. Part of his job is negotiation with persons across the world.

"But…you never speak of your money. Where you have it invested, how much you have in savings. That sort of thing."

"What you see is what I have and a little money, and of course, the hospital. But you know all those things," I say, with shrugging shoulders, hands held out in demonstration of the completeness of my statement.

"You don't trust me." It is a statement of fact rather than a question, as he looks at me inquiringly.

"Trust. That's a good one." I laugh, standing to clear away the dishes. This could in fact be yet one more of "those conversations," where I talk and he listens. Truly curious and interested.

"You don't trust me?" he asks, truly hurt, bringing his dishes to the kitchen sink.

"Peter, you of all people…the only one I trust is God, and I can't always hear Him."

"Really?" he says. "You don't trust anyone?"

"Well, it isn't so cut and dried as that, but we each have our own agenda, do we not? And in my experience, they are seldom, if ever, overlapping."

"So…you think I have an agenda, merely because I am asking you about your money?"

"No, we were talking about trust."

"So…go on."

"Well, money to me is a horizontal expression of God, or infinite intelligence, if that is an easier explanation for you. And I would like to think that my path is vertical. So I really don't think much about money. I am certain I will have all I need, as long as I am responsible in my use of it and keep it in circulation. In that I 'trust,' I trust my teachers and my guides, my unseen ones. You know."

He's laughing now. "Your unseen guides?" The laughter becoming a resounding chuckle as he repeats himself, "Your unseen guides?"

"Yep," I tell him, undaunted by his disbelief and his laughter. He hasn't been the first to laugh at me, and I feel certain he won't be the last.

"Do they talk to you? Really, with voices?"

"Well, sort of, you know, I get the message, or feel a 'presence,' or a dream is clearly a message."

"So…you're not going to tell me about your money."

"I did, I told you how I feel about it."

"That doesn't tell me how much you're worth or what you believe to be a good investment."

"Peter…" I laugh yet again. "I don't have a plan other than the one I just told you of. And as far as what I am worth, it changes with any given day. I had a friend tell me that you are only worth what you can get your hands on right now. That would be about a hundred dollars in my purse."

"Okay, so you don't want to tell me about your money."

He is wringing his hands, pacing the kitchen floor, and making little purring noises at Daisie. "So, tell me a dream you've had. Is it about money?"

"Well no, it's about fear, but, isn't that why you need money— because you are afraid?"

"Hmph…" issues from his mouth. He raises his eyebrows and, standing back from me, says in very measured monotones, "I… don't…think so…okay, okay, tell me your dream, the one about fear of money…" He's laughing again.

"I will…" I said with conviction. "No more laughing until I get through."

"Okay, okay…" He is really laughing now. But his hands are up in rapt surrender. "Come on…tell me your story of money."

"Well, I had this dream years ago. And it was all black and white, with the exception of a very few things. There was a big man with a black hat and cloak, and he was the devil."

"I thought you said last time we talked you didn't believe in the devil." He is still chuckling.

"Peter…anyway, this devil is taking everything from me. Not things, but people I love, one by one, making them disappear. It was so real, I thought I woke up, and it was still happening. I kept telling myself 'it's a dream,' and I just couldn't make it go away. I have never been so frightened in my life, or more alone, and 'he,' one by one, took Tony, then Jillian and Samantha, and put me in a pen. I could see for miles, and there was no water and no trees, nothing, and everything I loved was gone. I was alone. I was certain I was really awake, and I told him to stop, that I wasn't frightened anymore, there was nothing left to lose, so why would I be frightened. I told him to go away. He wouldn't go away, and came closer and closer to me.

"But I truly saw no more he could take from me but my life, and without all of them, it had no meaning, so I stood up and told him to leave now. He sort of evaporated into thin air. And as he left, I felt something in my hand. I looked, and it was one very beautiful, perfect, long-stemmed red rose. And it was red. Not black, or white, but red.

"And as I looked at it, I knew that fear was really the only enemy. That the only thing to fear was fear itself."

"So…I guess I don't get the point here. What has fear got to do with money?"

Good grief, this man has a one-track mind. I shrug my shoulders, and say, "Well, if you are not afraid, and if you trust in a higher being, you won't be afraid. Then what is the big deal about money?"

"But…you have all these things. Why aren't you living in some little dump?"

"Because I need these things, I need beauty, warmth, comfort. So, He has seen fit to give them to me."

"And the red rose, was it a symbol to you of money?"

"No, of beauty. Of the beauty of my life, the perfection of the universe."

"I don't get it, but if you say so…" He is laughing again.

"Well, you can't say you haven't had a very entertaining breakfast."

"True, true, but you never told me about your money."

"Yes, I did."

"Okay, give me a hug," he said as he puts his jacket on to leave. "Anything I should know about Mom and Pops?"

"Just that the faucets are leaking in the kitchen and bathroom, and it would help if you could fix them."

He never did. I called the plumber.

4

As the third person my mother has fired leaves, in frustration I tell her, "Mother, you are a tyrant. You have to tell them what you want. They can't read your mind. Either that, or you have to let them do what I tell them. Or tell them what 'you' did, you know, how you ran the house."

"I don't know what I did. I just did it."

"Oh, Mother, get real, think about what you did when you got up in the morning, what you did all day. That's all you have to tell them."

I can't believe that she can't remember what she did…or I won't believe it…that is just too frightening.

This went on for thirty-seven days, and on the morning of the thirty-seventh day, I arrived, and my mother was sitting in her chair—the big, purple, dirty chair with the food spills and skin cells all over it. She smells strongly of urine and is sobbing as if her heart will break… Daddy is sitting in his recliner, a few feet from Mother, and he too is crying. His head hanging on his chest, tears plummeting in profusion from his clouded eyes, saliva dripping from the slackness of his mouth.

"Oh, Mother, what's the matter?" I say, as I kneel in front of her chair, my hand on her face. "It's okay, we'll get you cleaned up. It's okay, Mother. Don't cry."

She's sobbing uncontrollably, leaning her head back on the chair and hanging it down rhythmically, holding a tissue in hand. Tissues litter the chairs, floor, and all recesses within the house.

I pivot toward my father. "Daddy, why are you crying?"

He lifts his head and dejectedly states, "Because she is crying."

My heart wells with pain. These once-strong, capable people, reduced to an incapacity beyond words.

I go to Daddy's chair and hug him, so frail, so small. I go back to Mother's chair.

"Okay, it's going to be okay, we can fix this," I say as the tears stream down my face. "It's okay, it's going to be okay."

I hug Mother and tell her, "I'll clean you up, and we'll start all over today."

"No! They chipped my plate," she sobs, her words slurred from the many strokes and the sobs of a shattered life.

"What do you mean, they chipped your plate?"

"That girl who was here this morning to fix breakfast. She chipped my plate."

The sobs are uncontrollable now as I pat her and shush her. "It's okay," I sigh. "It's okay."

"No, no," she says, shaking her head back and forth, her words of despair whispered. "It's never going to be okay again."

"Let me see," I tell her.

I enter the kitchen, my mother's domain.

And on the counter sits a lone salad plate. One of a complete set of eight. They are porcelain, with that grayish-white look that makes up the background, with little blue flowers around the edges. The dishes are perhaps fifteen years old. I can remember when she bought them, as she couldn't find any she liked, so we shopped, and shopped.

A plate with a hole at its edge the size of a dime.

It isn't just a sliver of porcelain gone, that is indiscernible at a glance; it is a hole.

I pick it up and am immersed in grief and foreboding.

It portends the future. I can feel its despair, its legacy of ruination, and the end of all my mother has known.

My mother, so careful with things and so proud of her home-making skills, her ability to cook and can foods fresh from their own vegetable garden. The aroma of everything delectable wafting from the kitchen when you entered their home. Pies, jellies, preserves. Roasts with potatoes and carrots, pork chops with homemade applesauce and pickled beets, and green beans fresh from the garden. Clam chowder, fritters, and fried oysters.

This woman, who had come to fix breakfast, had unknowingly altered their lives forever.

For in that chipped plate lay the remnants of my mother's life, the very essence of her being. The means by which she judged herself. Her accomplishments.

I dropped my head and watched as the tears slid down my face, splashing on the chipped plate. My grief is palatable and real, my knees are weak with dread and fear as I gaze at this plate.

A plate that represents my mother's life. My hands are shaking as I place it under the rest of the dishes in the cupboard. Knowing as I did so that the die was cast, the inexplicable chain of events was not within my power to control. The plate was beyond repair, ruined, could not be replaced.

I cannot bring myself to throw it away. The prophesy involved in that, unbearable.

Resting my hands on the counter, I pray, "Lord, please fill me with your compassion. Allow the strength within me to flow through to these two people I love so dearly."

I sigh deeply and return to the living room.

"The plate *is* chipped, Mom, but I just tucked it under the rest of them. It'll be all right. You have lots of plates."

My mother lowered her head and, stifling a sob, said, "Yes. I guess, *if you say so.*"

The sarcasm brings me back to reality, the ever-present illusion to my profound knowledge, experience, and capacity for meddling.

What did she expect me to do, leave them here by themselves? No one else was paying their bills or seeing to it they had clean clothes or food, or someone to help them. As Peter so aptly put it, "They seem fine to me." My siblings, they have many excuses, or none. Can't they see these people who have been there for them all their lives, now need them, or are they so selfish they can't be bothered? They know I will do it. I always have. You would think they could see how hard it is for me, and offer to help. Some people cannot deal with this, to be sure. And they certainly do not want to incur Mother's wrath…these thoughts better left alone, as it takes only more of my energy.

"Come on, you guys, let's get cleaned up. We'll all feel better."

Who ever thought of that sentence? Miraculously, it always works. We do feel better. Clean, dressed, and fed.

I didn't return the following day. I simply could not face what awaited me there.

I couldn't identify it; I couldn't put a name on it. But it was something I could not face.

I weeded, and washed floors, and tried to control my surroundings as best I could.

Tomorrow was another day, a trite expression also profound in its accuracy.

I slept deeply and serenely that night, vowing that I could fix everything the next day.

They would have to come here and live. It was the only alternative. We have been through all sorts of people, and it simply wasn't working.

The first glimmer of daylight is lifting its head, the phone is ringing, and I glance at the clock lighted in its red coloring. It states it is five minutes before five o'clock.

I reach for the phone, deep foreboding in my heart.

"It's your dad, Cara. I just had them come get your mother."

"Who?" I ask, not knowing, not wanting to know.

"The aid car," he says. "I waited as long as I could. I think I did the right thing."

"I'll be right there," I tell him. "Do you want me to pick you up?"

"No, I'll drive."

I dress and put on minimal makeup. From experience, I know I won't be home until night. If then.

———~᠊ᢦ᠊ᢦ᠊ᢦ᠊ᢦ᠊ᢦ᠊ᢦ᠊ᢦ᠊᠊——

The doctors and nurses all acknowledge my presence as I walk into the ER.

Countless times over the last ten years, I have sat in these rooms and waited and watched as they have passed judgment on my parents' well-being.

"She's in the last room at the end," Janie says, recognizing me. "Just go on back."

I see Daddy sitting in a straight-backed metal chair in the corner. He has his hat in his hands, hanging between his knees. His chin is resting on his chest, as it rises up and down with each sob. His shirt collar is turned in on one side, and the shirt has been buttoned wrong. He has slippers on his feet.

The room is small, and has all the usual ER supplies and necessities.

On a gurney right in front of me lays my mother. The gurney is raised up waist-high, and she is lying on her side, her head turned away from me.

She looks enormous, I think. In fact she is thin at 180 pounds, from a previous 300 pounds.

Everything is quiet, and we are alone. I walk around the gurney, bend, and, rubbing Daddy's back, kiss him on the top of his head, with his white, dirty hair.

Mother's eyes are shut, but loosely so. Her mouth is hanging open.

"Hi, Mama," I say as I stroke her hair.

"She can't talk. She can't open her eyes, or close her mouth," Daddy says, his sobs stifled, fighting for control, rolling the brim of his hat in his hands.

"Oh, Mama, I'm so sorry." I stroke her brow. So smooth, not a sign of a line or wrinkle.

I take her flaccid hand in mine. "Can you hear me, Mother?" I ask.

She strokes the back of my hand with her thumb.

"Do you have any pain?"

No response.

"Can you open your eyes?"

No response.

"So you are in no pain." I am insistent. Again, she rubs my hand with her thumb.

It is funny, how life is; you never think the end will ever come for someone you love.

Isn't that a profound blessing.

I smooth her forehead and pat her hand. "Oh, Mama," I say, the horrendous pain of helplessness, the anguish flooding my very soul.

In the background, I can hear the hospital's "canned Muzak" and it suddenly floods my mind with my mother's voice, so lyrical, so melodious, singing and dancing with us as children.

She shudders and starts to vomit through a mouth that will not respond.

"Help! Help!" I scream.

A male nurse comes in and says, "What do you want me to do?" He looks twelve and is mortified by my mother's obvious vomiting.

"I don't know what you should do, but do something now!" I scream. "She's going to choke on her own vomit!" I quickly move around the gurney and try to push her considerable weight over to the side so she can let the vomit roll out of her open mouth.

The music is playing "Charmaine," and I remember my parents dancing to it and looking so happy, my mother's voice floating through the air as they danced past us as we sat on the floor playing.

This can't be happening.

A short nurse enters the room. She steps to the front of my mother and says, "I think she's had another stroke. They often vomit then."

I look up to speak to her, still holding Mother up. Suddenly I am swept by nausea, a weakness that invades and somehow diminishes my very being. I am so weak I am unable to stand.

Oh, no…I remember that feeling. The moment my child died, far more intense, but…it is their life…their very soul leaving mine…she's gone.

I struggle to breathe, to hold my head up. I hear the nurse telling me, "You should get some air."

I turn, see that there is an open door to the left of me, go to it, and slide down the doorjamb. Holding my head between my knees, I silently ask the Father to give me strength to go back in there.

As my prayers are answered, I return to the room. The nurse looks at me and says, "They'll pass a nasogastric tube and suction so she won't choke anymore."

I take Daddy, and we go eat lunch, returning to the hospital room where they have moved her. To stand vigil once again.

Nothing changes. She can't open her eyes or close her mouth.

But she can understand, and rub my hand for "yes." She is in no pain, she indicates. I tell her, "I've called the rest of the kids, and they are coming," and she rubs my hand.

I kiss her forehead and tell her, "Mother, you can go if you want to." Remembering the last time I had told her that, not six months ago, she said, *"He didn't want her."* Her words had broken my heart.

He's waiting, I am sure. *Lord, receive my mother, for I have loved her so.*

I wept in my soggy pillow that night and plead with the Lord to help her, to take her home to Him. *Please, dear Lord, help my poor mother. Take her home to you.*

"She has to come willingly," He softly stated. I was filled with peace. I was humbled before Him, grateful and filled with thanks and praise.

And I slept.

In the next seventeen hours of my mother's life, her children came, and her beloved Samantha sat at her bedside.

The man she had spent her whole life with, her best friend, the little boy of seven who told the little girl of four that he loved her, her lover, her husband, sat at her side.

I went home, picked green beans, and gave thanks that He had taken her home, where she was safe and no longer frightened.

For in those hours of waiting, I knew that what had indeed spurned her anger to such heights was fear.

What we manifest in life is— what we fear, what we desire.

Desire promotes a feeling of joy, excitement, and anticipation.

Fear promotes a feeling of anger, a "dis-ease," sleeplessness, a lack of balance.

I would wait now for the inevitable. Daddy would go soon. He is so frail he can't possibly exist on his own, to do those things that need to be done just to survive, and he is certainly as confused as she was.

To my great surprise, as well as everyone else's, he rallied. His grief seemed nonexistent. Within two weeks, he had thrown away every stitch of clothing, every handbag she had owned, and some articles of clothing with tags from the store that she had not even worn.

"I could take those back, Daddy," I tell him one day.

"Nope, they're gone," he said.

I asked, "Can I help you?"

"No, I'll do it myself."

He threw away a new leather coat I had given her for Christmas, gloves from Italy that I had brought back, and things she had bought for him that he didn't like, or just didn't want to have to remind him of her.

He has gone through the cupboards and refrigerators and threw away all of the foods she liked and had eaten. His reasons his own, and he shared them with no one.

My siblings and I stood by and watched, as her existence in the house was abolished, all but the table next to her chair. Her writings, with every illness they each had had, and the treatments and surgeries to correct the same, documented in detail. The only words of emotion, noted on a day Daddy had collapsed in the garage, said, "They said he was old and frail—oh my."

Their travels as well. Her pens and pencils, her crossword puzzles. All these he leaves undisturbed.

When I asked if I could have a small something of hers, he thought for a moment, "No, it's better this way."

Is he trying to forget her? No, there is a shrine to her in the bedroom on the dresser. A picture of her, some flowers from the funeral I dried and took to him. Five of the two dozen red roses he had sent to her for her funeral. A small plaque with a pretty little poem about friendship.

The bed had been saturated in urine. But he won't part with it; they had shared this bed, and he didn't want another. So, I had it cleaned and turned it over.

None of these expressions that he has shown of grief, did I feel when my child was killed.

Grief—what a small, insignificant word to express such a multifaceted emotion.

Elizabeth Kubler Ross said it came in stages: anger, depression, rage, denial, grief, bargaining, and finally, acceptance.

Ah, finally, I understand.

The montage of emotions colliding within him refuses to be denied. It resides in his mind, his heart, his solar plexus. Anger, relief, happiness, freedom, shame, and guilt—such diminutive words to express feelings.

That he could feel this way about someone who has meant the world to him for all of his life.

His anger is profound.

His despair and loneliness, pushed to the back of his mind by busyness. Anger at the lost years of his life, of her life. Reason and understanding, once so much a part of his nature, gone.

For him, perhaps it has been accumulating for years. Years of verbal abuse, years of tolerating her enormous mood swings. And in the last years of her life, demands on his physical and psychological being.

He was simply emotionally and physically depleted. She had used him up.

He has freedom, and money.

And will.

An amazing proliferation of what was just, months past, nonexistent.

As the cocooning is of the butterfly, he has emerged.

But time passes, and the reality of his loneliness embroiders his life. Despondency overcomes him. He stops making plans for the future and is frustrated by her lack of ability to communicate with him from the "other side."

He thinks she's mad at him.

5

I've lost him, *Tony*, lost him forever. The sheets are all wrinkled; I hate that. The clock just chimed midnight. *Lord, why can't I just go to sleep?* I flip and flop, get up, and straighten the sheets. You'd think after all these years that this would be over, and now I think it is. Am I heartbroken? Too late for that, my heart has been broken for so many years, it's probably hardened like Pharaoh's.

I can sense that Tony's mother just died. I could be wrong…I know how strange that is, but seldom am I mistaken. I can't seem to shake the feeling.

Is this an ego trip on my part? A loss of power, at least a power I thought I had.

I have loved him for so many years, or the idea of him, I don't know how to stop. Talk about crippling your life. But, when you have those shining moments, moments beyond words, moments that have only happened between the two of you, a connection that no one else can touch, it is just too hard to let go.

His mother has been the single most important person in his life. She gave him life, and immediately, she was too preoccupied with her own to care for him. She left him with her mother for the most part, slept with strange men with him in the bed beside them, was a raging drunk, and called him a "dirty little bastard." He cried when he told me this.

This giant hulk of a man cried, heartbroken. He wanted nothing to do with her, he'd say. But I knew different. He just wanted her to love him.

Isn't that what we all want from our mothers? If your mother doesn't love you, how valid can you be as a person?

I had hired her when she was out of work.

I invited her to dinner; she would show up drunk, spouting obscenities not heard in a barroom. "Leave the old lady out of our life," he'd say.

But I truly thought he'd be happier if they could be reconciled; after all, she had introduced us. I knew in her own way, she loved him. Her life was just so hard.

Now as Myrna lay on her deathbed, it is Marsha who will hold him in her arms and console him. It is Marsha who will care for her, and see to her needs, leaving him forever in her debt, a debt of gratitude and relief, a relief that he is not alone, a relief that someone has spared him the responsibility of caring for his aged mother, and the peace of knowing he, too, was a part of that. Because Marsha was strong enough to do what must be done.

Would I have done that? I think I would have, but perhaps not; he was insistent Myrna not be a part of our life, and I, seeing a white knight and not a man, believed him.

Too, I am generally not motivated by greed, and Marsha has everything to gain. Tony for one, the house and money for another. That should do it. Marsha has saved him, protected him, sheltered him, loved him. She has seen him as a man. My hat is off to her, and for him, I am happy. Laying here in this hot, messy bed, on a cold winter's night, I wonder why I didn't know to do that…still the scent of his masculinity engulfs me, and as I think once more of the touch of his thick, strong hands as they caress my body, a single tear drips to the pillow beneath my head.

I know nothing can be more painful that losing a child, that I would survive this. If I was going to die from emotional pain, or a broken heart, I most certainly would have already done so. At last, I sleep.

With the unmitigated glee of a small child, I rise from my bed, the previous distress obliterated, as even in the deep slumber of exhausted sleep, I sense the serene calm that has shrouded the earth outside my bedroom.

Tiptoeing across the plush white of the carpeted floor to the window, leaving Daisie sleeping peacefully on my bed, I look out of the large paladin windows into the softness of falling snow. The flakes as large as those of feathers, as white as if they had been plucked from a dove. The full of the quickening moon, lending a bluish cast to the snow, leaving a dancing fairy like light in its path, blanketing the earth in drifts of resounding wonder. Covering the scars of the winter earth and blanketing the majestic emerald green of the trees, the enormous trunks of gray-brown leaving it to look as if it were wearing a coat of ermine. No longer apparent are the brown, withered fronds of the sword fern, the dried dead of trimmed perennials are covered by the purest of white.

The sounds of chirping birds have been silenced. The scurrying of the raccoons and squirrels are no more, for they, too, have taken refuge from the bitter cold of winter and found solace and comfort in God's blanket, knowing that it will insulate them in their homes of fallen trees and small, earthen caves. The leafless branches of deciduous trees stand coated in an icy crust of diamonds that glitter as if by earthly light.

There is a small precipice to the west of the house, the denseness of the forest giving a perfect backdrop, as standing regal against the white purity of the snow, a great imperial buck stands, a custodian to his wondrous surroundings. His massive chest the nutlike color of his species, his antlers held high, as pride emanates from within him. The soft white clouds form as the breath from his nostrils, tell of the chill of the air.

I return to my bed and I am touched by the reverence of the scene before me, as once again, I fall into the blissful slumber of forgetfulness; I give thanks in silence to the God of this earth.

The brightness is astounding as I awaken to the snow-shrouded world of a bright winter day, the Westminster chimes of the great clock in the foyer, striking the hour of seven. It has snowed all night and continues its soft descent to the wondrous, white world below. The mountains in the distance glitter in the most extraordinary purples, pinks, and gold as the sunrise awakens the world.

Once more, the nagging premonition engulfs me, and I struggle to push it aside. I have also discovered that the electricity is off. I hate that. That means no heat, no water, so many things we take for granted daily.

As I boil coffee and build a fire, I notice that the weight of the snow has broken the branches of two of my gorgeous plum trees. I am heartsick, as there is nothing to do about any of that today. I am literally snowed in. The snow, with drifts of five feet, has even the bronze lions covered as they rest en garde at the entrance to the house.

The lights flash on, then off, on again…ah, I think they are going to stay on.

The phone is ringing as I start to reset all the clocks. It is Samantha; she is crying. "Oh, honey, what is wrong?"

"Daddy just called, Gramma Myrna died last night."

"Oh, Samantha, I am so sorry, is there anything I can do for you?"

"No, Mother, I know she was old and sick, but…I will miss her so much." Great sobs come, uncontrolled now. My poor, darling daughter. Death is such an unwelcome fact of life.

"How is Daddy doing?" I ask, knowing the answer.

"He's really upset, Mother, I think you should call him. I think he would like that."

"Yeah, probably, but right now, I think I should come down and be with you."

"No, Mother, come after you call Daddy, besides, the snow is too deep to even walk through."

"Okay. Maybe I should."

I am afraid to call. I have to make the phone call immediately, or I will lose the courage. Samantha said, "Mother, it is the right thing to do, and if it makes him mad now, he will be glad you called when he thinks about it later."

"I just don't want him to go off on me, or to go ballistic because I called."

"Oh, Mother, just call him."

She is right; it is what I want to do, and the right thing to do. It is a lack of courage that keeps me from wanting to do it. The fear of hearing his voice, the pull of my heartstrings as I picture the softness of his lips, the very essence of who he is, was, to me.

"Hello..." Marsha has answered.

"Is Antonio there?" I ask.

She hesitates. "Who is this?"

"It's Cara," I say.

"Tony, phone," she says, making no attempt at being polite.

I hear his voice in the background. "Is it the ex?" he says.

His voice is soft, a sensual baritone, which after all these years makes my heart catch in my throat, and I feel weak. I love him; I will always love him. I feel the pull of our connection even as I speak to him, and I feel he feels it too. Nothing will ever come of this, I think, the emotion flooding the very depths of my soul.

"Hi, you," he says.

"Hi. I just wanted you to know how sorry I am. I just talked to Samantha, and she said your mom died last night."

"It's better," he said.

"I know, I just went through that with Mother, but it is still hard."

"Yeah, I know you did."

"Okay...I won't keep you. I just wanted you to know I was thinking of you."

"Okay, kid, take care of yourself."

"I will. You too."

I hear the click of the receiver, and immediately feel lost and alone. What a trite conversation for two people who could always talk for hours. Hours of conversation about everything and everyone. To fall asleep in each other's arms, not from a lack of anything more to say, but from sheer exhaustion, or because the early light of dawn was creeping in the window, both of us having to go to work.

Is it just my imagination…I can feel the pull of emotion between us. I can feel the fright in Marsha's voice.

The fear that all will be lost in an instant.

6

Tony replaces the receiver back in the cradle of the telephone—what the hell? *Jesus, I think I feel sick. Why the* fuck *didn't she wanna talk to me?*

I need a drink. Christ, I need a drink. Dammit! I don't care if it is nine in the morning!

He walks the few feet it takes to enter his mother's small but serviceable kitchen space. It is all white. White paint, white cabinets, white tile, with the dirt that has ground into the grout of the tile over the many years being the only color in the room, along with the occasional chip in the old tile, leaving a feeling of a shabby uncleanliness about the room. There are no curtains that hang at the small window above the old kitchen sink. Nothing sits atop the white tile counters. *She was like that,* he thought. No frills, no subterfuge, what you saw is what you got.

His hand shakes as he pours the bourbon in the glass. No water, no ice. Just booze.

The sweat trickles down the side of his forehead. With the heel of his hand, he pushes it into what used to be a mane of black hair, but is now only a white, balding stubble.

When the fuck did that happen? When did I get this old? When did things go wrong with "her"?

She's probably still pissed off at me. She said I'd turn into a rock if I didn't quit screamin', "Fuck you, God, you son of a bitch!" *So it's like Job, is it? Take your children, take your wife—well, screw you, God. The devil's got me. And I don't give a fuck.*

His throat tight with emotion. Damn her... *God, I love her. I've never stopped loving her. I hate her. Why did she have to do that? Leave me. Leave me all alone, and now she calls to say she's sorry my mother is dead. Can't we just talk like regular people? Hell, I'd talk to her.*

Nothin's ever good enough for her. She has to have it all her way, all the time. She hated my mother.

He takes a hard, long gulp of the fiery hot liquid and leaning against the counter bangs his head on the cupboard door, the tears coming now in an avalanche of despair.

That's not true, he thinks.

The old lady was a royal pain in the ass, and "she" was such a high-class broad, I should have known it would never work. I drank too much, and then the women. That time in the Ranchero, Christ, that was the shits, and then Inger, Jesus Christ, what was I thinking?

And nothing was ever good enough. We have to have a new house. You can't be drunk all the time. You have to come home for dinner. I want another baby—like I needed another kid. You have to quit drinking. Tell me you love me, why can't you tell me you love me?

Crazy little bitch, I married her didn't I? I'm here aren't I?

I did tell her some wild stories, crazy little bitch believed me too. How can such a smart woman be so stupid?

Yeah, I'm better off with fat little Marsha. She is a good woman, not so demanding. Grateful…stupid, but grateful.

He takes another long drink and clutches the side of the tile counter.

It'll be all right. I'll be all right. I need a smoke. Just one. After all my ole lady just died. She's laying there right now in her bed, dead. My mother is dead, the ole bitch finally died. How many times when I was a snot-nosed kid did I wish she would just die, and now, look at me, I'm all fucked up.

And then *she* has to call. I knew she would. I was afraid she wouldn't. I love her. He could hear the sound of her voice echoing in his head. I love her, I miss her. The soft silkiness of her skin…like satin. Snow white, and so soft. Those deep, mystical, turquoise eyes, slanted like she was some kind of cat. Her hands, her beautiful, tall, thin, graceful body. That flaming red hair. That woman…that woman no man ever could take their eyes from.

And she was mine. She is mine. *She will always be mine.*

'Til death do us part, they said. What death? The kid, that did it. I just couldn't do that…oh, Christ, I just couldn't do that. Shit, what a bitch life is. And all that crap about God and where the kid was. Just let it go. I told her. But, "No," she said. "If she was in Europe, wouldn't you want to know about Europe?"

"She's not in Europe," I told her. "She's fucking dead. Let it go." The kid was always in trouble, running away from home, climbing out of the window at night. Shit, I told the old lady then that she wasn't long for this world. That she needed to be scared. The kid isn't scared of anything, but no, she says she just needs to be loved. Loved my ass, she needs the fear of God pounded into her thick little skull. Ditchin' school, getting caught smokin' pot on the school grounds, how stupid is that?

"*I try, Tony, I just can't. I really do try. And you're gone, or drinking all the time doesn't help.*" She had said.

Whining, women, always whining. Yeah, it was always all my fault. "Other people lose kids, and they just get on with it, why can't you?"

What did she say? I can't think what she said now, just now over the phone. Did she say she loved me? I can feel her lips as they touch my cheek, her hand as it caresses my face, just months ago when she brought Samantha to stay with the ol' lady.

Pissed me off. Where the fuck does she get off coming here, and *"Don't leave because of me, I'm leaving,"* she says, like I cared what she did. She left me. She knew I loved her, and she left me…threw me out like an ole shoe. Women. One damn thing, you mess up a few times, and they just get up and leave you. Even fat little Marsha, one time, and man, I'm out the door. I call

Samantha, and ask if I can come stay with her. She acts like her mother—"No way, Daddy no way."

What the hell do they expect me to do? I have to stay with this one. *Be a good boy.* Women. *Go to work, don't drink, don't screw around. Watch your language, Tony, change your clothes, Antonio. Take a bath Tony.* Shit!

Those other women didn't ever mean anything, I told her that, and it's not like I really cared. You know, you just get in situations that you can't get out of.

Like that time at the Ranchero—boy, that was bad. He takes another long drink, thinking of that fateful day. I'm standing in the back, making out with this chick, really an ugly little thing. But they all dared me, and at ten in the morning, in walks the ol' lady. What the hell is she doing here? I don't see her, but all the other guys do, and she, so calm, so cool, and collected, sits down clear at the end of the bar, just watching me. Orders a straight shot, so I guess you could say she wasn't calm, cool, or collected, since she doesn't usually drink, and she just watches me, watches me make an ass of myself while Bob and all these guys are trying to get my attention. Geez…I looked up and saw her and thought my knees were gonna give out. But I'm not beggin'—okay, I was wrong, but I'm not beggin' for forgiveness; she'll just have to get over it. I told her it was a bet, and she just gave me a look, tears streamin' down her face. She got up and walked out. Christ, that was a bad day. But I was drunk.

Then there was the big, fat, old broad, the one I met at the bar, took her over to meet Cara; she sure screwed that up. I just wanted her to meet my beautiful wife, and my beautiful fuckin' wife thought I was bangin' her. Would she listen? Hell no. She couldn't understand that I loved *her*, and those other women, just didn't mean a thing. I just get tired of the nose-to-the-grindstone shit. I needed to have fun, not have to think of all this shit all the time.

Sure, it was my idea she work until we had some cash in the bank. But like everything else, she has to make a big deal of it. So she goes and buys a hospital. Without telling me. What the hell is that all about? I try to help her. But hell no! I get chewed out for doing one thing to help her—well, never again. Her excuse is, if I want money, and she has to work, she is going to make money.

What the hell, another belt of this stuff should take care of it. He listens to the gurgle of the booze as it fills the glass. *I just want that dead, old lady out of my house. It is my house now.* I could shit-can Marsha now, but what the hell, she's all right, I'm used to her. But things are gonna be different…

The kid, Samantha said she was coming, that's good. I like her, hell, I love the kid…got a lot of spunk, like the old lady…even looks a little like her. Pisses Marsha off, but what the hell, I'm tired of her shit too.

He pours himself another drink, a short one, his mind acknowledging that he is becoming incoherent even to himself. Hell, I'll be fine. I knew this was coming, and Samantha will be here soon. That's okay. I love the kid, but she knows that.

My life hasn't been worth a fuck since that shit with my leg. One automobile accident after another. First, I pile up the Cougar, then the ol' lady totals the Jaguar, and then that shit in Wyoming. The pain…nobody understands how bad that was. How in the hell would they like it to be crippled for the rest of their lives?

Oh, she said she understood, but it was always, "*Tony, you have to do this, you can do this.*"

I tried to tell her, "I can't. I'm nothin' now, I'm nothin' but a goddamn cripple. Leave. Get the hell out of here, get yourself a real man."

"*I don't want a real man,*" she'd scream at me. "*I want you!*" How the hell is that supposed to make me feel? I'll never be the same again. I am a cripple. I should have just had them cut the god-damn thing off. Doctors don't know shit. They said I'd recover if I exercise. Well, who can exercise in all this pain? And she leaves my wheelchair home. God, how I hate that self-righteous bitch…

The doctor said to do it, she tells me. Like she did everything someone tells her…what about what I tell her? Life…fuckin'… sucks.

But things are gonna change now. I'm gonna have some money. And piss on everyone else. I have my friends; I don't need her, or my mother, to tell me what to do.

None of this cryin' and wailin', none of this "Tell me how you feel, Antonio." Feelin' gets you nowhere.

Suddenly, Tony feels the hand on his arm. He jumps. Marsha is there, and he's shocked; he thought it would be Cara.

He wanted it to be Cara.

"Tony, are you all right?"

"Yeah, I'm fine."

"They're here for your mom."

"Yeah, sure, I'm coming." Tony says, as he drains the glass, takes a stifled breath, and closes his eyes for just a second. Thinking, *Why can't things be like they used to be? I miss them. Her, the brats. That freckled redheaded little kid who was so smart, and my little blonde sidekick who wanted to do everything with me. What happened to those days? The house was warm and felt happy. I was in love, and I was loved. God, if you existed, you wouldn't have taken that from me. What have I done to deserve this?*

He feels the tears streaming down his face, raising his arm, he wipes at them with the back of his hand.

"Tony." Marsha hollers. "Are you all right? They're here."

"Yea, I'm coming."

7

Cara

It is early morning; the pale light of dawn still hours away, as it is January, and dark is a peaceful shroud here. The living room is lovely in the softness of the lamplight, as if it were candles glowing on the silver that sets atop the polished, ornately carved table. The room is peaceful, surprising to me, since I rarely sit in here. I'm so busy making things orderly and beautiful that I rarely take the time to enjoy them. I can hear the clocks striking the hour, and I love the simplicity of time and order. I find I count when I am upset, or even when tired. I sense I am attempting to get back in touch with universal order. After all, wouldn't it stand to reason that clocks would tick rhythmically to the energy of the universe?

I ask the angels to surround me as I am writing this, as I do for nearly everything I do. I need help, Lord, just in my everyday living. Life to me is so sweet and so foreign. I am always profoundly shocked at people, what they do, and how they think. Interesting, as I really can't figure out what they think, if in fact thinking proceeds their doing.

And normal? What is normal? I am certain I am different than what is considered normal. I have worked most of my life. I have been so poor, I had nothing to eat. I have been very wealthy. I would be willing to bet that my neighbors and acquaintances are certain I was at one time, a high paid "call girl."

I have visitations from angels. Bands of angels. They have come frequently since the thirteenth of January of this year. Always at approximately eleven each night.

That's the time of night Jillian always came to say good night. And when she comes to me, it is most frequently at that same time now.

"We are the angels the Lord has sent. We've come to take care of you, to help you."

"But I don't know what to do."

"We'll help you. You are to take care of yourself. Rest. Get organized. Erase the confusion in your life. We will help. You are not safe with those you trust."

"What about Samantha?"

"It will be your greatest gift to her. She will no longer have to worry about you."

They fill the left-hand side of my bedroom, a soft glowing, a light that is a profusion of the softest gossamer of pinks and golds. They appear to be androgynous, and give the impression that they are floating. I am so deeply moved and grateful. They have given me peace. I will try to do as I am told.

I judge everyone by me. Is that bad? I am a good person, I am kind and generous and trusting, so much so that the Lord sends angels to tell me not to trust. I am frightened of my own intuition. I seem to sense how people really feel, what they really mean. And that frightens and confuses me. It is quite difficult to deal with. Is it fear, jealousy, anger, love? What are they really feeling? Or, am I merely projecting my own feelings on them?

Is it possible? Could people have a "survival" personality? A personality that personifies the sum of their experiences during this life and the lives they have led previously?

Of all the people I know, if you look deeply enough, you find that their true selves, the very essence of their being, is rooted in fear and/or guilt. Oh, I imagine there are those who are traversing backward in this life and are thought to be evil. But do I truly believe their souls are lost to God? In their totality, I do not.

Life is apparently a spiral, in which we "grow" to God, and in doing so, we encounter experience after experience that provides us with the knowledge and insight to go fearlessly further. Seeking not to justify us, but to justify the existence of our creator.

At the base of that spiral is all humanity grouped into a clannish population, by necessity, for sheer survival. We find it necessary to band as a group, to live, to eat, to be safe from the elements of the earth. The need for companionship, and the need to procreate, being inborn.

Life is meant to hasten our reunion with God, not to prolong it. And for each experience in life we engage in, we move closer to His ideal. For it is not what happens to us in life, but our reaction to it, that is important, and that which determines our position on the spiral of life.

Apparently. That word always reminds me of a joke my piano teacher told me, and for the life of me, I cannot remember what the joke is. But a chuckle is a chuckle, and so we will leave it at that.

Again, *apparently*, we arrive here at a specified place in the spiral with work to do; things to learn; and people, places, and animals to love. That, to be sure, is the operative word. *Love.* The fragrance of the flowers in the early morning dawn. The beauty of a sunset against the majestic mountains, as it is reflected in the waters. The soft, gentle caress of a loved one. The warm, milky smell of babies and puppies. The weight of a baby in your arms, signifying trust and dependence.

Did God create us so that we could experience the rose, to touch the velvety softness of its petals, to smell the fragrance that permeates its very essence, perhaps, even, He intended us to feel the very prick of its thorn. For, after all, is not that life itself, the beauty and the pain? Would we appreciate one without the other? Would we even recognize it?

There are times, in my most intimate musings, that I think: I shall so miss this earth when I am dead. I look at the beauty and the magnificence around me and thrill at its splendor. My heart is filled to brimming, and my very soul is touched by all the glory before me. I stand in awe of the world that surrounds me and wonder at its Creator.

Do others feel this rapture, I ponder in my heart of hearts. Do others recognize the depth of a being so powerful, so knowing, that such a creation can exist, let alone flourish? The organization of the world is profound.

It is with great relief to me, and to God as well, I am certain, that the so-called Hard Scientist and the Soft Scientist can finally work together, to be cohesive in their research and see that, in fact, it is just one science. The science of a creator so powerful and filled with such an abundance of love and compassion for this world. A world in such denial, an unfathomable denial, that a supreme being does in fact exist.

My own experiences in this exquisite world are profound by most people's standards. I was, without a doubt, shocked by my own arrival here. Do I belong? Hardly. I could not have been more shocked.

And where on the spiral to God did I begin? That has been my life's preoccupation.

And where do those souls, so intricately woven into my life like the threads in cloth, appear on that spiral? That, too, is a constant source of wonderment. Do I have the right to judge? No. Do I judge anyway? I try not to, but forgive me, Lord, I do.

I profess to a philosophical knowledge of things unworldly, intangible, leaving me with no one to discuss these things with other than myself, and how then am I to learn more? That has proven to be a conundrum, at best. So…I talk to angels and to spirits from the other side.

Does this make me strange? I think so. I think other people think so. Do I feel out of place? I do.

I have very few memories of my childhood, short as it was. For the essence of my soul arrived intact and has remained that way lo' these many years. I have never felt I grew up, only that I arrived here on this planet of so many splendors, in small human form. My thoughts and thinking have never changed over the years, and in fact, I came here knowing about Socrates, Plato, and a vast array of personages that I no longer can attest to knowing or relating to. Is it still imprinted on my soul? Yes, I think it is.

As a child, I often wondered what it would feel like to be special, to be so loved and cherished that you were deserving of love, of respect. To have everyone appreciate and accept you for whomever you are. To have them instinctively understand you. A few of my friends appeared to have that in their families; some did not.

As an adult looking back on this, I find that most people judge everyone by themselves, and therefore have little or no motive to look beyond that. If they are dishonest or untrustworthy, that is what they see in others and are threatened by this knowledge.

Love is such a profound and utterly selfless act, that it is found seldom, and even then, only in fleeting moments of time.

We love our children unconditionally, until they grow to be a more distinct personality. When they exhibit actions or opinions contrary to our own, so often that love is replaced by anger, dislike, and fear. Fear of losing control. For is that not what we love about little babies, their utter dependence on us for their survival, the replication of ourselves? Our very ability to think we can control them? Conversely, the moment we are inconvenienced by them and they exhibit an existence that is separate from us and our way of thinking and doing, our love dissipates to something much less admirable.

For control is an illusion at best. And control is what everyone is seeking. Control over their lives and the lives of those they profess to love. Control will eliminate the tragedy and despair in our lives, the treachery, the terrible fears of the unknown. We as humans are sure of this, certain we know all the answers, at the very least what is best for us and those with whom we share our lives. Fear of rejection, fear of loneliness, fear of hunger, of life. But isn't fear simply an arrogant lack of faith? How do we, as mere mortals, look around at all the splendor, the order, and dare to think we can control that which God has ordained. "Why do you fear O you of little faith" (Matthew 7:7).

Knowing this does not keep me from being fearful. That has been my quest, to trust in the Lord with all my heart, to give up my control to the Lord, and to trust that I am doing exactly as was intended for me to do. To follow the path that has been paved for me so that I may arrive at my proper destination.

I long ago gave up the thoughts of karma, the eastern belief of "you reap what you sow." For, in fact, that is why Christ died for us, so that we may be delivered from the consistent karmic pattern. We have been given *grace*. This earth experience is a valid one, one that will teach us to love unconditionally. It may take us many lifetimes, but in time, we will experience unconditional love, freeing us to transcend the spiral on this plane of existence.

I believe there is truth to every religion and every spiritual experience.

Religion was designed by man to control the masses. Man has created God in an image that suits his necessity. From the earliest of times, God was thought to be fearsome, creating disaster and havoc in his path. Then, as man became less manageable, God became loving and benevolent. Nothing on this earth is so powerful as that, that which we have no tangible proof of, or power over. And all the religious leaders of the world control those that are fearful, lonely, and lost. They have used those same fears to control the masses. They have amassed vast fortunes in the name of God, committed despicable crimes in His name, and justified their actions because they were serving the one God.

There are no lies, only half-truths. Nothing is new in this universe. Our Creator has only waited for the right person to "discover" that, that has always been.

Intuition is what you feel when you are hearing God's words. A hunch is what God wishes you to do. It is fear that keeps us from hearing that which He is telling us. Fear to be who we are. Fear that we are not good enough. Not intelligent enough. Not aesthetically beautiful enough. Not wealthy enough.

God does not wish us to suffer, but to be an example of his love and creativity. His promise to us is to "seek and ye shall find. Ask and it shall be answered." God gave us the gift of life, the ultimate present. He wished for us health, wealth, love of friends and family, and perfect self-expression. That is our divine right as his children, and ours for the asking. In asking, you must believe you will receive, giving thanks that you have received, and acting in faith.

How do I know these things? Let me take you on a journey— a profound discovery of life, of love, of acceptance…or not…

8

There are not many things I remember as a child. I remember standing between my parents on the front seat of a black Model T Ford on a warm summer day. My father is young and happy, the world before him.

My mother is listening intently as he is speaking to her. We are driving up the hill of a grassy meadow.

I am perhaps two years of age and am dressed in little short pants, and shoes and stockings, and my legs are firm and sturdy. Long-legged colt, they call me. I'm fair of face, with little wisps of golden brown hair and eyes of the clearest azure blue. My arms are planted firmly behind each of them on the seat, as I listen intently to their conversation. I can look through the windshield of the car and see the powdery blue sky, the puffy white clouds. I can smell the grass as we drive over it, crushing the fragrance from it. I feel happy, contended, as if I were a prized piece to their puzzle. I am where I was intended to be. I have foundation. I am loved.

Loved by this young man and this young woman. Unscathed by the life to come. Dreaming dreams of the perfect life that will unfold before them. Unhampered by fear of the unknown.

The next memory is of a shack, our home; the house is small and dinghy, sparsely furnished and dark. I can see the rooms clearly, there is no ornamentation, no order or cleanliness. An old wooden rocking chair with large flat arms that my brother has used a potato peeler on sits beneath a window, the ink-stained leather seat of an old, overstuffed couch worn colorless, is pushed against the wall to the far side of the room. The windows are cracked, and not adorned with curtains. There is a kitchen directly behind this room, with a woodstove for cooking and heating, a small wooden table that is chipped and wobbly, with chairs that match it perfectly. I am four years old.

There are two small closet-sized bedrooms on either side of these rooms. There is no bathroom—we use a pot in the bedroom to the side of the kitchen, and light a match if it smells too bad. I don't remember where it was dumped.

There is dirty, yellowish linoleum, with large gray patches of asbestos on the kitchen floor, the rest of the floors are just wooden planks, their cracks and crevices filled with dirt and food from the other children.

The house sits at such an angle toward the front of the house that we can stand on roller skates and coast from the kitchen to the front door.

The kitchen cupboards are tall for a four-year-old, and it is difficult to make the ascent. I drag a chair over to the counter and climb up to make mustard sandwiches. My younger brothers are hungry, and I don't know where Mommy is, or if she's coming back. Mustard and stale bread, sugar if I can find some. That will have to do, and "Don't get any mustard on you, it will stain," I tell them in my most grown-up voice.

I don't want them to be scared or hungry. Maybe we should go to Gramma's—she'd know what to do. I hate to be alone.

At Gramma's, it is always neat and clean and warm. And she makes good things to eat. She knows everything and is always happy. Most of the time, if Mommy has to go, we go to Gramma's. I don't know what happened today.

Maybe she is angry. I unbraided my hair this morning because I wanted Mommy to comb it today, and it was standing out all over my head. My hair is long and wrinkly after it has been braided for so many days. I had to go potty, and it stunk, and she said, "Light a match!" I did, but the flames caught my hair on fire.

I was screaming and running around in my bare feet and my flannel nightgown that Gramma had made for me.

"Stop it! Stand still," Mommy said, and she put her hands right in the flames of my hair and made it go out. But she said, "Why don't you be careful? Look what you've done! And stop crying. You have nothing to cry about."

But I was scared, and I didn't do it on purpose.

So maybe that's why she went.

I don't know where Daddy is. Gramma says he went to war. I don't know what that really means, but I think it's scary. He's fighting the Japanese. Why? Maybe he won't come home. I think Mommy misses him. I really feel sad when he's not home.

Things are different, quiet, and sad. I don't think there should be wars. Why would that be all right?

9

Daddy's home! Everything is going to be all right. Mommy went away for a long time, and she said Daddy was in the hospital, but he's coming home. And we're going to have another baby and we're going to move. I don't want to move. We won't be close to Gramma's.

But move we do, and Mother has a cute little baby.

I like the baby fine. But Daddy likes her better than me, I think. He really likes her. She is really cute and really little. We pass around popcorn, and she tries to walk from each of us to the popcorn. She is so little she can walk under the kitchen table.

Our house is attached to someone else's house. But it is really nice. And lots of kids to play with. There is a little black girl that lives next door. Her name is Betty, and she likes me, and we play all the time. And there are lots of other kids for us to play with. The girl down the street, Beverly, has a really pretty mother. She gets dressed up and wears makeup every day. I asked Mommy why she doesn't get dressed up and put on makeup and fix her hair. She was really mad at me, again. She screams a lot. The neighbors can hear her, and I wish they couldn't.

Daddy works at night and sometimes Mother lets me stay up, and Daddy brings home hamburgers when it's really in the middle of the night.

It's summer now, I am nearly eight years old and Daddy said if I picked beans in the fields, he would match every cent I made. Wow! I worked so hard that summer, and Mother and Daddy were so surprised. And at dinner, I got to have second helpings of dessert. It was worth all the itchy, sweaty work. But I think they needed the money, or maybe he forgot.

We're going to move again. To a house that's all our own.

I'm going into the second grade; I'm really tall and kinda skinny. I don't want to go to a new school. I feel out of place. Mother lets me have my nails long and paint them red. I think they look really pretty.

We're all real excited.

The house is in the country, and so we are going to move out of the projects, and no one will live in the same house as we do. We are going out to see it today. I hope it's like Gramma's house. Her house is quite large and has a porch with flower boxes, and every summer, she has flowers called nasturtiums and geraniums. She has a big yard that my uncle has to mow and a garden that has lots of vegetables, and she has gooseberry bushes too and apple trees and strawberries and rhubarb. And she picks flowers and has them on the table in the dining room. In the cellar, she has lots of jars of food she canned. And she makes pies and kills the chickens for dinner, and they run around with their heads cut off. It's kinda funny and kinda scary.

I don't think I want to kill any chickens.

And when we stay overnight, we always go to church, and I really like to go to church. Gramma sings in the choir. It's wonderful.

She has ladies that come for lunch, and they play cards called Bridge. And she makes cute little sandwiches with the crusts cut off the bread, and they talk and laugh.

Gramma's a big woman, not tall, but large-boned. Her hands are the hands of a woman who has worked hard all of her life. She dresses quite conservatively, and on Sunday, she always wears a pretty patterned dress with a brooch at the neckline and earrings that match, only recently deciding it would be acceptable to wear pants on occasion. Her hair is short, and she has a permanent, as regular as clockwork. She has a face that is reminiscent of George

Washington. Sad but true. Her eyes are deep set and hazel in color. There is sadness in those eyes, as well as resignation for what life has dealt her. But when she knew we were coming, she would be waiting on the porch, squatting down with her arms open wide.

But the new house is not like that. We go down a long dirt road. Through lots of brush, no big trees, just brush. Blackberries, stickery things. And the house is just plain boards on the outside. It isn't painted. And the yard is really messy and dry. The house inside is just boards, but Mother and Daddy say they will fix it pretty. I'm so disappointed. I thought it would be like Gramma's. And we have to use an outhouse because there isn't any water.

Daddy says there is five acres, and he is going to do lots of things with it. We are going to have a garden like Gramma and Grampa. And flowers in the yard. And he's going to dig up the stumps, and we can have pigs and cows.

Mother isn't too happy to hear all this, but she's happy to have our own home.

There are three bedrooms and a bathroom with a tub and sink and toilet. We just can't use them because there is no water. And a back porch that Mother has an old ringer washer in. There is a well right in back of the house, but most of the time, it's dry. Beside that is a big shed we use for a cellar.

I have my own room for a time with an old army cot, and the boys have bunk beds Daddy made out of canvas and two-by-fours and nailed them to the wall.

He put up drywall in all the rooms with Grampa helping him. He planted corn, bought pigs and some drop calves, and started hauling scrap metal to pay for all of this.

He just kept piling up "stuff" in a big pile. Old cars sat around the property that needed repair, and so we played in them.

The pigs would get out, and Mother and the boys and I would have to chase them back to the pen. She screamed and hollered, and I'm sure it drove her crazy.

Daddy would sometimes have horses there he had to break.

And clear land he did. He would plant dynamite under the stump of the tree he cut down, light it, and we would all run for cover. One time it landed on the roof of the house and, boy, was Mother mad.

We always had funny animals. The bull used to eat all the wiring off of the truck, the puppies my brother dropped down the well to see if they could swim. Poor Mother, hanging over an eighteen-foot well, fishing little puppies out with an old fishing net. Calves that needed to be fed by hand because they were not yet weaned and could be had for little or nothing, and we needed the meat. Horse meat was available and so we ate it, but beef was preferable, and so we raised our own. Daddy used to tie them up short to the back of the truck and say, "Go to the house now" to us children (of course we never really did), shoot it in the head with a .22, and then butcher it.

We couldn't eat the meat for months, even if it was served.

On Saturdays, Daddy would take the truck and go get big milk cans of water that would have to last the rest of the week. We would put a big washtub in the middle of the kitchen floor, and we would all take our weekly bath, with the cleanest child being able to bathe first. It was my fervent goal to be the cleanest at the end of the week. The thought of having to sit in someone else's dirty water was more than I could bear. Mother would have to heat the water on the stove and would pour it in slowly over your hair and body.

I would wash the dishes at night, and with the dirty dishwater, wash the kitchen floor, whenever it got washed, which was infrequently. I vowed I would live differently. If cleanliness was next to godliness, as I was told often by my great-aunt, then surely, we were living in sin.

There were neighbors about a mile away that were much dirtier than we, but that only made matters worse for me.

It must have been so hard on Mother to live like this, as she was the only girl and the only granddaughter in very large family.

She was given to having headaches and all sorts of maladies. It seemed to me, she was constantly pregnant and would spend days in bed or simply reading.

Housework was never important to her, or she never had time, so I was assigned most of those duties.

I weeded the flowerbeds and cleaned the house. I made lists to facilitate my abilities to get all these things done.

I was absolutely in awe of God's greatness as I looked at a bearded iris and thought of the intricacies of its very being. The subtle changes in the colors, the ripple of its petals, the way the little beard always stood straight up. And I was so thrilled when, with weeding and water, they were even more beautiful. We had one red rosebush, and the fragrance was beyond belief. So remarkably beautiful. The petals, soft and supple. What kind of creator could do all these things and keep them in order, each and every thing? The day and night, the spring, summer, fall, and winter. The perfection of even the little bugs. The corn. Gramma said that for every piece of silk on an ear of corn, there would be a kernel of corn. What a miraculous thing that was. I think it took more than six days to make all of this, or it was perfect planning. No one, not even God, could do so well in six days, and I am only ten, and think of the things I don't know. But I read about Plato and Socrates, and they seem to have it pretty well figured out. If I could talk to anyone in the world, it would be them, and Christ. They would know all about God.

Most Sundays, we go to one of the grandparents. Daddy's mother is really tall, with great big bosoms. And such pretty, happy eyes. Daddy has eyes like hers. And she has beautiful hands with long, tapered fingers and pretty fingernails. Her hair is long and gray, and she wears it braided and all wrapped around her head. They have a big farm, and there are always lots of people and lots of food. She bakes all the time, and when you wash the dishes, you just set the table again. She says this saves time. She really loves us, you can tell. Grandpa is a great, tall man that always has a suit on with a white shirt and tie. He works away as a boss of a mill. And Grandma takes care of the farm. Her house has lots of rooms, but the kitchen is the first thing you come to, and it is very large, and everyone just stays there.

But most of the time, we go to Gramma's on Sundays and on Christmas.

I have to walk about half a mile to the school bus stop each day. One day, one of the neighbor boys threw a snake at me and called me four eyes (I have to wear glasses; it's from reading so much, Mother says.), and the snake slid down inside my coat, and I was screaming and running, and Mother had to get it out. Mostly I don't think she likes me very much, because nothing I do is right, and she screams at me all the time. But I would have been afraid to get the snake off me; by then, it was in my clothes, but she reached down inside my blouse and got it out. I hugged her, and sobbed for a long time. I was so frightened.

I have lots of friends at school and go to their houses often to spend the night and sometimes the weekend. Mother doesn't seem to care, but they don't come here. I don't know why.

Janet wears a bra, and all the boys tease her. But I wish I could wear a bra. You can see "them" through my sweaters, and it is embarrassing. But Mother says, "You need a bra like you need another hole in your head. I'll tell you when you need a bra."

I was glad to get my glasses; I was so surprised to find that the leaves on the trees were separate on the tree. Not just when they fell on the ground. And the road had little pebbles of rock and wasn't just a gray mass. More important, I can see the blackboard at school; I had been missing *so* much.

Sometimes I go to Donna's house. I really like it there. Everything is so orderly. The house is big and finished and clean, and the yard is mowed. And they have dinner every night. And they say grace before dinner and breakfast. And go to church every Sunday. They are Catholic, and Grampa says that is an awful thing. But it seems good to me. I like to go to church, and besides, he doesn't like "spooks" or Indians or Japanese. And he always laughed at me if I fell down or got hurt. So I don't think I'll listen to him.

Years later, he would tell me that he was a member of the Ku Klux Klan. I was appalled and asked him why in the world he would do such a thing. He said, "You don't understand, times were different then, it was the thing to do." He always scared me, and actually I think now, he had no intention of doing so. He was a short, stocky man, and I used to try to imagine what he looked like when he was young. He was bald, with a fringe of white hair that Gramma cut for him. He had dazzling, big blue eyes and a look of mischief in them—intelligent eyes; he sort of rolled when he walked, perhaps because he was so bowlegged. Never very ambitious, he was a salesman, a carpenter, and an accountant.

Daddy says I'm old enough to babysit, *and I can keep the money*.

I can buy clothes. My shoes are always dirty and old, and my socks keep sliding down in my shoes. I hate that, and I only have three outfits to wear to school, and I make a list so I don't wear the same thing twice. It would be wonderful to have my own money.

The details are foggy, but the first person I babysat for died.

Her parents went to a party, and so I stayed with the children. I fed them dinner, and they went to bed; the little girl had on a big, flowing flannel nightgown. About two in the morning, they came home, and then took me home.

She got up and was standing in front of the woodstove. Her nightgown caught on fire, and she had third-degree burns all over her body. She died two days later. It certainly wasn't my fault, but how I grieved for that poor little girl and her mother. Her mother just cried all the time.

Little did I know I would one day know what that feels like.

10

I wasn't going to tell you this, but I feel I must.

I'm lying on the bed with Deborah. *She sort of my cousin.* We are looking at movie magazine, and doing other things I never do at home. She is very grown-up. I came home with them from Gramma's last night, and it is the first time I've ever spent the night with her. We are having a good time.

All of a sudden, standing at her bedroom door is my uncle. He isn't wearing any clothes. I don't know what to do—should I run and hide? Should I cover my head?

I just look down at the magazine and try to ignore the fact that he is there.

"Get ready if you want me to take you girls to the show," he says.

"Okay," Deborah says.

He turns and leaves the room.

"Oh," I say to Debby, "why did he do that? I am so embarrassed I could die."

"Oh, he does that all the time," she says. "Doesn't your father?"

"No," I say. "Never."

We have something to eat, although I am so upset that I can hardly eat.

He says, "Come on, girls, get in the car."

I start to get in the back with Deb. And he says, "No, Cara, you get up front with me. Company always gets to ride in front."

"I'm frightened to ride up there with him," I whisper to Deb.

She rolls her eyes. "That's silly," she said. "Besides, he'll be mad if you don't."

He's around on the other side of the car now, holding the door open for me to get in.

We drive to the theater, and he pulls up in front and stops the car.

"Deb, go stand in the line and see what time the show is over so I know when to pick you up."

She opens her car door, and I start to open mine.

"No," he says, "Cara, you stay with me. She'll be right back."

I close the door. And he pulls me over to him. He smells of whiskey. And sweat. He puts his arm around me and pulls me so close to him I can't move. He puts his other hand up my sweater and is pinching my nipples and squeezing my breasts.

I am crying; all I can do is cry and whimper, "No, no, no."

Now his hand is inside my panties, and he has his finger in my bottom.

I am perfectly rigid with fear. Praying, *God, please don't let this be happening to me. Please make him stop.*

He's whispering nasty things to me and telling me never to tell anyone or they will just think I am a bad girl.

Finally, after perhaps fifteen minutes, the longest of my life, Debby comes back. I jerk away from him, and he leers at me and licks his finger.

I want to throw up. I just want to go home. Now! Now!

I am crying, and Debby says, "What's the matter?"

I tell her; I tell her nearly all of it.

She puts her arm around me and says, "I know, he does that to me all the time."

"Have you told your mother?" I say.

She says, "Yes, I've told her, but she says I'm making it up. She thinks it's because I don't like him and want to go back to my father's."

"Well, I am going to tell my mother, and I am going to tell Gramma. She will make him stop doing that. She is his mother."

I barely slept at all that night. And when I got back to Gramma's, I told her and Mother what had happened.

"What a horrible thing to say about someone," Gramma said. "Nice little girls don't talk like that. You should have your mouth washed out with soap."

"But its true, Gramma! Mother, don't you believe me?"

"I don't know what to believe," she said. "You've always had a very vivid imagination."

"No, Mother, it's the truth. And Debby says he does it to her all the time. We have to do something."

"Sometimes, things are what they are, and are better left unsaid," said Gramma.

So at eight years of age, I learned that men are untouchable, and women are pretty much powerless against them.

The most important rules are left unspoken. Is it out of fear, or is it lack of understanding?

Understanding that the fear and powerlessness even exists, I am not certain that women even realize that they live in fear of men.

Is it a "boiled frog" theory—it is said that you can put a frog in a deep pan of cool water and slowly turn the heat up until you boil the frog to death. He never makes an attempt to leap out of the pan.

Stupid women—where would men be without them?

So over hundreds, maybe thousands of years, women have let it become ingrained in their very being that, that is the way life is.

Men provided financial security, physical safety, and social acceptability, and were therefore beyond the rules of proper etiquette.

Years later, I would read that it was common practice in many European countries, in and before the eighteenth century, for the male members of a family to "indoctrinate" the females of the families, until they "came of age" or began their menstrual cycle, thinking that they would make better wives if they were schooled in the art of lovemaking.

Did that make it right? I thought not.

Yet my life went on.

We went camping and had family picnics. We went to the ocean and played in the water. We went to the lake, and I learned to swim. But never very adeptly. We dug for clams and ate salmon and bread and salad, with strawberry shortcake for dinner. Afterward, we would always play cards or games.

Mother and Daddy went to parties and had parties. They had a wide circle of friends and family, and everyone was in the same financial and family circumstances.

The war was over, and once again, America was the land of opportunity.

Optimism was higher than it had been in nearly twenty years. This generation had survived the Great Depression and two world wars. Hitler was dead, or so they thought. The stock market was rebounding. American Savings Bonds were a sure bet. There were jobs to be had.

The women of America had entered the job market during the Second World War and found they could juggle the jobs of child rearing and housekeeping, and supplement the family income.

Industry that had once provided only machinery and equipment for war now made washing machines and automobiles again.

Airplanes that once carried troops to foreign countries for destruction now carried whole families to visit and to "vacation"— a new word in the vocabulary of a war-torn world.

Telephones and televisions became something that every family had access to. What was happening in the world was made available to anyone interested and not dependent on the static-filled radio or what the neighbors "heard."

People were learning again how to play and be happy. To dance and to sing.

And Mother wanted all of that. She wanted to go to California. To bathe in the land of milk and honey. She wanted an automobile that was beautiful. And to see something beyond this land of "Paul Bunyan."

She wanted to see the world and all it offered.

High society, perhaps she would not attain. But she was well equipped to do so.

As a young woman of seventeen or so, she was sent to live in servitude, as her mother had done before her, to help care for the children of women who were of a higher society to prepare their meals, and set their tables, to wash their linens and fine things.

Exposure to these things left her well-equipped to entertain with a knowledge and flourish that was without question what she was born to do.

So it was on a daily basis, I was instructed as to what was proper and improper for a "lady" to do and say. How to set a table. How to plan a menu. Which side of the person to serve from. That the very presentation of the meal was of primary importance.

When in doubt, wear black—it was elegant, stylish, and always acceptable. And never, never, wear white after Labor Day.

I took all of these things very seriously and was a fine student of all these womanly attributes.

I could cook, clean, and set a beautiful table.

Gramma taught me to garden, to can vegetables, and fruits. And to make beautiful bouquets of flowers for the table, as fresh flowers were something necessary to the inviting atmosphere of any home.

Gramma would decide something looked shabby, and off we would go to the general store. To buy paint, to paint the cabinet. Or fabric to make new curtains. And, if she needed a new shelf for something, and Grandpa wasn't quick enough to build it, out we would go to the shop, and Gramma would saw and nail and build the shelf herself.

Being of a very esoteric and intuitive nature, I readily identified the wealth and results of all of these subtle nuances.

Play was something you did after your work was done, and it simply never seemed to be done.

I believe you must learn to play, to be given permission to do so. Many activities you engage in during your lifetime are enjoyable, but to enjoy yourself and not be productive is something learned. It is your God-given right to enjoy the life God has given you. I never learned as a child and as an adult it has been a difficult transition.

To be productive is my goal in life, and there is nothing productive about the pursuit of happiness. The message was loud and clear.

Loud and clear also was the fact that I was pretty much on my own when not under the wing of my dear grandmother.

Daddy could do little to protect me and his profound love for my mother outweighed any and all interference in her behavior toward me.

11

I cannot bear the screaming the belittling, not one moment longer. She has been screaming at me since…since…"Please stop, Mother. Please stop," I cried, as I sat huddled on the bed, hands over my ears.

"Who do you think you are?" she screamed. "I can't stand your sullenness—you will do as you are told!"

"But, Mother," I said, "I have cleaned the house and done everything you wanted."

"It's not good enough. There are spots on the windows."

I run from the bedroom. I don't know what to do, and Daddy is gone. I run out the back door. It's cold and snowing out. Where will I go? I see the cellar and run in and lock myself in.

She's outside. Screaming again for me to come out. She has been screaming at me all day, and I have had to wash all the floors and dust all the furniture and change all the beds and do the laundry, and I am afraid of the wringer.

"I won't," I tell her. "I won't until Daddy comes home."

Finally, she's gone, no longer screaming and pounding on the door.

The cellar is dark; it smells bad, musty, and damp. There is only one light, and I am too little to reach it. I can hear the rats scurrying around, and they are making little squeaking noises.

There are shelves with jars of food, and sacks of potatoes on the floor. The tears stream down my face as my body is racked with sobs.

I huddle in the corner between the sacks of potatoes.

The terror creeps over me like a cloud over a summer day. I shall die in here. I shall never survive the fear of this dank, dark place. But I cannot go back in there. I can't. I have made her madder now than she was before. I try so hard to please her; I don't know why she doesn't like me. Sometimes she yells at the other kids, but mostly it's me.

What if Daddy never comes home? She yells at him, too; I wouldn't come home if I were him.

Lord, please take me to heaven now if Daddy isn't coming home.

Hours go by, and I can't seem to quit crying. And as the hours go by, I become more and more afraid to go out. Now I can never go out. I'm hungry, and there is nothing to eat. Food all around me, and I'm afraid to eat it, as I know that will just make her madder.

I can see through the cracks in the walls, and it is dark now.

Oh, please God, let my daddy come home. I don't want to stay in here any longer, and I don't want to die alone, or when I am only ten.

I hear the sound of a truck. Daddy's home, and now I'm crying harder. What if Daddy's mad at me too? I didn't mean to be bad; I don't even know what I did wrong.

There's a knock at the door.

"Caralee, it's your dad. Can I come in?"

I say nothing. All I can do is sob, great heaving sobs, of fear, of relief.

"Cara, please open the door. She's not mad at you anymore. Let me come in. It will be all right."

"She hates me, Daddy. I can't come out."

"Open the door for me, Cara. I love you, and it will be all right."

I go to the door and pry it open. In the moonlight, I can see my daddy's face, and he too is crying.

"I'm so sorry," he says. "I am so very sorry," as he takes me in his arms. My whole body is racked with sobs, as he holds me to him, stroking my hair and saying, "It's all right, baby, it's all right. Tell me what happened."

Through great sobs, I tell him. "I am bleeding, Daddy, I am going to die. And Mother just started screaming at me, and I was so scared I couldn't hear her. I kept telling her to stop, but she wouldn't. She said I was being ridiculous. To clean the house and never to go near boys again. I don't know what that means, Daddy, and the bleeding won't stop. She hates me, and I am going to die."

"Shhh, shhh, don't cry anymore. You have just become a woman. It happens to all women, and your mother just didn't know what to do or say. You are too young, but sometimes, it does happen that way. And it is nothing to be ashamed of."

"She said I was dirty. She hates me."

"She didn't mean that. She has a hard time saying what she feels sometimes. But she didn't mean that."

"She's not mad at me anymore?"

"No, she's not mad anymore."

"But she doesn't love me, Daddy."

"She does, Cara, she just has a hard time showing it. I think she doesn't love me sometimes, too. But she does."

As his gentle hands dried my eyes and wiped my tears, he said, "Try to understand her, she doesn't always mean what she says.

"Come now, let's get you washed up and have some dinner. She saved you dinner, and you can eat with me."

12

When I was in the fourth grade, I told my teacher I thought my standards were too high. Miss. Kenny said, "Never, ever lower your standards for anyone."

In the fifth grade, I received the most prestigious of all honors, at least I thought so—most likely to succeed. And I got a little gold pin that said just that. Mr. Morris was my teacher, and it was based on my skill in dealing with my fellow students and my scholastic ability. Wow! I was happy at school and with my friends.

By the time I was twelve years old, I could perform any household task with the ease generally given a woman of thirty or forty years. I wanted to please, to be accepted, to be loved.

I wake in the middle of the night. I can hear her screaming at Daddy. "I'm sick and tired of this. You said we could go. I hate your family, I hate the way we have to live. I won't put up with it a minute longer. You do something now!"

I'm so frightened. I can hear Peter sniffling in the next room. I sometimes think he is more frightened of her than I am. She seems to take turns as to who she is mad at. Is that possible? I am secretly relieved when I hear her screaming at him, as I know I am safe for the time being.

Daddy's telling her, "Be still, you'll wake the kids."

"I don't care" is her reply. "I want this done."

What does she want done? I wonder. I'm frightened. Maybe she wants us gone. We are a whole lot of trouble to her. I hope she leaves us with Gramma if she is going to give us away. This is the third time in as many weeks that we have awakened in the night to their fighting.

It frightens me beyond words, and in the morning, I'm afraid to look at her. What is she going to do?

Daddy looks tired in the morning.

He has two jobs and is gone all the time. I really miss him.

Today, a nice man and lady came, and Daddy brought them in the house. They said they wanted to buy the house and would move in, in two weeks.

I can't believe my ears. She is going to just leave us here with strangers. Why would she do that? Is Daddy going with her?

The people leave, saying they "will return next week."

I run, sobbing, to my father.

"Daddy, are you and Mother going to leave? Where will we go?"

"No, we wouldn't leave you, you know better than that. Didn't your mother tell you? We are going to move to California."

I look at Mother's face. She is happy, smug, smiling. She has won.

There is a beautiful red and white station wagon in the front yard. Mother and Daddy say it is ours. And we are going to drive to California in it.

I can't believe this is happening. How can this be happening? What about my friends, my school, Gramma? I can't go, I won't go. How can they do this to me?

I run to go outside, the fear gripping me as the bile rises in my throat. I vomit on the grass outside, wrenching my body with each convulsion of my fear.

God, I cry out, what can I do? How can you send me so far away from Gramma, to be alone with Mother? I'll never survive. How can you do this to me? Please help me, Lord, I whisper to the silent evening light.

I am kneeling in the back seat and looking out the back window of the beautiful red and white car, and I see the snow-capped mountains, of such majestic beauty, the sun leaving shimmering gold highlights cascading over them. The ancient, emerald green forest towering above us as their arms sway in the gentle breeze of the soft wind.

The crystal-clear beauty of the midnight blue water of the sound glistens as the sun touches the snowy white caps of the small, gentle waves. This gentle green and blue world, gone forever. How can she have done this?

I turn to sit in the seat as a single tear gently rolls down my cheek. My life is over. Defeat is imminent. I apologize to you, Lord, I beg your forgiveness.

I cannot go away from everything I am familiar with, all the people I love. What will become of me? What will become of the hopes and dreams I had?

The large white house with the pasture laying green, and clean around and in front of it. The beautiful dairy cattle grazing there. The six children I plan to raise, to love, and to cherish. To surround them in love and security. That is all I ever wanted, to be a mother. I have no desire to be rich and famous, only to love and be loved, to be a good wife and mother. I will never, never scream at my children or my husband. I will always do the right thing. Lord, I promise.

We travel for days, it seems, and the forests give way to golden, rolling hills, with a sky so big and blue, and the sunlight is intense. There are massive old oak trees, and the golden grasses blow in the gentle breezes. I never imagined a world so different could exist.

The heat is oppressive, and we stop to fill small pans with ice to place on the floor of the car. But the heat is so intense that the ice melts almost immediately.

Mother and Daddy buy bread and bologna and cheese, and we stop in parks to eat lunch and dinner. And in the mornings, we go to restaurants for breakfast. I don't think I have ever been in a restaurant before. It's really quite exciting.

We sing songs. Old songs and popular songs of the day. Mother has a very nice voice and is so happy to finally be going to California. All her prayers have been answered, if in fact she does pray.

I ask her if she prays, and she says, "What a question to ask. Shame on you."

I don't say anything more about it.

I liked to go to Sunday school with the people down the street. But it really scared me. They talked about the trials and tribulations of the second coming and the anti-Christ. They said that he would be marked with the sign of 666, and that there would be terrible famine and pestilence. That you would be made to take the mark of the beast, or you couldn't have food, clothing, or anything, no house to live in, no work to do. The only way to salvation was to pray to God for forgiveness. And hope he takes you to heaven. I decided it would be better to die than to take the mark of the beast and live in eternal damnation. Besides, I don't think you really die; I just think you change form. You know, like maybe become an angel of the Lord.

I know it's really childish, but will the Lord be able to find me all the way in California? I would ask Mother, but she doesn't want to talk about that, I guess.

We are on a small road, which seems to wander aimlessly through the smooth, golden hills. I wonder if we are lost, but Daddy knows how to go there, he says.

But it is taking so many days. And it is so very hot. How do people live in such heat? You see cows and horses grazing on the scrubby grass. And I wonder if they get enough to eat, but they are really big, so I guess they do.

We pass through an enormous city. A city the size of which I have never seen. And lots of roads they call freeways. Daddy says this is Los Angeles. The houses are colored blue and pink and beige. Strange to have houses that color. And the trees are very tall, with large tassels on the top; they call them palm trees, and they have bananas and coconuts in them.

Outside of Los Angeles, there are miles and miles of orange and lemon groves, and the fragrance is absolutely the most wonderful thing I have ever smelled. The leaves on the trees are shiny and thick, and the little balls of orange and yellow are beyond compare. There are big trenches filled with water to water the trees, and I wonder where they get all this water, as I have seen no rivers and no lakes.

What a wondrous adventure; every sense alive with the sights and smells, thousands of cars and people, and all the colorful houses they live in. Truly a foreign land.

As the orange and lemon groves disappear in the distance, something even more exciting comes into view.

Never have I seen anything so beautiful. The Pacific Ocean. With its billowy white foaming waves beating against majestic rocks, larger than any I've ever seen. Palm trees blowing in the wind against the magnificent azure blue of the water. The soft gold of the sandy beach, stretching forever along the rocky coastline.

I can smell the brine of the sea, and forever will remember the depths of emotion I felt at these new and immovable treasures.

I was going to be all right. Gramma said, "God didn't give you anything you couldn't handle, and when he closed one door, another one opened."

The handle had been turned, and the door had opened. Beauty was everywhere in the world. And this was my new world.

In that one moment I felt free and grown-up. I would be able to do this. I would.

Maybe Mother was right all along. This was a new and exciting adventure. The "land of milk and honey," the big billboards said. And I could see and smell the truth in them.

We are finally there. La Mesa, California, certainly not by the ocean, and hot and ugly, except for the orange and lemon groves. But as we pull up in front of a pretty, white Spanish-style house, Daddy says this is it. I am so excited I can barely be still. The house is big and clean. With shiny, soft, yellowish brown wood floors, with paint on the walls, and pretty arched doorways leading to each of the many rooms. There is a bedroom for the girls, and one for the boys, and Mother and Daddy have a real big bedroom.

There was a room like Gramma had, that you only ate in, a real dining room. And the living room is big, and the sunlight flows in through the beautiful big windows. I like the floors best, I think. The kitchen is clean and has a modern stove and a real refrigerator, one that doesn't need ice. The bathroom has a tub, shower, a sink, and a toilet that really has water. I flush it tons of times. What miraculous things.

"Mother, are we going to run out of water here too?"

"No," she says. "There is city water here."

Running water all the time, it is really the most wonderful thing. Everything around us, as you peer over the tops of all the houses set in rows, is barren hills, no trees, no lakes, no rivers or mountains. Just a rolling sea of brown scrubby brush. But here, we have water and an indoor bathroom.

I can go barefoot all the time and only have to wear shorts and a little top. There is freedom in not having to wear so many clothes.

And having water is the most important thing in life, I decide.

The yard is all green, and the landlord said we couldn't walk on it.

"It's dichondra," he says. "And they'll kill it if you let those kids play on it." He was an old man, bald with a fringe of hair. It looked as if his head had just grown right through his hair. As he raised his right thumb to press on the right side of his nose and blew hard, making snot fly out onto the lawn.

Oh yuck, I didn't like him.

Well, neither did Mother.

We lived there throughout the summer, but it wasn't long before I heard she and Daddy talking about moving again.

Fear again, rigid fear, seeping throughout my body. Not again, I just couldn't move again. Peter and I decide this will be our lives: moving all the time, looking for someplace that Mother will be happy. The search was on. Where would we live? Would we go back to Washington? Would we move to the ocean? It seemed there was more money. How else could we afford all this water?

But when they would come back from looking for a place to live, Mother would always say everything was too expensive. I continued to clean and babysit my brothers and sister. And plan for the daunting experience of going to a new school and meeting new friends.

We move several more times over the ensuing months, but nothing Mother can be happy with. Each time, there is something or someone that makes her unhappy.

Finally, in the fall of my thirteenth year, we move to a house nearer the ocean in San Diego that is ours.

"We bought it," Mother tells us. "It's small, but will do nicely."

It is small. Only about nine hundred square feet for eight of us. But there is water and a nice bathroom. The floors are tiled, beige squares of tile all throughout the house. There are three bedrooms, a living room, and a kitchen with an area to eat at the end of it. With high windows in the bedrooms that you can't see out of, unless you stand on the bed, and that is, of course forbidden. There is a small yard with plants native to the area. I didn't know the names of any of them. Maybe Gramma would come and tell me. The streets were lined with houses that all looked the same. Some turquoise, some beige, some green and gray, but essentially all the same little cracker-box houses.

Gramma and Grampa do come, and life is wonderful for me. The house is clean, and when we come home from school, there are cookies baked, and the laundry is off the clotheslines and all folded. And she changed the sheets on all the beds. Mother only washed them if you took them to her, and not too often. Sometimes the sheets on the beds in the boys' room were brown, they'd have been on for so long, and colored sheets were yet to come.

Gramma would say, "Now when you get a home of your own, it's important to keep your bedding clean. You will be healthier if you are clean."

"Did you tell Mama that?" I'd ask.

"Yes, I did," she said. "But sometimes children want to live their own life, and don't wish to live their parent's life."

"Boy, I don't wish to live my Mama's life," I tell Gramma.

She laughs and hugs me. I think Gramma misses us as much as we miss her.

But the house is small, and with ten of us, now the boys have to sleep in the garage. The garage has no windows, and the walls show the boards, the floor is only cement, and is cracked and smells musty. I was glad I wasn't a boy.

We started school in the fall. To say it was frightening is an understatement. To get there, we had to walk about a mile and a half, on busy streets lined with house after house, tall slender palm trees swaying in the gentle ocean breezes, with oleander bushes in vibrant reds and purples and whites filling the four-lane highway divider, and the cars just flying by. The smells of the balmy salt air created a peaceful feeling, but I was overwhelmed by the noise and the busyness. People all around, and they looked different, to be sure.

We were country bumpkins, to put it mildly. Our clothing was different, our general bearing was one lacking in self-confidence. And everything was intimidating to us. We were familiar with gravel and dirt roads, country lanes, and outhouses.

The girls were prettier than I was, with beautiful clothing and clean, polished shoes. Many of them even wore makeup and had chic little haircuts. And in gym class, we had to take off all our clothing and shower with everyone looking. They shaved their legs and underarms and had pretty underwear with lace and ribbons on them.

I just wanted to go home.

And if I couldn't go home, then I desperately wanted to belong.

Meanwhile, at home, Mother was having coffee with neighbors. Gramma and Grampa had gone back home to peaceful familiarity. Mother and Daddy had met couples through Daddy's work and in the neighborhood and had picked up where they left off. Their life seemed to be the same. They partied and had company over and went to other couples' houses.

And it was warm and sunny every day. Mother loved it. She was happier, and so life was better for all of us.

Daddy wore a suit with a white shirt and tie every day. No more logging trucks, scrap metal, or breaking horses to get by. No more baths in dirty water or in the washtub.

No more long, cold winters or snow.

Was he happy and contented?

Daddy wanted Mother to be happy and deemed it his duty and goal in life to accomplish just that. If Mother was happy, life would be better.

Every blue moon, he would drink too much, and boy, would she be mad. He was not to swear, drink, or smoke. Not because she had a specific reason, she just didn't think it was conducive to a respectable life.

I tried to be happy. After all, what alternative was there?

I tried infiltrating the camp of girls at recess, but they seemed to be divided into three divisions of hierarchy. There were the dorks—generally homely girls, fat, slovenly, or just plain quiet and shy, bookwormy, and belonging in the band.

Or, there were the *bad* girls. They wore lots of makeup. Wild clothing, smoked, generally did not give a hoot about school or their grades and were reputed to be loose with the boys. Now, mind you, I had no idea what "loose" implied, but I was certain it wasn't good.

Then there was the society crowd—they were generally from upper-crust families, wore very nice clothes (clothing being the tantamount deciding factor among the youth of our time), wore makeup, but with taste, had nice hair cuts, and were generally very attractive, in the case of Inga and Eva, downright gorgeous, and also got good grades in school. Of course, these girls were the cream of the crop as far as boys went, as they had the power.

It was *Grease* in reality.

Who did I want to be? A society girl, to be sure. I was smart, but sometimes that was a bad thing too. I took stock of my wardrobe and my looks. I was redheaded, with thin, fine, frog hair, freckled face, one eyebrow, no eyelashes, glasses, and my face was just plain boney, with a jutting chin and prominent cheekbones. I had a nice nose (which probably didn't account for much in the way of acceptance), and my eyes were a pretty color, a deep turquoise blue, and almond shaped, but it didn't look very promising. And my clothes were just not "hep."

So I joined the band and played the clarinet. Oh, was I bad. The dorks weren't so bad. I liked them. And they liked me. I got good grades and made a few friends.

I was not miserable but close. Gramma had left, and so I would come home from school, and Mother would be in the reclining chair they had bought, reading and watching the new invention called a television, still in her nightgown and robe, exactly as I had left her early that morning.

I would have to vacuum and clean up the breakfast dishes, bring in the laundry, and fold it. And help with dinner.

We older children shared in the washing of the dinner dishes, and because we fought, we had to hold water in our mouths. And dare not swallow it. We'd punch each other, then laugh and invariably spit out the water, which of course we had to clean up—leaving that the only clean spot on the kitchen floor, always.

Then the most exciting thing happened. I got a letter from Debby, and she said her parents said she could come and stay with us in the summer. I begged and pleaded, and Mother said yes.

What a summer! She probably fell into the *bad* girl category. But remembering what she had endured as a very little girl, I was not surprised.

We went to the little shopping area every day and talked to boys in cars, bought watermelons and went to the city shopping, all with my mother's consent.

She was having as good a time as we were. She took us to the beach every day, after we cleaned the house and did everything she wanted done.

We shopped for sexy bathing suits. Mine was a black one piece, and it looked stunning, Debby said. She showed me how to wear makeup, and we each plucked our one eyebrow to two exquisite arches over our now heavily-mascaraed eyes. We both had our hair cut in DA's and we now "rode" with boys in cars. Deb was fearless. Wild and carefree. Really, what else could happen to her?

The boys would drop us off at home and come and pick us up. Deb would sit on their laps in the car and wiggle around and wink at me. I never got it. I was entirely certain that Mother would have a fit, but she never said anything.

Deb thinks we really need to meet some "real men."

She has an idea—we can go to San Diego.

"This is a sailor town, isn't it?" she says. "Just tell them you're eighteen. You look eighteen."

She was right. In one afternoon, we had dates that night. Two sailors. Wally and Johnny. Wally was very tall, over six feet. Thin, with no shoulders, and kind of straight up and down. A soft-looking face, like he was very shy. Dark brown eyes that were framed by my old eyebrow. Heavy lips, and the biggest hands and feet I had ever seen.

Johnny was short. Shorter than me, but with nice broad shoulders and a narrow little waist and hips. The most beautiful blue eyes and the happiest smile. Blonde, with almost movie-star good looks. Both of them had short, short hair as deemed regulation by the Navy, and they of, course, wore navy whites.

"You get Johnny," she said.

Now I was fearless as well. And it seemed Mother didn't mind at all; she just wanted to know all about it. Seems I wasn't the only country bumpkin.

They, Mother and Daddy, even took us to a fancy nightclub in San Diego. We all had dinner and danced.

I had made a navy blue, linen shift with a draped neckline, bought high heels, and thought I was beautiful. Johnny thought so, too, and he was an older, experienced man. So it must be true.

I danced with Daddy that night, and he said, "Be careful, chicken, I don't think this is such a good idea. But your Mother seems to think it's fine. Just be careful."

Don Ameche, the actor, was there, and he came over and asked me to dance. Of course I said yes. Dancing was the most wonderful thing I had ever done.

We had a wonderful summer. We went water skiing, lay on the beach and got golden brown, the salty sea air softening all my anxieties and slowly formed a new life. This handsome man loved me, I was sure.

His parents had a big wheat farm in North Dakota, and I was sure he would take me home with him. I would have six children, and life would be close to what I had planned.

This was just a soft, foreign interlude to what my real life would again be.

He's kissing my forehead, my eyes, his hands touching my breasts, cupping them in his palm. His breath, hot and sweet, as his lips rest ever so close to mine. His voice, deep and husky with desire. "Cara, you must not ever do this. You are such a nice girl, you mustn't ever let anyone do this to you. Not without the promise of marriage."

"I don't care," I say. "I do love you, and we will get married. I know you will marry me."

"No," he said, as he pulled away from me, his arms outstretched, his hands holding each of my arms. "I won't. Debby told me how old you are. You're only thirteen years old, you have your whole life ahead of you, and I am going to war. You'll forget about me.

"Deb is wild, and will lead you down the wrong path. I know you are kinda lost, but this is not what you need right now."

"But I love you," I say through sobs, the tears flowing down my cheeks.

"You aren't ready to love anyone yet. You have to experience life yet. Finish school. You can do anything. You are smart, and you're a beautiful young lady. I would love to see you when you are all grown-up."

He kissed me softly on the forehead, reached up, and released my arms from around his neck. Turned and left me standing in the front yard.

Deb went home late that summer, and life picked up where it had stopped.

I started school that fall determined to be happy. Whatever that meant. Acceptance! I decided. Acceptance of whatever life had in store for me.

I would go on without Johnny. Obviously you won't die of a broken heart.

A new girl, Margie Grisome, was in my class that year, and we became fast friends. Her parents were old, and her brother had cystic fibrosis.

She, too, was pretty much alone. She was tall and thin, with the cutest upturned nose. With big, blue, happy eyes, and a smile that was pretty much constant. With a quick, easy, infectious laugh. She loved my family. Probably anyone's family, as hers was pretty stressful to say the least.

Mother had borrowed a sewing machine, and I had bought material with my babysitting money, and we made school clothes. And I bought two matching skirts and sweaters. "Dyed to match." One deep lapis blue. And the other emerald green. I looked really cool.

All of a sudden, I was "in" with the society crowd. Inga, Janet, Marilyn, Margie, and I were a team. We were nice girls, we got good grades. We didn't drink, smoke, or go all the way. Actually, we didn't date. After Johnny, I had no desire to expose myself to that again.

But we did go to occasional parties. And at one of those parties, I had my first real kiss. Maynard something, I can't remember his last name. We were just standing around talking, and he asked me to take a walk with him.

It was in front of someone's garage, and he kissed me. He wasn't anyone I was remotely interested in. Just a guy. Not even a very popular guy. But he kissed me. Deep and long. Soft and gentle. It was like the Fourth of July. An explosion of my senses. Felt to the very tips of my toes. A kiss to last a lifetime.

I never talked to him again.

13

We all went shopping, the gang and me. We went to pool parties and to the beach. There were lots of boys I had a crush on, and my mother always yelled that I was boy-crazy. Perhaps I was. All the girls I knew were too. It was the way things were. We were all crazy for boys; their approval was what made our world go 'round.

There was a boy named Jimmy Watts, and he was dark and swarthy, a bad boy to be sure. He smoked and had a car. Inga really liked him. But so did I. However, I knew if Inga liked him, he was all but lost to me. She was blond and beautiful. With dark perfect eyebrows and skin that was clear and golden. Her lashes, were so long they fluttered when she talked. And her family was rich. Rich beyond anything I could imagine. They lived in a big, beautiful house with a swimming pool, and her father was a doctor. I didn't stand a chance. I, with my glasses, and freckles and my red hair. A little mascara and two eyebrows weren't going to change a thing here.

Summer has come and gone. And with it, Deb. I now had two eyebrows arched to perfection, eyelashes made thick, dark and wispy, compliments of Maybelline. Accentuating the already-beautiful turquoise color of my eyes. And enhancing the strangely-almond shape. My haircut is fashionable. I now know I have long, beautiful legs, not like a colt as I have always heard. But like a woman, firm rounded hips, and a very tiny waist. And more importantly, I have breasts. Not enormous breasts, but they will grow, I'm sure. And gleaned from the earnings of my industrious babysitting and housecleaning and my ability to sew, I have four beautiful new outfits to wear.

Finally, success is attainable, acceptance is at hand. I can finally "be like everyone else."

All these many years later, I find this a strange and humorous preoccupation.

Having explored all the sects of pubescent society, I have accumulated many friends and acquaintances. The nerds, who are brilliant and devoted in their quest for success with their unequaled need to excel. If you wish to have position and riches in this world, marry a nerd, or be one.

The bad girls who smoke, wear sleazy clothing and go out with bad boys, and know that if you douche with a shaken-up Coca-Cola after sex, you won't get pregnant. Appalling to me and not very effective for them, as time pointed out. But the girls were really very nice, just tough. Usually from poor and ethnic groups whose parents didn't have the time or energy to supervise their many offspring.

But I was enamored of the girls who were well-spoken, well-mannered, and well-dressed. The society crowd and gradually the others fell by the wayside. Sad, but true.

There were a few cute guys who liked me. But only Jimmy Watts inspired me. But I wouldn't "put out," even though I really didn't have a clue as to what that meant. So he soon lost interest in me. As he really only had eyes for Inga.

But he had a friend, an older "man" that lived down the street from him that would occasionally grace our company. He was a senior in high school and had his own car. He was tall and thin, had strawberry blond, curly hair, and was a fine-boned beauty that reminded me of Ashley in *Gone with the Wind*. He was from Texas and had the most wonderful Texan accent and a funny little laugh, almost like a girl.

He thought I was beautiful and would come by after school and take me home. He smoked, and still my mother thought he was nice.

If I couldn't have Rhett, I would have Ashley. Unlike Scarlett, I would have preferred Rhett.

We went to parties and hung out with the crowd. We fought and made up.

And his other friends told me I was too nice for him. But I was in love. And true to form, blind.

Do we all wander so aimlessly looking for love and acceptance?

"Please take this ring," he said as he gave me the most beautiful diamond engagement ring. It had a large diamond in the center and two smaller ones on either side.

"I can't. My parents would never let me do this—I am only fourteen years old."

"But I love you and want to marry you, please, we'll keep it a secret."

So I put the ring on when he picked me up in the morning and took it off when he brought me home in the afternoon. I felt loved and grown-up.

Margie and Inga and Janet and Marilyn all thought I was crazy, but that didn't seem to have any effect on my decision to marry him. I wasn't going to do that any time soon, and this was fun.

Summer comes and goes again, and I spend as much time at the beach as I can. Rick hates the beach. It's dirty, and he is so fair he burns easily.

In the fall, school starts again. I really have no aspirations to aspire to, as all my sights are set on accomplishing one goal: I am going to marry and have children.

School is fun, though, I like the social aspect, and I have made the drill team. Wow! I love it. And as the weeks pass, I find I'm not so in love with the big, tall Texan. He has gotten kicked out of school and won't go to Delta, the "bad kids' school." And he says he doesn't want a job either. I don't like that. What kind of future is that for our children and me?

I'm giving his ring back, I decide angrily.

We fight, we make up. We don't hang out with the gang anymore. He just wants to be alone and make out. That's okay, but I miss the parties and the fun, and we fight more and more.

Each time it happens, he gets more insistent. "If you really loved me…" he says.

"I don't know," I tell him. "You have to go back to school or get a job."

"I will," he says. "I love you, and I'll take care of you."

My girlfriends are really against all of this. But, I just can't decide.

"There's a party tonight. Let's go," I tell him.

"No, I hate those parties, nothing but a bunch of stupid little kids."

"Well, I'm going," as I threw the ring at him. "And you can keep this."

I have on a white corduroy skirt, tight, with little slits on each side at the hemline, and a little white sweater, three-quarter-length sleeves, and a stand-up collar with a V-neck, and red flat ballerina shoes. I'm tan, and I feel almost as pretty as Inga. The party is fun; I'm so glad I came.

The music is loud, and there is lots of food, and I'm dancing a slow dance with a very handsome dark stranger. I did the right thing. I am glad I came with the crowd.

Someone is tapping me on the shoulder. I turn and look up, and there he is. Rick.

"Please, Cara, dance with me, I'm sorry," he says.

The tall, dark stranger drops my hand and moves away; Rick takes me into his arms.

"Please come and just talk to me," he says.

"No, you've been drinking."

"I'm fine, really, I'm fine. Just go for a little ride with me."

—⁓⁓∘⌒⊙⊙⌒∘⁓⁓—

Days fall into weeks. I am so sick, I can barely get out of bed in the morning.

I have PE first class, and I am so sick, all I can do is vomit.

Drill team is exhausting. Standing, marching for hours. Baseball. Running the bases. I love baseball, and I'm good at it, but I simply am too sick. I don't know what is the matter with me. I feel confused, frightened.

I do know what is the matter with me. Deep, deep down in the very recesses of who I am. I do know what is the matter with me.

On that night when he begged me to go with him in the car, "it" happened. It just happened. He wouldn't stop, and I couldn't make him stop. I tried, but he just wouldn't stop. And to make matters worse, I liked it. It was as if everything else in the world had no other meaning. Only this sensation, this feeling, this reality. Explosions of the senses as if it were the Fourth of July. In my mind and in my body. My mind and body, exhilarated and weakened all at the same time. Hot, steamy, sweating, flesh sliding across one another. Only knowing the moment. Only caring about the moment. All the novels I had read didn't do it justice. But truly how would you put "that" into words?

Words of love and commitment spilled from his lips as he consumed my body.

That night after he had taken me home, I stood in the shower scrubbing, scrubbing, praying to God that the guilt and shame would wash down the drain. Please, God, I beg. Forgive me. I will never see him again. I won't think of it again.

Mother has had to come and get me from school twice. But by afternoon, I am fine. She's angry and says I'm just trying to get out of school, but that is not it.

He calls; I won't talk to him. He comes over; I won't see him.

The sickness is worse, and weeks go by. The school nurse wants to see my mother.

It must be really bad. I'm going to die. But I really don't care.

Mother screams, "You're pregnant, aren't you? You are, aren't you, you dirty, dirty little girl."

"How can you think that?" I scream back at her. "How can you think that?"

"You had sex with him, didn't you?" she screams at me again. "That's why you won't see him or talk to him. I knew it." She's hysterical. Screaming, crying. "What will people think?"

I don't know what to do. It must have been sex. How can I say? I didn't know, when really I knew. Even though she hadn't ever told me, I knew. I knew from the girls at school. I knew, it was wrong. I knew I shouldn't do it.

Daddy's home now; the screaming has stopped, and I am clinging to him, and he is holding me, and I am sobbing, "There, there, chicken, it'll be all right."

I am so sorry I have disappointed him. "I don't know how it happened, Daddy, it just happened. I am sooo sorry. Please forgive me. I won't tell anyone, you don't have to."

"But you see, Cara, you're going have a baby. Everyone will know."

A sense of peace enveloped me, as the realization flowed through me.

A baby, a baby, I always wanted a baby. Lots of babies. I love little children.

My mother is screaming and crying, all at the same time. She slaps my face, hard, the sting and jolt of it a shock. "You little slut."

"I know what that means. It is not like that," I tell her.

Daddy is patting my mother's arm and telling her he will take care of it.

I barely hear as he tells me to go to my room. "We'll get someone to give you an abortion," he says.

I feel suddenly sick again. "No, no," I tell him. "No, you can't make me do this. I want this baby. You can't make me kill my baby."

Poor Daddy, Mother is screaming at him to "do something."

I am wailing and crying that "I won't...I can't do this thing."

A week went by with the terrible tension invading the house.

Finally he arrives home from work one night and tells me he has it all arranged. And the problem will be taken care of.

"No. No…" I sob. "I can't, Daddy. It's wrong, and I can't do it."

We were married on Christmas Eve. I was three and a half months pregnant and very, very ill.

We moved in with his parents, Vera and Amos. Within two months, he joined the air force, eventually going to Korea, where he would stay for nearly two years. His parents and my parents were wonderful.

Vera taught me to drive. Going the wrong way up off-ramps and bumping over the empty sand dunes surrounding San Diego's Miramar Naval Air Station.

When I was feeling unwell, Vera's solution was to go shopping, and I would sit in the potted palm trees, trying to get over the all-consuming nausea. Or cling to the escalator as it careened to the second floor of the department store, fighting for the overwhelming dizziness to subside.

Vera, laughing all the time, encouraging and accepting.

Mother would make me cornstarch pudding and cucumber sandwiches when I visited her. Amos would go to the closest restaurant and buy me shrimp cocktails. Those were about the only foods I could keep down.

Cigarettes and Coca-Cola would send me into the depths of vomiting.

I walked on the beach and planned for my perfect baby. I made pretty little outfits in pink, blue, yellow, green, and white. Everything had to match. This baby would have everything I could ever give it. Love, love, and more love. Clean, pretty clothing. Dance and piano lessons.

And I would tell her how pretty she was and read to her and take long walks with her.

How did I know it would be a girl? I simply knew. And her name would be Julia Marie or Samantha Jeanne, whichever one suited her best. And if by chance it were a boy, well, we would name him after his father.

Mother had a baby shower for me, and all my school friends came.

It was a nice shower, but I had crossed a threshold. One of the many I would cross in my lifetime.

From carefree youthfulness to adulthood, to parenthood. More than that, I was different again.

My friends one by one disappeared, and with them, my youth. In their place came worries about money and marriage.

I was alone again.

Rick was overwhelmed by the responsibility. He hated me, I was sure of it. He took the only way he could: out. He had joined the air force.

He hated boot camp, and in his letters to me, he said he was going to go AWOL. He spent time in the brig. Would he ever grow up? I was certain he would. But in the meantime, we needed money to live. Vera and Amos were wonderful to me. But I needed a place of my own to bring my child home to. There simply wasn't room where they lived.

By my seventh month, I was feeling much better and went to work as a dental assistant.

I still didn't have enough money to live on.

Mother and Daddy said I could come back home if I paid rent, and Mother would take care of the baby, and I could go back to work.

What I was going to do was beyond me; pregnant girls couldn't go to school so I would forever remain uneducated. I was devastated by this knowledge.

I made up my mind that I would go back to school as soon as all the children were in school. But one thing at a time, I thought.

The time just flew by, and I was so excited. A baby! It was more than I could ever want. I bought a used crib and dresser, sanded and painted it, and put little decals on it. It was perfect.

Mom and I washed and folded all the little clothes. Everything was so little and cute.

I wrote to Rick. Every night. I got only an occasional letter; he was excited about the baby as well and wanted to come home.

He promised to send money. But something always happened. A poker game. He paid for a party for everyone…it went on and on.

Finally, the big day is here. I am the mother of the most beautiful perfect little pink and white baby I have ever in my life seen. She has the softest, curliest, pinkish-red hair, and the biggest, bluest eyes I have ever seen. Her little hand closes around my finger, and I am more in love than I ever knew was possible.

The minute I saw her, she was Samantha Jeanne. She has a little bite out of her ear, and I think the angels in heaven must have loved her as much as I do because they bit a little earlobe. Just a tiny, tiny piece. They just couldn't help themselves.

She smelled like only a baby can. She had long little legs and perfect hands and feet. And the cutest little button of a nose. And her tiny little shoulder blades looked exactly like that is where her wings would go.

I have never been happier in my life. We could do this, and everything was going to be fine.

Her daddy sent her a silver baby cup. And granny and granddaddy showered her with love, attention, and gifts.

And her gramma and poppa, they just plain adored her. I think my mother loved her more than her own children.

She filled our house with love, crying, and dirty diapers. I had never been happier.

Now if only my husband would come home. Life would be perfect.

14

It is dark, and the road seems to be straight ahead and flat.

Texas appears to be a godforsaken country. There are no trees, no canyons.

No rivers, with the exception of the Rio Grande. Just dust and powdery sand that covers the windshield of the car in such profusion that I have to use the windshield wipers.

The inside of the car absolutely reeks of vomit. I've fed the baby green beans, and she has vomited all over. It issued forth like a rocket, filling every crevice in the automobile.

I stopped at a gas station and tried to clean us both up, but still, we are a mess.

I left at four this morning and have driven all day and into the night. The country is desolate, and I can't find a town to stop in for the rest of the night.

It enters my mind that I could be lost, but the map lies on the passenger seat, and I seem to be going in the right direction. East to Biloxi, Mississippi.

Will he be happy to see us? He doesn't seem to be too excited when I speak to him on the phone. I know he has to call from a phone booth, as they have no phones in the barracks, still…his letters are few and far between.

He says he has rented a place for us to live. So I am excited. Our first home together. Our beautiful baby girl. All pink and white. Her hair is even more pink than red. She's a good baby, now that the colic is over.

I stood in the shower and cried for the first six weeks of her life, nearly every night. I was so tired. Working and having a child was hard.

He's never seen her. His daughter. What a wonderful gift to give him. This beautiful child.

Will he like her? Will he hold her and talk to her? Like my daddy does.

I'm a little frightened. This probably isn't what he had in mind for his life.

I've decided that love is a state of mind and that you can love anyone who is good to you. And we have this beautiful child in common to love and care for. And as parents, that is our first responsibility.

Mother always said my father came first. I don't know. He is an adult. I think your first responsibility should be to your children; after all, they are the innocent party involved in all of this.

I stopped finally at midnight and slept for several hours in a fleabag motel just outside of Louisiana, bathed the baby, cleaned out the car, and took a shower. At least it no longer reeks of vomit, or perhaps I have simply gotten used to it.

Now the dirty diapers from the trunk are invading the inside of the car. He is so clean. And so fussy about this car, he'll most likely be mad.

His parents gave us this car for a wedding present. It is a black Plymouth, with grayish-blue interior, and the seats are cloth. With a baby, that's not good.

I again decide water is the most valuable resource of the earth.

It is seven in the morning, and the sun is up, and it is beautiful out. The sky is blue, and it is verdant green here with moss dripping from the trees, just like in the books.

I think, oh, Scarlett is finally back at Tara.

If Texas was deplete of the scenic, Louisiana is not. All around me are rivers, and the vegetation is lush and a resplendent green. There are riverboats, with men and boys standing in them with big poles.

Am I coming to the land of Tom Sawyer?

There are small storefronts with people sitting around in old, wooden rocking chairs, and the smell of the river is pungent.

A much better smell than the diapers.

We are coming close to Mississippi, and my heart is nearly jumping into my throat. With each mile I drive the fear mounts, *the cause of such fear*, I find I am unable to distinguish. It is the only thing to do, I decide. Get on with it. I must think of other things. Samantha has been so good. Such a good little baby.

Maybe I should get gas. I still have about fifteen dollars, and at twenty-five cents a gallon, I can fill up.

I do have some money hidden, as I am sure he will have none.

I shipped all the dishes and linen railway express. And I am so happy to finally be able to use my things.

As I traverse the Mississippi River I am so surprised that is just a regular-sized river…until I get just above New Orleans, and there I see why it is called the Great Mississippi. The water is muddy and brown. With no white water or the deep green of the rivers in Washington. But I am not disappointed. It is beautiful. I skirt the outside of New Orleans and travel on Highway 10 to Biloxi.

I wonder how they decide where the borders are.

The Gulf of Mexico is at my right, and I am once again disappointed in the way it looks. I was expecting the ocean. With its big billowing, thundering waves, with the sparkle of diamonds cresting on them. But it, too, is brown and still, with but a gentle lapping at the shore.

There are beautiful, big, Southern mansions on the left of the highway, and I see a sign that says "Thomas Jefferson Mansion." I thought he lived in Virginia or someplace else.

I'll have to go there.

My hands are sweating on the steering wheel. Am I scared or just excited? The sign says ten miles to Biloxi.

I had better stop and feed Samantha and get cleaned up again. I find I am looking for any excuse at all to stave off the inevitable.

I see a Mobil gas station ahead and decide to stop. I pull up to the gas pump, and a young man comes out to help. I roll down the window and tell him I need ten gallons of gas. That should be plenty, and I'll still have money left.

"Sorry, ma'am, I's can't give you no gas," he says with a deep Southern drawl.

"Why?" I ask him.

"We only s'posed to serve the coloreds," he says.

"What coloreds?" I ask.

"You white, ma'am, go to town."

Oh my lord, this is just like Texas—crazy people.

But I do as he says and decide to go directly to the base. Now if I can just find it.

Find it I did, driving up in front of the barracks with my precious child in tow.

The barracks are white, in need of painting, but white. There are men standing around talking and smoking. All are dressed in fatigues, army green, starched and pressed. With creases down the front of the pants, and the shirts, creased to military precision on each side. Their combat boots are laced outside the pants, allowing them to blouse up. They all have on billed caps of the same color. They all look the same. I'll never find him. I watch as one man turns, and, taking off his cap, begins to walk toward me.

I had forgotten how tall he is and how curly his blonde hair is.

He seems excited as he comes toward the car. He is thin, with pretty blue eyes, and a straight, perfect nose. With pretty teeth and a nice smile. Actually, he is as handsome as I remembered. It has been nearly a year since I have seen him, and I will be here for only six months, then he goes back to Korea, and I will go back to California.

What will he think? I've had a child and probably changed a lot. I feel dirty and sweaty, with a sleeveless blouse tied up under my breasts, and bermuda shorts on. All of a sudden, I want to run.

Does he think I'm pretty? Does he still love me? Will he love Samantha?

"Hi," he says, bashful and blushing. "I can't believe you drove all this way by yourself. Were you scared?"

"Hi." I look down. Doesn't he want to kiss me or anything?

"Yeah." I shake my head and try to look alluring. "I'm fine. We're both fine… Do you want to meet your daughter?"

He reaches in the car seat and pulls out this beautiful child, and you can tell he is in love, at least with her.

"Look at her little pink fingers," he says as she curls them around his finger… And she really does have curly red hair, I thought you were kidding me.

"What a pretty little girl! Are you going to be daddy's little girl?' he croons to her.

Thank God.

"I rented us an apartment," he says. "Come on, let's go and get some lunch, and we'll go see it. It's the best I could do with the money I had, but it's pretty bad."

"It'll be fine," I tell him.

He hands me the baby and slides behind the steering wheel. I go around and get into the car.

The street is old and quiet with enormous oak trees lining it, with a few palm trees scattered in the landscape. Oak trees that are magnificent in their grandeur, veiled as a bride with Spanish moss.

Magnolia trees and lilac trees that are massive, with sidewalks broken from the years-old invasion of the lovely old trees, the cement protruding up.

The grass is sparse and is badly in need of mowing. The houses are all big and beyond recognition as to what color they were. With what paint *is* on them hanging in curls, as if it were a decorative adornment.

There is a hushed, heavy silence, and the smell of musty age mixed with the heavy fragrance of lilac and magnolia permeates the car, through the open windows. I have seen no town yet. And wonder where it is.

We've not said a thing to each other. He has looked at Samantha and smiled several times, but not a word.

He pulls up in front of this ancient mansion and says, "This is it."

"Oh my gosh, it's so big," I tell him.

He laughs and says, "Oh, we only have the lower left side. But it has a bedroom and a living room."

There is a porch that surrounds the whole of the house, and to the left of the house is a once-beautiful, overgrown garden. In the center of the garden, a chipped, scrolled wrought-iron chaise lounge sits. An old woman of about sixty reclines, sipping iced tea. I would soon learn that it indeed was a mint julep, and iced tea had never crossed her lips.

As I get out of the car, I can smell the gardenias in the air, thick, sweet, the humidity at about 90 percent and the air something you can almost touch. It is so like all the books I have read about the South, and I love it.

The steps are broken, and weathered, and the porch is slanting in the direction of the broken sidewalk, with the railing missing many of the supporting soldiers.

This is my first home, and I am happy. Soap and water can do wonders.

The front door is massive and has an oval, beveled, leaded glass in it that takes up the whole door. I have never seen anything so beautiful, or so ravaged by time.

The hallway is massive and dark, with raised paneling in mahogany mounting four stories up. I see no light fixtures. The stairway to the left of us is wide, with a plain, dark wooden railings and stairs that are split and sagging. The floor is dark hardwood with piles of dirt in the corners, and worn, sagging spots, light from wear. To our right is the biggest chair I have ever seen, with hooks for coats and a big, foggy, cracked mirror in it. The odor of mildew and mold permeates the meager air.

I hold my baby closer, heave a heavy sigh, and look up at Rick.

He steps some ten feet forward, and there is a blackened wooden door. He slides the old skeleton key in the lock, and the door swings open, revealing a room with the same blackened wooden floors, walls of green peeling paint. With two windows framed in the same black wood. The windows look out onto the small overgrown garden. Something skitters across the floor as we go further into our new home. The furniture is Greek-looking black, with torn cushions, and the sofa a wood-framed Victorian style with shredded maroon brocade. There are two chairs and a small lamp and table.

I follow him as we go through to the bedroom, which is in the front of the house. It has a door in it that must be behind the big chair in the outside hallway, at the head of the bed are four windows. There are gaping holes in the floor, that I would, over the months ahead, sweep the dirt in and fill with newspapers to keep the lizards out.

The bathroom has a large-footed porcelain tub that is chipped and stained with big, yellow rust stains. There is a washbasin and a toilet in the same condition. "At least there is water," I say.

"Oh yeah," he says.

The toilet would be used to flush the dustpans full of cockroaches. I would stand and watch the water swirl to be sure that they all went down and didn't come back up. A room that had a lock on the door and would mean safety in the months to come.

But I didn't know that then.

We proceed back the way we came, about thirty feet through the living room, and arrive at the kitchen.

There is a large porcelain sink with a drain board attached that is hanging from the wall. The faucet is dripping, and the porcelain is again chipped and stained.

A small, dirty, white drop-leafed table sits in front of the window at my left, with two equally beat-up kitchen chairs flanking it. There is an old-fashioned, built-in buffet behind me. The walls are green enamel, and as with the rest of the apartment, the paint is peeling. Little did I know that every evening after I turned out the one hanging light-bulb, that the walls would become golden, golden and moving with cockroaches.

The floors are linoleum that is so worn, there is no color left. There is a door that leads outside to a small porch, and you can see clotheslines in the distance. Clotheslines that I will hang my baby's diapers on, and when I bring them in, they will be covered with lizards.

I reach up to kiss him. "It's wonderful," I say.

"Ah, none of that," he says. "Y'all don't want to start somethin' ya can't finish," as he pulls back.

"What do you mean?" I ask him. Thinking this was what he wanted. Would want.

"I have to stay at the base another month, but I'll come to see my baby."

I was aghast! "Why," I ask him. "Why didn't you tell me?"

"Couldn't, they just told me. Come on, let's go get something to eat. Did you bring any money?" he asks with a sheepish grin.

So things weren't how I thought they'd be.

Nothing ever has been. So get on with it. I'm so disappointed and a little scared to think of staying there all by myself.

"Well, do ya?" he snaps me out of my reverie.

"Do I what?" I ask him.

"Have any money?" he says again.

"Only a little, but we can go eat. And I'll take you back to the base."

"I'll need the car," he says.

"Oh no, I can't be here by myself without a car with a little baby. No. Is there telephone?"

"Yeah, at the drugstore in town or the landlady said in an emergency you could use hers."

We quarreled, but briefly concerning who would take the car; however, when it concerned Samantha, he would never win.

I spent the next two days at the railway station in the wrong waiting room. "Oh no, ma'am, youse cain't be in here, that other side there is fo' white folks," a uniformed sweating black man proclaims.

I go outside in the sweltering heat, thick with humidity, bend to take a drink out of the fountain, feeling eyes upon me, I look up and spy a sign over the fountain that says "colored" in big black letters.

Arranging for the five hundred pounds of household goods to be delivered to the house, I proceed to find a Laundromat.

As I drive through winding, dusty roads, the trees get bigger, the grass more sparse, and the houses now look like shanties.

But a Laundromat I find. I pull up in front, and notice I have the only car that is devoid of dirt, rust, and peeling paint. The sidewalk in front is boards, unpainted, weathered boards. Better than the dust I guess, as I pack the baby in and sit her in her stroller and back out to get the laundry. There is a small grocery store next door; I should go there after I get the laundry done. The storefronts are ancient and badly in need of repair and paint. The windows are dirty, and there are old Coca-Cola signs in them with the red and white of Campbell's soup cans stacked high, and meat lying on an open counter. Maybe I didn't want to go there. But I hadn't seen another store, so…

The Laundromat is busy, and people are bustling about with small children playing, and women laughing and talking.

There is a hush. "That there y're baybe?" a large, black woman points to Samantha and speaks to me. She looks just like Mammy in *Gone With the Wind*.

"Yes," I tell her. So proud.

"She's a right pretty little thing," Mammy says.

"Thank you, I think so too."

"Honey, does y'all know where's yous is?"

I look around. Everyone in here is black. Oh, Lord, I think. Now I have to haul all these dirty clothes back to the car and look for a *white* Laundromat. Are these people crazy or what? "I'm sorry," I say. "I didn't realize it made a difference. Is it against the law, or can I just stay and do the laundry?"

"Honey, youse in colored town, and white folks cain't be here. Youse go back where you came from."

They are all talking now, and I'm about to cry.

There's whispering, and finally, "Girl, git youse washin' done, and youse go on home."

I did.

There would be many more incidents of a like nature, but slowly, I learned that the South, for all of its genteel ways, was steeped in mystery and separateness.

Everyone else, however, seemed quite happy with the situation. They all knew their place and stayed there.

With of course, the exception of me.

I liked the little shanty town, and on several lazy afternoons, I found myself idly crossing the railroad tracks and watching the women sitting on their slanting, unpainted porches, the smells of fried chicken wafting through the air, pots of water boiling on the porches with piles of crayfish waiting to be thrown in. The pretty little children run barefooted in the dusty roads and play under giant trees, and yes, while eating watermelons, peaches, and cucumbers.

Rick finally came home to stay, but life was not easy. He was moody and hated the lack of money and the structure of military life.

Some evenings he would not speak a word and would rock in the rocking chair from the time he got home till the time he went to bed.

"Are you mad at me?" I would whine, wounded that he didn't even answer me.

Bed was not a pleasant experience for either of us.

He was frightened by my passion, or revolted, I couldn't distinguish the two, and I, upset by the lack of his. Each condition, compounding the next.

Time passed slowly, and we made friends with the people renting the other apartments and a few guys from the base. I would make spaghetti, and we would play pinochle. We went for drives on long, hot Sunday afternoons.

I would go to the beach, but it was polluted and condemned. Lord, how I missed the ocean.

We went to the movies once, but the rats were so thick, I buttoned the baby in my coat. "Never again," I told him. He went by himself. He went by himself a great deal, at least he went *without* me.

In the evenings, I would listen to the radio and dance round the kitchen floor with Samantha, crooning in her ear. She'd smile that big, happy smile, and I too would be happy.

I wrote home to my parents and sent them pictures of the baby.

She was still colicky and would scream for hours in the night. He would scream at me to "shut that fuckin' kid up." Pushing me, slapping me and shaking me so hard my head would hurt. Some nights threatening to hurt us both if she didn't shut up.

On those nights, I would lock both Samantha and me in the bathroom and wait for him to go back to sleep or for her to hush. Some nights I would bundle her up, and we would drive around in the middle of the night. There was an old Catholic church on the highway, and we would go in there and sit until three or four in the morning.

I was so homesick, I was literally sick. But to call home made it worse, and the cost was at least a dollar. A dollar we didn't have.

One evening late, the lady next door, with whom I had on a couple of occasions shared a mint julep with, came to tell me my mother was on the phone.

My uncle had blown his head off with a shotgun.

I thought I would faint. I sobbed into the night, my poor grandmother, this was the third child she had lost.

Finally, the day came when Rick got his orders to go to Korea; I would have never thought I would be so glad to have this over.

I packed up our things, sent them railway express, and the three of us got in the car and drove back to San Diego.

The tears spilled off my cheeks, and I sobbed quietly as I looked out the window of the car. The Pacific Ocean. Crashing, billowing white waves wash up on a beach of clean golden sand. The relief is like an ocean wave as it washes over me, cleansing my heart and mind lifting my spirits.

Home.

15

I was certain we would be married forever. That we had only to learn about each other, and we really hadn't had an easy start.

When you are fourteen and pregnant, you are just frightened.

I suppose, really, he was very frightened too.

My daughter is the most beautiful little princess in the world. She has soft, thick, strawberry-blonde curls, like her father, and my pretty turquoise eyes. The prettiest turned-up little nose. And she is smart. She is clean and dressed up all the time, and we have a good time. I take her shopping and we go to the zoo and to the beach on my days off.

It is a good life, and again, it is about to change.

After two years, he is coming home.

Am I excited? No, I am terrified. But I can make this work. I can.

He arrives in San Francisco at 11:45 PM, and I am going to drive there to pick him up, leaving Samantha with my grandparents in Sacramento.

At the ripe, old age of seventeen. I am terrified, there is no other way to describe it.

It is dark, and June. And although the road is devoid of almost any other automobiles, the Tulle fog is terrifyingly thick. Like pea soup. I should have come earlier in the day. I have no idea where to go. I have a map, and that is it.

With the radio blaring. I am, after all, only a teenager. With prayers said in continuum, I proceed with all the valor of a warrior.

Through the valley and into the beautiful city of San Francisco. The lights of the city sparkle, and you can see the bridge as it spans the waters of the San Francisco Bay. Funny, terror, or excitement are all the same to me.

I arrive in one piece, and better yet, at the proper destination. And there he is.

But there is no flutter, no thrill. I am terrified of this man. He and his many moods. Will they (the demons of his soul) be abated with time, or will they become more extreme?

Remember, I tell myself, "for better or worse," I promised.

We stay a short time at my grandparents and then travel to Washington to see my parents, as they have once again moved back. They would, over the ensuing years, move every two or three years. Once beleaguered and burdened by my mother's wander-lust, I can see it now for what it is…simply a desire by an intelligent woman to seek new information. To travel the world and experience different cultures, to see firsthand what her geography books had shown her. I am certain she would not be able to fathom my, or that of my siblings', need for a sense of security and permanence. She only understood our needs in response to her own. I can to some degree acknowledge that, "what we wish for ourselves, is often what we give those we are entrusted with."

So…our mother imbued in us an ever-present thirst for knowledge, and a sense of adventure that replaced the sense of security and permanence we so desperately wished for.

We drove on, up into Canada, and across to Toronto. The country is beautiful; the golden wheat fields flowing in the breeze, like waves on the ocean. Miles and miles of them, as far as the eye can see. I love the traveling, and Samantha is so good.

We don't seem to know what to say to each other, and the only time he has touched me was the first night he came home. But with time, I think, this will get better.

From Toronto, we follow the St. Lawrence River along to Niagara Falls. It is breathtakingly beautiful. The Lord in all His glory.

Back down into Michigan and to the air force base he will be stationed at for the next three years. Three years of stilted conversations, assured poverty, arguments, beatings, and loneliness, I think to myself, as we pull into a motel.

The country is green and flat. I have never seen such flat country. The lakes are beautiful, and the trees are mainly deciduous. So unlike any place I had been.

We rent an apartment in the little town of Mt. Clemens, and it is beautiful. All hardwood floors, two bedrooms, a very nice kitchen. With a view of all downtown. And the town is lovely. Neat, clean, and orderly. The apartment is on the second floor, so we can see everything. There is a basement with washers and dryers. And the nicest people living in the other apartments.

The lady, Mrs. Liebowitz who owns the house lives downstairs and is old, probably seventy or so.

It was their home originally, but her husband died, so she had to split it up into apartments to continue to live there.

She is wonderful. She has had Samantha and me down for lunch, and she would have silver, china, and white linen tablecloths, with napkins and silver candlestick holders with white tapered candles in them. She served chicken salad sandwiches with the crusts cut off. The chicken salad had a strange taste to it. It was good, just different.

"What is this?" I asked of the small, round, brownish-looking thing on my plate.

"Why, my dear, they are capers, and they will add a tantalizing flavor to nearly any salad such as this."

Umm, I thought, as soon as I can afford to, I am going use capers. This is nice.

Her home was filled with exquisitely beautiful things from all over the world. And the atmosphere gave a soft, peaceful feeling of safety and security. I loved going to visit her, and I think she enjoyed the visits as much as I did. We played cards, sometimes in the evenings when Rick was away. She told me of books and encouraged me to get a library card.

The very first book I checked out was *Atlas Shrugged* by Ayn Rand, then *The Fountainhead*, and Leon Uris's *Exodus*, the last being to shocking too read but for a while each day.

We would discuss them for hours. She, and the books of Ayn Rand, made a profound metamorphosis in the way I felt about life and my role in it.

Now, upstairs, was the opposite end of the spectrum. Zora was a massive woman. Loud and boisterous, happy and somewhat crude. She would come lumbering down the back steps to my back porch, claiming victory over this or that. Television was her primary interest, and since I didn't have one, (no one I knew had a television with the exception of my parents) we found we didn't have very much in common.

But a truly interesting person, and a good friend when you knew no one.

The rest of the military personnel lived on base, and we didn't see but a couple of them.

Money was a big problem. I was certain that if we had money, everything would be all right. That, and another baby, would make everything all right. Money and children: the worst things for an already failing marriage.

How do people live like this, day after fearful, sad day?

16

I am pregnant again. I am sure. I haven't been to the doctor yet; I can't go until I tell him. And I just can't tell him.

What about all these movies where the husband is so thrilled to find out he is going to be a father? Even Rhett Butler was happy Scarlett was going to have a child.

I am so sick I can't keep anything down, and this morning he came into the bathroom, as I was raising myself off the floor from the toilet. I turn and there he is.

"You're knocked up again, aren't you?"

I look down at the floor.

"Aren't you?" His hand flies through the air at my face, hitting me with the back of it. The metallic taste of blood fills my mouth. I look at him, the words won't come out. I raise my hand to my bleeding mouth and wipe the blood away, looking down at the floor.

"All we need is another screaming kid," he says as he shoves me against the wall.

"I'm sorry," I say, but I don't mean it. I want this baby. I love Samantha so much, and I love this baby too. He just needs to be around when they are born, and he'll see how precious they are. Things will be better. I pray to God things will be better.

But things are not better.

This is a big responsibility for someone who has really never had any responsibility at all. But things are different now. I'm eighteen, and he has been gone for two years, and I am under the impression that life will get better.

He has slapped me, pushed me, and choked me, at least every other day. I worry for the child I am carrying. Also for Samantha; has she seen him, has she heard us?

I wonder what a two-year-old child's memories are of.

This evening I was in the bathtub, and he wanted to know where the twenty-five cents was. "I gave it at church this morning," I say.

He reaches down into the bathtub. His hands close tightly around my neck, his thumbs pushing so hard on my throat that I can't breathe.

"You fucking little bitch, you make me sick, this bathroom makes me sick. Who ever told you pink and green go together? I'm sick of the whole fuckin' thing."

I can't breathe and am starting to pass out. With my heart racing, all I can do is flail around in the water.

Finally, he lets go of my throat, grabs my hair, and pulls so hard I think it will come out. He's banging my head on the back of the old porcelain tub. The sobs are coming hoarsely from my throat.

"Please, please stop. I'm so sorry. I'll never do it again."

He pushes my head under the water. And as he's leaving the bathroom, he stops and turns to look at me as I am struggling for self-control and trying to cover my body.

"You goddamn right you're never doing that again."

I hear the door slam and know he's gone for the night.

Where does he go… I don't know.

I would be frightened here by myself with a small child, and pregnant. But truly, I am more frightened when he is home.

I have to give Mrs. Liebowitz the name and address of my parents, so they can come and get Samantha. Just in case he kills me. Maybe she could keep her until they get here.

I dread him coming home at night.

Of being alone with him.

I try and have Samantha fed, bathed, and in bed early so she can't hear what's going on or even have to endure the atmosphere.

None of my clothes fit, and I have no maternity clothes here. Mom is sending them to me. But I remember what I have, and that, too, is limited to about three things.

I bought a lovely little piece of pink cotton today at Woolworth's. It has tiny little white flowers in it. I made it up this afternoon, and I feel quite pretty.

I have done my hair and scrubbed my face clean, and Samantha is all dressed up for her daddy. I'm making spaghetti, so he'll be happy.

I hear the back door open. The table is all set, all I have to do is make a salad.

He puts his lunch pail down on the kitchen counter. He looks at me.

"What is that?" he says with a cruel voice.

I think, *Is he mad?* I'm just going to pretend everything is all right.

I twirl around. "Isn't it cute? I made it today and had enough to make Samantha a pinafore."

"Where did you get the money, you been holdin' out on me?"

"No, it was only two dollars," I tell him.

"Only two dollars…only two dollars…" He hits me with the back of his hand. My glasses fly off my face and across the room.

My hand flies to my face. My hot, stinging face. I reach out and pick up my glasses and put them back on.

Samantha is crying and clinging to my leg.

I will not let him ruin this day, I think to myself, as I pick up my baby daughter and croon to her that everything is all right, Daddy didn't mean to frighten her.

I look at him, anger and defiance obvious in my eyes.

I see the anger in his and put the baby in the highchair. "Mommy is going to fix your dinner now."

"Mommy's going to fix your dinner now," he mimics me as he grabs my shoulder and spins me around to face him. The fear rises in me, full blown. I can't speak as he grabs my smock at the neckline, holding it tight in his fist. He shoves me into the refrigerator, pulling me off my feet as he does so. I hear the fabric rip and feel the coldness of the refrigerator on my back as the tear widens.

I can feel the tears as they stream down my face. My new top is ruined. I'll have to just make a seam down the back. I want to laugh at the ludicrousness of the entire scene. As if in slow motion, the rest of my life unfolds before me. Years of fear, guilt, pain and sadness loom dismally.

He drops me and storms out the back door.

From previous scenes such as this, I know he won't be home anytime soon. Again, the relief floods my heart—also guilt. Do I want him to go? I knew he would be mad. But I need something to wear, and it's not like he gives me any of the money they give him every week.

He expects me to pay for everything with my allotment, and he keeps all of his money. He says that's what my money is for.

I retrieve my glasses after some searching, as I am in fact nearly blind.

Samantha offers me my glasses and waits for me to put them on in the morning before she says, "Mornin', Mama." Profound insight, this wondrous daughter of mine.

I feed her, and I find that I am too upset to eat, I clean up the dishes, and decide we can eat this tomorrow night, knowing full well that this too will start another fight. As his majesty does not eat leftovers.

On thirty dollars a week, he can't eat leftovers.

The air outside is getting more still by the minute with the sky darkening; it has happened frequently throughout the summer. You can hear and feel the silence.

Samantha and I go out onto the porch to see. It's true, I've witnessed it before. "Come, let's go inside," I say to her. "Mommy will read you a story, and then we'll have a bath."

A tornado is coming, I think to myself, and the feeling of excitement and fear well up inside of me. I love the storms.

We sit in the rocking chair, and I rock her and read to her. About the three little pigs. We sing "The Tiny Little Spider" and "Kkkatie, Beautiful Katie."

It thunders, the lightning flashes, the air gets heavier, the sky black, and the stillness is incredible as the evening wears on.

We rock and talk about what we will do tomorrow, and she feels the baby kick, and we talk about the baby.

"It's my baby," she says.

"Yes, it is your baby too," I tell her.

"I doesn't want a brother," she says. "He'll just be mean like Daddy."

My heart breaks that my daughter thinks her father mean. And that he doesn't seem to care or at least consider what she might think.

It's stiflingly hot, and the humidity makes it hard to breathe. We're not afraid of the thunder and lighting. Considering our household, thunder and lightning are commonplace.

I try to decide if I should take Samantha and go to the basement. But there is no wind yet, so I'll wait. We are on the second floor, and the beautiful trees outside are massive, so when the wind starts, I have to go.

I tell her stories about the thunder and lightning. Frightening stories, really, about God being angry. Silly, senseless, things to tell children. But that is what I was told.

A booming crash of thunder, a blinding flash of lightning, with a bolt that zigzags through the sky, and the rain comes in an onslaught of water.

We go through the house closing windows and doors.

There will be no tornado, and another frightening day is over.

Tomorrow is another day.

17

We had to go to the commissary today. All the while we have shopped, Samantha has cried. She's hungry and tired. I try to console her, but nothing will do. She just cannot stop crying.

"Shut that brat up. I'm so sick of that constant crying," he says as he pinches my elbow tightly with his fingers.

"I'm sorry," I say. "She's tired and hungry…" But I hate it when he's mad. He just sits and rocks in the rocking chair and doesn't say a word for sometimes as long as three days. The drive home is horrific. And I'm so nauseated. I was never sick this long with Samantha. I'm in my fourth month. And I am still sick about every other day, all day long.

We carry all the groceries up to our second story flat, and I get her something to eat. But she is still crying. Probably the tension. I'm sure children can feel that horrible tension. It permeates the very air we breathe.

He comes in the kitchen and, with a cold, quiet look, says through clenched teeth, "Shut the fuckin' bastard up or I'll kill you both."

I'm so angry and so scared. How dare he call her a bastard. She may have been conceived out of matrimony, but we did get married. I have a no. 10 can of peaches in my hand.

I yell back, "Don't ever, ever call her a bastard again." And hurl the can of peaches at him, missing him by the hair of an "angel," I am sure.

He comes toward me, grabs me by the smock I am wearing (a new one I just made and one of the only two I have), and slams me into the wall; he then hits me so hard I slump to the floor. He hits me again and again. There is blood on the floor, but all I can think about are my children. Will he hit Samantha? Is the baby I am carrying all right? He's yelling at me, screaming like he was crazy. "I never wanted all these brats, I fuckin' can't stand the pressure, I hate your fuckin' guts, you make me sick, I wish I'd never met you. What the fuck you doin' getting knocked up all the time!"

He leaves, slamming the door after him. I know he'll be back; it always ends the same. I don't know why he doesn't love me. I try so hard to do everything he wants: keep the house spotless and have his meals on time. And budget, my God, we have no money, but he says that is my fault too.

It is nearly midnight, and I hear him coming up the stairs. Oh, Lord. Let him be sorry. And, Lord, help me be a better wife, I pray. "Cara, Cara," I hear him calling me. I stay in bed, pretending to be asleep. He sits on the edge of the bed, leans so close to me I can smell his aftershave, and the fragrance of him, and... he's been drinking.

He brushes the hair off my face, bends down and kisses me on the forehead, the tip of my nose, my eyelids...I roll closer to him, and he pulls me to him. "I love you, Cara Leah, I'm so sorry. I'll never do that again, I promise."

"But you always say that," I whisper to him. "And you always do it again." He kisses me again, this time with longing, and I return his kisses through swollen, bruised lips. Lord, I want to believe him. Please let him be telling me the truth. I love him so much...*Do I? My mind terrified to venture there...I remember thinking, "you could love anyone that was good to you, that love was a state of mind," I certainly didn't think he was good to me or our children. But, what was I to do?* Because of my *dallying* as Mother would put it, he was the father of my child, my children...I *had* asked him to stop, I had begged. I had pushed and shoved at him and who would have thought you would get pregnant the very first time.

He undresses and slides into the bed with me. Kissing me and caressing my breasts, entering me, and for a few short moments, all our problems are gone.

The sunlight awakens me, and I stretch and yawn. Today will be a good day, a new day. Things will be better now. Maybe if we can find someplace cheaper to live—I'll talk to him about that when he wakes up.

We have declared a truce of sorts. Most of the problems stem from money or the lack of it. We decide that however nice our apartment is in town, a cheaper place would be better.

18

We move about twelve miles outside Mt. Clemens to a cement block duplex located on a very large farm. It has four rooms and a bath. The floors are linoleum, with hardwood in the living room. Across the road is a very fancy red brick house that is surrounded by beautiful green, flat pasture with Holstein milk cows, forever dubbed the dirty brick house and the pink and black cows by Samantha.

I was moved in and had homemade curtains up at the windows in two weeks.

He was gone on some sort of special training. TDY, they called it. Peace at last.

The family that lives next door are very nice. Ruth and Erick von Urston.

They have a little girl Samantha's age. Sherry Lynn. We share a common laundry room, and she is as busy being a wife and mother as I am. He is a great big Danish man who is very kind to his family.

We are again in debt up to our eyes. New seat covers for the car. New tires for the car, new clothes for Rick, beers, and whatever else he wants, but I do not have any new clothes for the baby. And I have no friends here to give me a shower, just Ruth and Mrs. Liebowitz in town.

He won't leave me the car, saying, "My place is home." I have no money anyway, as I have to give him my allotment check now.

If I want money, I "can ask my fuckin' parents," he says.

So food is scarce, as is everything else that costs money. I can have fifty dollars a month for groceries, and I have saved thirty dollars in the last six months. Alleluia!

The flat land so long covered in God's winter blanket of snow is starting to show signs of spring, as the snow seems to dissolve in a muddy slushy mess. The cows are covered in mud, and the trees are fat with buds.

So I am going to plant a garden. Samantha and I are thrilled as I crawl around in the earth weeding, with my belly dragging on the ground and the laughter that ensues as I struggle to a standing position again.

On the evenings he is home, he drinks and rocks, often not saying a word to either of us for days at a time.

Dinner, he pushes away as "slop" and goes out, leaving us at home. We haven't had sex for months, after all, I am "disgusting." And he'll "be glad when this shit is over."

Still, I am happy. Stupidity is a life-saving grace at times.

The summer heat is nearly unbearable, the humidity high, with rain and thunder every afternoon.

We have vegetables out of the garden, the corn is three feet high, and the green beans are starting to blossom.

I am finally over being so sick, and life is somewhat better. We have conceded to the fact that money is an issue. And he has once again asked his parents to help us.

They arrive laden with gifts. With toys and clothes for Samantha, money and clothes for Rick, with clothing for the new baby, and two beautiful rocking chairs. One for me to rock the baby in, and one for Samantha. A cute little black rocking chair with Peter Pumpkin Eater on it and a little music box on the rocker that plays the song.

Samantha has a new snowsuit; with her beautiful curly strawberry blond curls, she is darling. And the crowning jewel in their lives. She is adored by them, and they want nothing but the best for all of us. I will forever be grateful to these kind, caring people.

As I am with child, and enormous. I wash the dishes standing sideways to the sink, as I can't reach the sink otherwise. I can no longer see my feet nor put my own shoes on. So every morning now, Samantha puts on my old worn-out pair of shoes, and ties the laces and states, "There, Mommy."

My shadow. My little friend.

She told me today, while eating lunch, she had to go potty.

"Okay," I said. "Just remember to wash your hands." With little panties down around her ankles, she comes shuffling out of the hallway. "Mommy, don't eat my sandwich, okay?"

I laughed and laughed and hugged her. And assured her that I wouldn't eat her sandwich.

It's true, I'm starving, and eating anything and everything. I already weigh more than I did when she was born and still have two more months to go.

Last week I had four molars pulled without any anesthesia. I have had a toothache since we moved, and it got to be unbearable. I simply could not wait to have the baby first. The pain was excruciating, with the sweat of the dentist mingling with my own, as he leans into my body for leverage. His knee on the edge of the dental chair, trying to work around my very-pregnant body. Alas, this too shall pass, and the pain of *this* shall be gone.

There are twins in my family, I hope that isn't why I am so big and so sick. The thought of giving birth causes me to break out in a cold sweat.

I have all the baby clothes washed and ready. I have repainted Samantha's crib, and we bought her a bed. She's so excited: everything is "my baby," when is "my baby" coming.

We both take naps now; I am so tired. This afternoon, we are going to play outside with her new trike her grandparents got her. The day is long and hot and balmy, as we pluck four-leaf clovers from the grass and make crowns for our heads. She laughs and runs on her fat little three-year-old legs, and we plan the things we are going to do with our new baby. We hear a car coming down the road.

"Daddy's home," she says and runs to stand behind me. Please, Lord, make her not be afraid of him. I reach out and take her little hand in mine and tell her "Yes, he is, and he'll be so pleased to see what a pretty crown you made out of the beautiful clover." We would run to meet him, but the best I can do is wobble, I am so very large with child.

He says, "Come on, we are going to go to the city for dinner. Get your money."

"I don't have any money. We don't get paid until next week."

"What did you do with it?" he says.

"I paid the rent, and that's all there was after the seat covers you bought for the car."

"You mean you pissed it away, that's what you mean."

"No, I didn't, I paid bills with it. We can go out next week, besides I already have dinner fixed. It's your favorite. Spaghetti."

"I don't want spaghetti. Give me the money. I know you've got money stashed."

"No, I don't have any money stashed. We don't have enough money to stash."

He's starting to get mad now, and I can feel the terror climbing in me. I clutch Samantha's hand tighter. Hoping I don't scare her, I quite suddenly let go.

"You said when we moved in this hole we'd have some money, well, where the hell is it?"

"We do have more money, but it only means we can pay the bills, and with the baby coming, there are just more bills," I say apologetically.

"The goddamn baby, I'm sick of that fuckin' kid already. Get your ass in there and get me the fuckin' money."

"I told you I don't have any money. I'm telling you the truth." He is out of the car. He's coming toward me now, and the fear is clutching at my heart. *Please no, Lord. Please.*

He's shoving me in the house. He goes to the stove. The pot of sauce is setting on the burner. It's been simmering all day. And I see him lift the lid. He sniffs, looks up at me with utter revulsion.

"You expect me to eat this shit?" as he slings the pot. Spaghetti sauce all over everything. My newly washed and ironed curtains. The floors, the walls, everything. God, thank you he didn't throw it on us.

"I'm sorry," I tell him. "I'll fix you something else."

"You're fuckin' right you will," he says as he is poking me hard in the chest with his finger.

I make him a hamburger, clean up the mess, and feed and bathe Samantha, all the while sobbing quietly. If he hears me, he'll just get madder.

What am I going to do? I am so frightened. I really don't have anywhere to go. My mother is of the opinion that *you made your bed, you lie in it*, and I just can't ask his parents for help; they've helped so much already, and I'm three thousand miles from home.

It's Sunday morning and a beautiful day. I would so much like to go to church, but that is no longer allowed.

Samantha is playing outside in the sandbox with Sherry Lynn. Sherry Lynn is two, and they get along pretty well.

Rick is washing the car. He seems to be in a good mood today. I have no idea what time he came in last night. He didn't wake me, and I'm so relieved.

I stand washing dishes, my body to the side of the sink as I wash them with one hand. It's so funny, I haven't seen my feet for what seems like weeks. I go to look and see how Samantha is doing. There is a big beautiful elm in the enormous expanse of front lawn. It is sparse of flowers, but the grass is nice, and they keep it up nicely…it has a pretty white picket fence surrounding it, so it is nice for the children to play.

Rick is still washing the car. Polishing every nook and cranny.

One of these days, we'll have a nice home of our very own. With lots and lots of flowers and trees and swings for the children and their friends to go out and play with. He will get used to all this, after all, he was never there when I was pregnant with Samantha. So this is all new to him.

The girls are squabbling over something. Maybe I should go out there. Oh my God…

As if he was Superman, I see him out of the corner of my eye, as he seems to fly over the fence. Clears it as if it were nothing. He's running across the yard, what the… I see Samantha look up. She is stunned. She has little blue shorts on and a little pink blouse I made her, she is standing in the sandbox with a shovel in one hand and the little yellow bucket in another. Sherry Lynn and she both have little clover crowns on their heads, Sherry Lynn is sitting down in the sandbox, crying. He stands at the sandbox now, yelling something at Samantha, he towers over her, all six-foot-two of him.

I see his hand raise—oh my God, please!

I sling the dishtowel over my shoulder and run as fast as I can to get out there.

Samantha is lying slumped over the side of the sandbox. He's hit her with such force, she seems to be unconscious. I'm so stunned. Oh, Lord, help me. I've never felt such sheer terror and anger in my life. I kneel down and pick her up. Thank God, she is alive! I stand up and scream at him to get away from her, "Don't you ever, ever do this again. They are just little girls. How dare you hit her like that!"

"I won't have that little bastard throwing sand at people," he says.

"No!" I say. "But you'll hit her like the bully you are." I hit him with the wet dishtowel. He's backing away from me. "You stay away from both of us. Just leave, now," I tell him. "Don't you ever, ever hit either one of us again, do you hear me? Never."

I look at Samantha and her face has swollen so badly in a matter of minutes. The top of her ear on the left side of her face is level with the bottom of her ear on the right side of her face.

"Get out of my way," I shove past him, taking both of the girls with me. I get the car keys out of my purse, put both of the girls in the car, and start to back up. He has his hand on the car now.

"You get out of the car! Where are you going?"

"I'm going to the hospital with her. You've probably broken her eardrum. Get out of my way, or I'll run right over you."

I wait in the hospital waiting room. *How could he do this?* I think over and over again. How can we live in such fear and terror? I can't believe that God would let this happen to us. Surely things will get better. He hates the military. They make him so mad, and he seems to be always in trouble. He has already lost rank one time, which means money, and although I say I don't care about the money, we really need it to live on.

He wants me to get a job, but then, who will take care of my children? It isn't fair for them to have to have someone else raise them. Oh, Lord, help us. Seems I have spent most of my life praying.

Thank God, she's all right. The doctor said she would be fine. That apparently the "fall" she had had, hadn't hurt her near as badly as it could have. We were very lucky, he said, looking at me strangely, but I just couldn't tell him that her father had hit her. What would he think?

I took Sherry Lynn home, telling Ruth nothing of what happened and hoping Sherry Lynn wasn't old enough to think to tell her mother.

I walk in the house, and he has dinner on the table. And has shelled the peas. "I'm really sorry," he says. "Is the brat…I mean, Samantha, all right?"

I just look at him… "Stay away from us," I say. "She is not to sleep until tonight. Then we have to talk."

"Did you tell him I hit her?" he asks.

I know his real concern is that it would get back to his commanding officer, as I had gone to the base hospital. "No," I say. "I didn't want them to know what kind of monster you are." My fear and anger unwilling to absolve his sins.

Samantha and I spend the rest of the day with me reading to her and playing in the yard. We have dinner, and I bathe her and put her to bed. Sitting by her beside until she is asleep. Fear for my child clutching tightly at my heart. The "sins of the fathers," I think to myself. What in the world has this tiny little girl done to deserve a life like this?

I bend and kiss her lightly on her smooth young forehead and smooth away the tiny mass of strawberry blond curls.

The humidity in Michigan at this time of year is oppressive, and she sleeps with only a small nightgown and a sheet to cover her tiny, perfect body.

As I enter the living room, darkened now in the twilight of a summer's evening, I hear the rhythmic rocking of the rocking chair, and my heart skips a beat.

That is never good. Always a sign of his anger, his despair, his hatred of the position I have put us in.

The beer bottles clutter the coffee table, and I know it is to be a fight I will not win.

But for the sake of my child and my unborn child, we must talk.

Anger, fear, and the desire—no, not desire, but an inborn need to protect my children—pushes me beyond the depths of my fear of him.

"We have to talk," I say.

"I got nuthin' to say to you," he says, taking a gulp of his beer.

"Well, I've got quite a lot to say to you," I tell him as I sit my mammoth body on the couch across from him.

"Yeah, and I've heard it all before. You're always fuckin' right."

"Do you think what you did today was right?" I asked him.

"Yeah, I do, she has to learn not to treat other people like that."

"Really, isn't that what you did to her? You could have killed her. Caused her irreparable damage. What were you thinking? What are you thinking when you are hitting me and pushing me around."

"Yeah, well, maybe if you'd do what you're supposed to do, I wouldn't have to do that."

"And just what is that, exactly?" I ask him. As I am truly perplexed.

"How the shit am I supposed to know? Fuck it, I'm getting the fuck outta here. I need some space."

He is out of the rocking chair and into the kitchen at the back door before I can extricate my pregnant self from the soft cushions of the couch.

"But, Rick, we really need to talk about this. You can't ever do this again. I need you to promise me," I say as I am lumbering after him.

"Ya, well, we'll just see about that. Won't we." He pushes me in the chest with the heel of his hand.

As horrible as it is that he won't talk about it, and that I feel certain nothing has changed, I am once more relived that he is gone. For the first time, I understand that this is who he is, it would always be about him.

At least for the time being, we are safe.

I pick up the beer bottles and straighten up the house before going to bed.

What is it I read the other day?

Choices, discipline, responsibility, and acceptance.

19

Days pass, and Samantha's face heals, leaving no damage to her hearing.

I have been to the hospital on two different occasions, in the throes of false labor.

I am huge. I am giant. I can't get out of bed, and my feet and ankles are swollen and beyond recognition as well as my face. I am told I have "toxemia," whatever that is.

I feel wonderful. The best I have felt in months. Ruth next door said she would watch Samantha while I am in the hospital. I was really worried about leaving her with him.

I've washed and ironed all the curtains and scrubbed and waxed all the floors in the house. The baby's things are ready, and Samantha and I are excited.

I thought maybe Mother or Gramma would come and help me, but I live so far away, and they are too busy. And Vera has a job, so she can't come.

I am two weeks overdue and have trouble getting out of bed, let alone getting dressed.

"There is a possibility you'll have twins," the doctor says.

That is a little overwhelming, and something I haven't had the courage to tell Rick.

God doesn't give you more than you can handle. I will just put one at each end of the crib.

June 24, 3:00 AM. The labor has started, I am over being terrified; I just want this over. I get up and scrub the floors and iron his fatigues. Wash a load of clothes. Watching closely to see that I don't get my smock, or my mammoth breasts caught in the ringer.

I wash my hair and set it so it will be dry. I was in labor with Samantha for twenty-six hours. So I have time. But it is so hot and humid outside.

I go and wake Samantha; she will stay with Ruth.

I hold her close and tell her, "We are going to go get the baby today. And Mommy will be home soon just like we talked about." She sits in her high chair, chattering away.

"'Member, Mommy, no boy babies."

I have seen this baby in a dream, with blonde soft curls and in a baby blue one-piece pajama set standing in the crib. I think it must be a boy. I have carried it so much different than Samantha.

We've held the needle and thread above my enormous belly, and "it" can't seem to decide back and forth or around in a circle. So I really can't tell what this baby is, male or female.

"You will love it no matter, girl or boy," I tell Samantha as she eats her scrambled eggs. "I am going to go get Daddy up now."

"Can I have what Daddy has for my breakfast?" she asks.

"No, honey, Oreos and Coke make you sick to eat in the morning."

"But Daddy does, and it doesn't make him sick."

"He's used to it, though," as I think to myself what a ridiculous habit that was. And, I was certain his eating habits perpetuated his already-schizophrenic behavior.

The pains are harder now, and it is 7:00 AM. Maybe this labor won't be as long.

"Are you all right?" he keeps asking me.

The car careening through early morning traffic.

"Yes, I'm fine," I say, with tears streaming down my face. A mixture of pain, anxiety, excitement, *and relief.*

For the baby, for the fact that he does care, he does love me. He is here now, now when I need him. He is here.

It is a beautiful day to bring a child into this lovely world.

The sun is shining, the trees and flowers a reflection in the lake as we whisk past them. Thank you, Lord. Thank you so much. I knew you would hear my prayers.

We arrive at the base hospital at noon on Sunday.

I am whisked off to the labor room, and he is to be sequestered in the father's waiting room.

I am dripping with sweat; this is the fourth saddle block they have given me. Shoved… what looked to be enormous pie servers up *there*, while I vomited over the side of the gurney, all with no results.

The doctors say they are going to transfer me to St. Joseph's Hospital in Mt. Clemens. As they have no air-conditioning in the operating rooms here. And it has been far too long; they are going to do a cesarean.

The pain is excruciating. I really don't care if I die.

I just "want something for the pain," I plead to the nurse standing holding my hand.

"We can't, it will harm the baby. It is in a 'military position' and already so weak."

I sob. "Is my baby all right?"

"We're not sure" she says. "You've been in labor for more than forty-five hours, so we can't be sure."

I pass in and out of consciousness for the next hour or two. There is nothing else to vomit, but the nausea is overwhelming, the pain never-ending.

I am on a small gurney now, on the ground, it seems. I look down the length of my body, and I can see my toes. Amazing, I haven't seen my feet for months, and they are little again.

I see my belly and you can see the outline of a baby there, right under the skin.

A wave of pain comes again. I scream. My throat, raw from screaming.

The doctor kneels beside me. "Try to hang on a little longer, we are going to take you to the hospital in town, and it'll be over."

"Rick…"

"Your husband is going to follow," the doctor says.

We are in the ambulance. The doctor is being so kind.

I, who have never had a profanity issue forth from my mouth, am screaming everything profane I have ever heard. The doctor is patting my hand and smoothing the hair back from my sweat-soaked head, and I am telling him, "Please do not do that, you're messing up my hair."

Vanity knows no limits.

There is a priest in the elevator. He is holding a Bible with a rosary hanging from it. "Domini…" he is giving me the last rites.

I am incensed, through the fog of pain and utter exhaustion. "I am not Catholic," I tell him, "and I have no intention of dying."

"Rick, am I going to die?" He is crying. My God, what the hell is *he* crying about?

"Tell him I am not going to die. And who is going to pay for this?"

He just stands there.

Thankfully, I pass out again. It's hard to be in charge of things when you keep passing out.

I am draped all in green, stiff cloth, and it is freezing cold. I hear the cutting and feel the pressure.

I am so very, very tired. I can't do this any more; *I am just too tired.* I lift my hand, and the blood drips from my fingertips.

I feel myself floating. I am very high, and there is no pain.

There is white light all around me, but with edges, like a tunnel. The light is so bright and still not blinding.

I have never felt such profound peace and acceptance. A feeling of well-being and love—that is what it is; it is love. This is what love is. Ineffable.

The light is brighter at the end of the tunnel, and I seem to just be moving in that direction. Like you move through someplace familiar, unafraid, with excitement and anticipation I approach the end of the tunnel.

There are all sorts of people whom I have known forever. They know and understand me, accept me. I am so happy to see them.

Suddenly, in front of my line of vision is Gramma. She has on a white nightgown that comes down to her feet; I can see her feet. Her hair, the same salt and pepper it always was, braided in one long braid, that hangs down her back. She is so happy to see me.

Her hand is stretched out to take my hand in hers. "I've come to help you across," she says.

There is no fear as I instinctively understand what she means.

I understand that this is the most wonderful thing that could happen to me. That all this on earth is a learning experience so that we can grow to God. I sense His profound love for me, and the safety of what is offered. That this is where I belong, have always belonged.

Relief floods my very soul. It is over...this long and frightening experience is finally over.

I stretch out my hand to take hers. "My children," I say to her. "I can't leave my children. Not with him. I can't."

"Your life will be so hard," Gramma says. "*So very hard.*"

"But my children, Gramma, I can't leave them."

I look down, the baby is being held by a nurse, and she is black. The room is large and cold, so very cold, men and women with green clothing and masked faces, scurry around, lights bouncing off of chrome and stainless steel.

"Why is she black?" I ask my grandmother. "Is she dead?"

"She will die without you," she says.

"I can't go. I can't leave them alone."

"It is your choice...it is always your choice. Know you are never really alone," she said as she drops my hand and seems to drift into the background.

The loneliness is overwhelming. But with it a sense of peace that brings courage.

Excruciating pain envelopes me again. I once again can detect the odor of alcohol, ether, and that ever-present metallic smell of blood. My eyes flash open to the greenish-white lights of an operating room and feel the bone-chilling cold. The total exhaustion.

I hear my baby scream. "Thank you, Lord," I whisper.

The nurse standing at the top of my head says, "She's back."

I awaken to the sickening sounds of someone vomiting at the end of the bed. My eyes try to focus as I search for the culprit. "For goodness' sake, what is the matter?" I say to this man who has the courage to beat me and a child and now stands fearful and vomiting. The cold metal surface on which I lay feels slippery, as I struggle to lift my hand with its tubes and needles. My fingertips drip blood as I raise it.

I try to raise my head to look, but the effort is too much. As I lift my other arm and examine myself, I find I am covered in blood.

I feel so angry. "Where is my baby? Make them clean me up," I tell him.

A nurse appears, and as I feel the needle slide into my arm, I hear her tell my husband, "There is a bathroom down the hall you can clean up in."

Blessed oblivion overtakes me.

I weep noisily as I push the baby back into the nurse's arms. It has been three days, and they haven't let me see her. And now they bring me this baby that looks like a frog. Her eyes are way too big for her head, and she is enormous. She is all hairy, and it's black hair, it is even on her back.

She has streaks of black running from her eyes down her cheeks, and her forehead is pushed back so far she looks Neanderthal.

"This is not my baby," I tell the nurse. "I want my baby, I want my baby. What have you done with my baby?" The sobs coming now uncontrollably. The hysteria rising.

"Please," I plead with her. "Bring me my baby. You've made a mistake, please." I turn my head away and sob, without solace, into the pillow.

I open my eyes to Rick, sitting on the edge of my bed. He is holding my hand and kissing it.

"She's dead, isn't she?" I sob. "I want Samantha, and I need my mother."

He lifts me tenderly from the pillow, "No, sweetie, she is fine, and beautiful, our little girl is beautiful."

"No," I sob. "She was all black, I saw her. I think she's really dead, and they are bringing us some other baby. I want my baby, please make them bring me my baby," I plead with him and cling to his arm.

He strokes my hair and shushes me, "There, there," as he rocks me tenderly in his arms.

"She really is our baby," he says. "She has Deddy's thumbs," his soft Southern drawl assuring as I look at him.

"Really?" I say.

"Yea," he said. "Our little girl has her grandeddy's hands. She even looks like him. And she's a whopper, nine and a half pounds. Two feet long. I'll show you."

"They won't bring the baby in while you're here," I tell him.

"Yeah, they will," he said. "And Samantha is with your mom."

The tears come in an avalanche of relief. "She is?" I sob. "How? Why?"

"They thought you would die. So I called your folks." The tears are streaming down his face, and I remember *I do* love this man.

He, in all his complexity, is a tender and frightened little boy.

"I thought I'd lost you forever." We cling together and I am so relieved.

"Can you get them now?"

"Not until you rest, they said tonight, okay?" He rises to leave.

I awake to the sounds of cheerful, happy chatter in a sun-lit room.

IV fluids coursing through my veins, as once again I lift my arm, the hospital band in place, and needles poking everywhere. But at last, the hand is clean and dry.

I roll my head on the pillow, and there in the sunny room stands Mother and Gramma.

The sobs come unbidden, my cheeks are wet with tears.

"Mama, Gramma, I'm so glad you came. Did you see my baby…she's dead, isn't she?"

"No," Mother says. "She isn't dead, Cara, you mustn't think that. Why do you think that?"

"Because, Mother, I saw her. Gramma McDonald. She came to get me, and when I looked, the baby was all black, and the nurse said she was dead. I saw her, Mother, I know she was dead." The sobs now beyond control as the grief overwhelms me. "I am so sorry. I am so sorry."

"Cara, stop that now, you saw no one, your grandmother McDonald has been dead for years." my grandmother admonishes. "This is not good for you, or the baby." Gramma has never lied to me.

"Is she really alive, really?" I say, trying hard to control my sobbing and to believe what they are saying to me.

"Of course she is alive," my grandmother says with great authority.

"And Samantha, is Samantha all right?"

"Yes, she's is at home with your dad and Denise. We will bring her to see you tomorrow. Now rest."

I again drift into a deep sleep and again awaken to the sounds of happy chatter and a baby crying.

But it is the girl in the next bed. She is nursing her child, and her husband is at her side.

"Can you ring for the nurse?" she asks me.

"Yes, I think so," I say.

"They wanted me to tell you to call when you woke up."

"Have I been asleep a long time?" I ask her.

"Yeah, for two days."

Oh my gosh, maybe this has all been a dream, maybe I dreamed she was alive. That Mother and Gramma were here. The tears plummet down my face as I reach for the buzzer to call the nurse.

She appears at the bedside, donned in a crisp white uniform, with a cute little cap.

"Sooooo are you ready to see your new daughter?" her voice filled with enthusiasm.

"Is she really alive?" I ask her.

"Of course she's alive. She is a big, beautiful baby. Let's get you sitting up and ready for your new daughter." The nurse returns momentarily with a small, pink bundle in her arms.

"Is that my baby?" I say through sobs of relief.

"Yes, this is your baby." She lays the tiny bundle in my arms.

She is a lot bigger than Samantha was, I think, as I cradle her in my arms.

I pull the blanket away from her face; it is not my baby. It is a trick, they have given me someone else's child.

"This isn't my child," I tell the nurse, pushing the baby toward her.

The nurse is shocked but gently says, "Yes, this is your daughter."

"No, no, it isn't." Again, sobbing uncontrollably. And pushing the bundle at the nurse. "Take her away, her real mother will miss her."

"Is this your first child?" the nurse gently questions me.

"No, and my other child is redheaded and was pink and beautiful."

The nurse sits softly on the side of my bed and pats my hand. "You've had a hard, hard delivery and emergency surgery, you are still in shock, and the baby has had a hard time. But you are both going to be fine. Look at her. She is beautiful," as she softly pulls the blankets from this tiny little new life.

"But the black line…"

"It's silver nitrate. We put it in their eyes, to protect them."

She is squirming and crying now, her fingers stretched straight out as she lets me know how angry she is that I nearly deserted her and her sister. To let her die and leave Samantha alone. *While I just went into the light.*

"Shush, shush," I croon to her, and her little hand curls 'round my finger.

Her thumb is exactly like Amos's. Long and thin.

I pull her close and sob into the soft folds of her bunting. Tears of joy and relief flood my very soul.

She is alive; she is my child. My beautiful baby girl.

Samantha will love her so.

During the fourteen days in the hospital, I cried at the drop a hat. I was unable to eat, and if I could eat, I couldn't keep it down, consequentially nursing was difficult at first. Mother and Daddy have brought Samantha outside the hospital, and I can go to the window and see her, talk to her for a little bit. Rick has moved into the barracks, so there will be room for them to stay in our tiny little house.

But finally we can go home…

20

"My baby, my baby," Samantha exclaims as we get to the car. We can go nowhere until she unwraps her and looks at all her little fingers and toes in wonder. She is especially excited about her little toes. Then I remember all the toes of her dolls are bitten off. Oh dear.

"Is she really mine? Can I keep her?" Her enthusiasm is contagious, and we are all laughing and happy.

"Yes, yes," I say. So happy to feel normal.

"What do we call her?" my beautiful little redheaded daughter looks up at me quizzically.

"Remember, we were going to name her Jillian Kaye. So that's what you call her."

"Darlin' Jillian," her father announces.

Rick has moved back home. My father and grandmother have gone and left my mother and sister to stay for one more week.

Samantha is sleeping in the baby crib, Mother in her bed, Denise on the couch, and Jillian in a bassinet that I borrowed from Ruth.

Ruth. What would I do without her? She has been so much help.

My breasts are enormous. I look like a chicken, all breast and legs. I weighed 164 pounds when I went into the hospital. Three weeks later, I weigh 110 pounds and at least fifteen of those seems to be milk.

I am terrified to leave the baby alone, and so the bassinet has gone from room to room with me as I try to regain my strength. She is a quiet baby. She sleeps and eats and makes little grunting noises. Soft and cuddly, she likes to be held tightly and close to you.

Rick has found someone to rock with him. And he seems happy to rock her.

Mother is planning on going home this next weekend. But she is going to leave Denise here. I try to tell her that it is unnecessary, but she won't hear of taking her back with her.

Denise is ten and is still a child, so I can't see that it is going to help me at all, but…I think perhaps Mother just wants me to care for Denise for the summer…as if I needed someone else to care for now.

I am washing dishes, with the bassinet only a few feet from me.

The baby gurgles then gasps. I look into the bassinet, and she is blue!

"Oh, God," I scream. "Nooooooo!"

My mother comes running from the garage where she has been washing diapers in the old ringer washing machine.

"What is it?" she screams at me.

"Jillian, look at her!"

"Oh, oh, do something!" she shouts at me.

I reach in and pick up Jillian. She is gasping for breath, her little head lolling to the side, her skin a sickly blue. I turn her upside down and slap her on the back.

Nothing, she is still gasping for breath.

"Go to Ruth's, ask if you can use their phone!" I shout at my mother. "Tell Rick to come here. We need to go to the hospital."

"Denise," I scream, "you stay with Samantha, stay in the house, and do not let her out of your sight. Go to Ruth's if you need something."

Rick is standing in the back doorway. "Shit! What the fuck now?" he says.

"Get the car, we have to go to the hospital!"

Mother is back. "They said to take her to emergency at St. Joseph's right now."

We climb in the car.

Mother, from the back seat, says, "Give her to me." Jillian is nearly black now, and all I can do is pray. "Oh, Lord God, please don't take my baby now, after all of this. *Please, Lord, please don't take my baby.*"

Mother is giving her mouth-to-mouth, saying, "Breathe, breathe, Jillian, just breathe. *Please* breathe, Jillian."

The car once again careens through the steaming, tree-lined streets of Mt. Clemens. Children chasing balls and women chatting across fences, unaware that our world is about to crash.

"Is she dead?" he asks about every two minutes.

"No, I don't think so," Mother responds between breathing into this tiny creature's mouth.

My litany of prayers, more insistent by the mile, as I hang over the seat watching my baby daughter as the blue slowly turns to black.

They are waiting when we arrive and take us immediately to the emergency room.

A nurse appears from nowhere and takes Jillian from my arms. "She really doesn't want to be here, does she?" She looks at me, and I recognize the nice nurse in the delivery room.

They suspend her in a T-shaped wooden "holder" and say they are going to take X-rays. I stand watching, waiting, as all of a sudden, she coughs and starts screaming.

The tears flow, in silent thanks. "Thank you, God, thank you, God," I said as I slide to the floor, fighting for consciousness.

My mother is weeping silently in the corner.

The nurse ushers us all to the waiting room.

Very shortly, they bring us our pink, screaming baby, all bundled up and ready to go.

"Intervened crib death. That is all we can think of. There doesn't seem to be anything at all wrong with her. Just take her home and watch over her," the doctor said as he placed my baby Jillian in my arms.

We took my mother to the airport in Detroit the following Tuesday, and the five of us returned home. Denise was to stay for the rest of the summer.

Jillian is thriving. She is fat as can be and makes little growling noises; no cooing for her, she growls like a little bear. She loves to eat, to laugh, to sleep. She is just a good baby. No colic, no crying all night. Now that she has decided to stay here on this earth, she seems to be the happiest of babies.

Denise and Samantha fight all the time, and the suitcase is still sitting in the two-foot wide hallway.

We are actually having a good time. But Denise is just a kid. She has no homemaking skills at all and is really more a tomboy than anything. So other than playing with Samantha, setting the table, et cetera, she is only someone else to cook for, wash for, and I am *so tired*. It is *hot* and *humid*. My shorts stick to me, and the sweat trickles down between my breasts, or is that milk? I have turned into a milk machine, having to pump my breasts between feedings. I feel really ungrateful, but there it is.

Jillian is such a good baby, but it has only been a month.

With no help, I struggle.

Rick is mad because he "hasn't had any in over three months." Every night, it is the same thing.

I have asked Rick to put it in the attic at least three times. The damned suitcase. I trip over it; it is hard to get the bassinet around it.

It is Sunday morning; cartoons are blaring from the television set, with Rick and Denise and Samantha glued to it. A television set that he had to have, at great expense. He is eating his breakfast of Oreos and Coca-Cola.

The girls are not going to eat oatmeal if he doesn't have to too.

"For goodness' sake, put the cookies and Coke up and take care of this suitcase. Please. I could use a little help."

I am standing in the doorway of the living room, and in an instant, he is out of the rocking chair.

I sense what is about to happen.

His arm flies up, and he smacks me across the face with the back of his hand—full force and moving.

I lose my balance and fall to the floor. "No, the girls!" I am whining.

He kicks me. Then, leaning down, he is yelling, "You fuckin' little bitch, do this, do that, but what do I get? Not shit, that's what. Not a fuckin' thing. An' now I'm supposed to feed three fuckin' kids? Did your ol' lady leave you any money to feed that worthless little brat? Fuck no!" He's hitting me, kicking me, my stomach, and my thighs. The pain is intense.

I see Denise running to come help me. "No, no, Denise, get back."

All of a sudden, he stops. He is looking at me, stunned. Whimpering, I turn on the floor and try to get up.

"Oh, Cara, I am so sorry." He is sobbing and crying, all the while trying to help me up.

It is then I see it. Blood, blood all over the hardwood floors. My white shorts, slowly turning red. The stiches from the surgery, torn and gapping.

We gather up the children and go to the emergency ward. Yet once again.

⸺ ⁂ ⸺

"How did this happen to you?" The doctors continue to ask me.

"I fell. I've just been so tired."

"Your husband didn't do this?"

"No, no, he wouldn't do this."

"You know you can tell us. We can put him in the brig."

The things that go through my mind…I shouldn't have asked him to do anything. I shouldn't be so tired. He was so sorry, that is all he said all the way to hospital; he said how much he loved me and how sorry he was.

If they put him in the brig because of something I said, he'll kill me when he gets out.

That week, I took Denise to Detroit and put her on the plane for Spokane.

Vera and Amos, the proud new granny and granddaddy, have come from upstate New York to see our new darlin' Jillian.

Two of the most generous people I have ever known. They are at the same time an enigma to me.

I have shared their home and their lives, and I have never seen them kiss or touch each other in an intimate manner. They are kind to each other generally, and occasionally, she will grin like a young girl and say, "Now, Deddy," as she touches him gently on the arm.

They are far older than my parents—in their fifties, at the very least.

She is a handsome woman. Just short of being beautiful. Large-boned and tall, she is thin, with sloping shoulders and a straight back, carrying herself nicely with long arms and legs. A small nose and downward-slanting amber-colored eyes set off by fine ivory skin and thick, light auburn hair, that is streaked with gray.

Laughter and a sense of humor come easily to her. Believing that a woman can always dress well no matter what her station in life. She has a black dress, a navy dress, and a beige dress, with shoes to match. All dressed up, she looks very elegant.

Prone to migraines, I have seen her lie in bed for three days in a darkened room, with her head wrapped in towels and plastic bags wrapped around her feet in eighty-degree weather.

Amos was once a Baptist minister and reads the Bible con-sistently. Never speaking of why he is no longer a minister. He is short for a man and paunchy to say the least, with wide hips and sloping shoulders, arms that are long and seemingly dangle at his sides, with hands and digits that are large and long. Bald, with a fringe of gray hair encircling his head, he has small, beady intelligent eyes that are filled with patience and humor. His skin, pockmarked and thick. Golf, fishing, and gambling, his only vices. The ever present cigarette dangles from his mouth.

Compared to my father, he dresses quite flamboyantly, in short-sleeved silk shirts of a patterned variety.

They are both kind to me and seem to think I am the answer to all of their son's problems.

They are obviously smitten with our darlin' Jillian, and they have been in love with Samantha from the moment of her birth. They have come bearing gifts of every kind for everyone.

We go everywhere to see everything in the area. We go out to dinner every night and shop until I, for one, could drop.

Samantha has the most beautiful white fur coat with red velvet trim and red velvet leggings. A little hat to go with it that is red velvet and has white fur trim. And to finish her look, she has the most darling white fur muff. She has new dresses and black patent leather shoes.

Jillian has the prettiest pale pink snowsuit and mittens and the prettiest baby dresses.

She growls like a little grizzly and squeals, to her grandparents' delight.

I have a new white cashmere coat. The most expensive and most beautiful thing I have ever had. And the most wonderful thing, a new pair of shoes. The first I have had in over two years.

Rick has new slacks, shirts, and sports jackets. I don't know where he is going to wear all these things, but that is what he wanted, so that is what they bought him.

It is truly Christmas in September.

"Butch!" Vera yells. "Don't you hit that baby!" as she rises quickly out of her chair and catches his hand midair.

Samantha slides away just in time, as, while clinging to my leg, she whispers, "Daddy hits Mommy too."

Vera turns to me.

The look on my face is all she needs in answer.

She is up and pushing him into the wall. Her anger a volatile force within the small kitchen.

"Don't you *ever* let me find out you are cruel to any of these girls! You're a lucky man to have such a nice family. I'll tell yur deddy right now," her thick Texas drawl belying her anger. Her finger poking at his chest.

"Cara," she says, turning to me. "You call me, girl, if he ever hurts any one of you girls. I mean it, Butch, you remember what I said, yur deddy'll have yur hide. Now let's put these babies to bed and play some cards."

They paid off the gas card and the seat cover bill. They paid our utilities in advance for three months and loaded the kitchen with groceries.

I was so overwhelmed by their generosity, I could not even begin to thank them.

She sat down at the kitchen table the next morning while the guys were watching cartoons.

"Come, girl," patting the table with her hand, "tell me about your money and what has been happening."

"Ninety dollars a month isn't much to live on. I'm gon' to send you money every month. I want you to use it for a babysitter, and go out to eat and to a movie every week. And don't tell Butch. And don't you never let him hit you or those babies again. Promise me, girl."

"I promise," I tell her, my head hanging over the kitchen table as tears drip on to the tablecloth.

She reaches across the kitchen table we sit at. Her long, strong, hard-worked hand reaching out to touch my arm. The freckles, and blue veins standing out as she pats my arm in assurance.

"Ah, Cara, it'll be all right. You'll see, girl, he'll come around. He loves you and those babies. I know it."

Amos and Vera have been gone for over a month now. And still, he is nice to us.

We do go out to dinner and to the movies, and he seems so much happier.

What a difference that twenty-five dollars a month has made.

A hamburger and a movie is all he needed, I guess.

21

Autumn comes quickly, with leaves the colors of gold and russet that dance from the trees in swirling whirls to the earth below and, as quickly, the colorful dance departs in the night. I am awakened by the stillness of the night; I slide over the side of the bed and tiptoe out to the living room. The big picture window shows a sky heavy with snow, the ground beyond a glistening winter white. The moon a shining presence in the white night sky. The snow falling softly in flakes as big as a quarter. Designs as intricate as a lace doily.

It is so beautiful, I can hardly breathe.

Samantha's "dirty" brick house standing bare in a white blanket of snow. The "pink and black" cows huddled in a lone corner of the pasture under a leafless elm tree.

I tiptoe in the kitchen. It's only 3:00 AM. She'll go back to sleep.

I go as silently as I can to the girls' room.

"Samantha," I whisper as I bend and sit on her bed. "Samantha, wake up, it's snowing. Come see." I lift my sleeping daughter into my arms, and tiptoeing back into the living room, I whisper, "Look, sweetheart, look. It's snowing." She smells of sleep and the soft, sweet smells of little children. Warm and soft.

"Oh, Mommy, look." Her fat little hands stretch out.

We kneel on the couch, looking out the window at a true winter wonderland. All clean and new.

"Mommy, can we play in it?"

"In the morning, darling, we'll play in it in the morning."

"The cows, Mommy, they look cold."

"They do, don't they? But I think they are used to it."

"Let's go get my baby, Mommy, let's show Jillian. She'll really like it."

"Oh, honey, I think she's too little to be very excited. We'll show her in the morning."

We sit in the dark and watch the snow as it falls gently to the ground.

I leave her on the couch and go to the kitchen to make cocoa.

We sit and drink our cocoa, and I rock her to sleep, with promises of snowballs and snow angels.

The morning light streams through the windows of the girls' bedroom as I go to get them up. The snow has not abated in the night, and it is piled in huge drifts against the house and the fence that surrounds the spacious front yard.

I have never seen so much snow and feel as delighted as Samantha as she jumps up and down in great enthusiasm for the soon-to-be adventure.

We eat breakfast and dress, which entails layer upon layer of clothing, snowsuits, hats, gloves, boots. While I am dressing one, the other child is hot and fretting.

Alas, our time has arrived, and out we go to make snow angels and a snowman.

Only to find the snow is already nearly three feet deep and carrying Jillian, with snowflakes coating her tiny face, I watch in laughter as Samantha sinks to her neck in snow. With no way to climb out.

Both of us laughing, we trudge through the snow, the sunlight glistening on the mounds of white before us. Samantha throws her little head back to catch the snowflakes as they softly fall to her waiting face. Snowflakes stick to her eyelashes and the small shock of hair that protrudes from her stocking cap.

Our adventure is exciting but short, as the temperature is fifteen degrees. And no amount of adrenaline can keep the cold away.

After no more that forty-five minutes outside, we go in again. To disrobe, have something warm to drink, and clean up the dripping water as the melting snow from boots and clothing puddles on the kitchen floor.

They have finally plowed the main roads and salted the road in front of the house, and I have taken the girls and gone to the commissary today. I enter the back door, hollering for him to please come and help me carry in the groceries. I am immediately sensitive to that familiar feeling, *something is wrong*.

The house is dark and quiet. No television, no lights.

"Rick," I say as I go to the doorway leading to the living room.

My heart skips a beat and my knees have that watery feeling, as I see him rocking in the rocking chair. His hands folded on his lap, the rocker going back and forth, back and forth.

I back out of the room, going outside where the car stands laden with groceries and children. As I reach in for a bag of groceries, Samantha says, "I can help."

"No," I say rather sharply. "You stay with Jillian in the car." *They will be safe there*, I think to myself.

Taking bags of groceries in, I get her a book to look at. "Read Jillian a story," I tell her in my calmest voice.

She smiles and says, "Okay." She can say the alphabet and count to one hundred and recognizes some numbers. So she thinks she can also read to her sister. With constant interjections of "Shush, Jillian" as Jillian growls and squeals in utter delight.

I carry the groceries into the house. And seeing the diapers hanging frozen in the sunshine, I go to retrieve them from the clothesline.

You need no clothespins; you only need to bend their corners over the clothesline. After several hours, you bring them in and lay them all over the laundry room, and amazingly, they are dry in a day.

I bring the girls in, and undressing them, I ask, "I am fixing the girls lunch. Do you want something to eat?"

There is no response, only the steady, rhythmic sound of the rocker.

I stand in the doorway. Again I ask, "Do you want something to eat?"

"Shut the fuck up." His voice, a menace in and of itself without the filthy words.

I busy myself feeding Jillian lunch and putting groceries away. Then of course there is "cleaning up" Jillian's lunch. At six months old, she is so fat she is unable to sit up. And she will not let you feed her. She is a hands-on kind of child and determined to have her own way. She wants the food on the tray of her high chair, and she wants to eat it by herself. So we have food everywhere. But she is happy as she licks her lips saying, "Ummm." All the while she eats.

What would I do without this wonderful diversion of children?

I have missed my period this month. Does he know? Is that what he is angry about?

I don't know what he will do if I am pregnant again.

I put the girls down for a nap. They get up, we play for a while. We eat dinner.

The din of the rocking chair steady and ominous, the room in which it sits, dark and silent but for the slow and steady creak, creak. The man that propels it…quiet.

I bathe them. Jillian has "pooped" in the bathwater, and Samantha is highly offended.

Funny, though, it may be, I can understand her dismay, and I bathe Samantha again, laughing all the while.

Still, he has not turned on the light or the television. Only rocked, and rocked.

I sew for a while and shower. My body clammy with dread.

"Can I get you something?" I ask. There is no response. "Then I am going to bed."

Still… he rocks.

My fear is palatable, and I know from vast experience to leave him alone. I rack my mind and can think of a million things I did or didn't do that would make him mad.

The starch in his fatigues wasn't stiff enough last week, but I told him I was sorry. Dinner wasn't good the other night either. He hates vegetables, and all I had in the house to cook was vegetable soup. I know I should be a better wife. But I really don't know what he wants, and I am so tired all the time.

Lord, please help us.

I can hear the creak of the rocking chair as it rocks back and forth, back and forth.

I know his company is going TDY for three months. Even though I will be alone with the girls, I have such a feeling of relief that I ask God to forgive me.

Finally, I fall into a dreamless, fitful sleep.

My eyes fly open as I feel the pressure of his hands around my throat. I can't breathe, and my heart is racing. He is leaning over me, and I can smell the beer on his breath.

Startled, frightened beyond words, I lay paralyzed beneath the weight of his hands and his body as he leans on me.

I think of Vera's words and bring my arms up quickly between his, breaking his grip on my throat.

For an instant, I, too, am angry as I roll to the other side of the bed, kneeling, shouting through clenched teeth. "You stop this insanity now, or I will tell your daddy."

I see, too late, the back of his hand as it connects with the side of my face, knocking me to the floor on the other side of the bed. I pull myself up as a fist connects with my jaw, now the middle of my face, and my head reverberates with a hard, crunching sound.

"I found your little nest egg, you bitch," he is shouting at the top of his lungs.

There are literal stars, and my world is black, as once again his fist plows full force to my jaw. I taste the coppery taste of blood, feel the little chips of my teeth, and the blackness engulfs me.

The silvery glint of the morning light filters through the bedroom window as I open my one eye. Is the other one gone? I reach up to feel it swollen shut but still there.

I am lying on the bed, still in my nightgown. A damp cold towel on my face as my husband strokes my forehead, and his tears drip softly on my battered face.

"I am so sorry, Cara Leah, I am so sorry. I love you so much, I am so sorry. I promise I will never, never do this again. I promise."

I turn my head away from his heartfelt apology, the tears spilling from my one eye.

"Leeze don'uch me," I ask, astounded at the difficulty of saying these words.

There seems to be something wrong with my jaw and my teeth, the sharpness of my remaining teeth, cutting my swollen tongue, as I attempt to move it within my mouth.

My head hurts so bad, pounding, ceaselessly pounding.

"I have to report to the base. You will be fine, just keep this on your eye," referring to the cold cloth he has folded on my eye. He kisses my forehead.

How long have I been out, and where are the babies? I wonder as I struggle to come to a sitting position. I look around the room. The sheets and my nightgown, a bloody mess.

I'll have to soak these in cold water and bleach, I think to myself.

So… insanity does run rampant in this house.

My head thuds as I try to get to my feet. The blackness once more engulfs me.

———⁓⁓⁓⁓⁓⁓———

Again, I am awakened by the sound of voices, my heart skips a frightened beat; no more, I think, no more.

But it is Ruth's voice I hear. "Cara, Cara, it's Ruth. Can you talk to me?"

I look, and she is kneeling beside me. "We have to get you to the hospital."

"Oh, di you ge he?" I say through swollen, unintelligible lips.

"Samantha came and got me. Can you stand up?"

I think of my three-year-old daughter going through the deep snow to Ruth's, and I am both saddened and amazed at her bravery. My heart breaks as I think of her childhood fraught with unknown fear.

"'Hey nee' to ea'," I try to mouth to her.

"I'll do that, but first, let's see to you."

"I 'av 'ush a hedahe," I try to say as I stand with her help.

We go to the bathroom. "Oh, gawd," I weep as I look into the mirror. My face unfamiliar, bloody, my nose obviously broken, and my jaw cocked to one side. Leaning on the sink, I try to part my lips; my teeth are still there, just broken off, my tongue so swollen I can not extend it, but I can make out small bloody holes where I must have bitten it.

Cuts and gashes line my face, and I look to see Samantha standing behind Ruth's legs, sobbing.

"Erick has called the police," speaking of her big teddy bear–like husband. "But they say they can't interfere in domestic disputes. I am so sorry. Can you go home?"

The pain is horrific as I slip to the toilet seat, tears streaming, sobbing uncontrollably now.

"I can't go 'ome. Bethides, he thes he will 'ill me if I try to leaf 'im." There is no place for me to go. If I was a better wife, this wouldn't be happening. I just don't know what to do, what he wants.

"No one should do this to you. No one." She is angry and sympathetic, knowing there is no one to help.

The emergency room in town is where we go. I am afraid to go to the base. They will take away another stripe and that means more money gone. To say nothing of his anger.

They straighten my nose and tell me the rest will heal. They tell me to rest and try and watch where I am going "next time," that this could very well have resulted in a miscarriage.

I sit sobbing for my unborn child and praying, *Lord, please don't let there be a next time.* I have tried to tell him to wear a condom if he doesn't want any more children, but he says it is his right as my husband to do what he wants with me. That has certainly held true tonight when the police would not intervene.

His proclivities in the bedroom have become bizarre in my estimation. He wants me to go "down on him," and when I was informed what that meant, I was appalled. He was angered and, climbing out of our bed, left.

My grandmother used to use a button, but that obviously did not work. She had nine children.

The emergency room visit is twenty-five dollars, and I rummage in my purse for the secret little place I keep Vera's money.

It is gone. So now I know.

I give Ruth Vera and Amos's phone number in New York.

"Please call them and have them come and get the girls if he kills me. Okay?"

"My gawd," she says. "This is as bad as those soapbox things on television."

22

During the three months he is gone, my face heals, the scars diminish, and my nose has only a slight bump on it. My teeth, however, remain chipped, and my jaw, slightly crooked. Ah, but the pain is gone. I have gained some much-needed weight and feel rested for the first time in what seems years.

It is still winter, but the roads are clear and the girls and I go to Mrs. Liebowitz's for lunch. We shop in the pretty little town of Mt. Clemens and eat at the soda fountain.

We even drive all the way to Chicago. It was quite exciting. But I got lost so many times that I vowed not to repeat that adventure.

The three months fly by, and rather than excitement at seeing him again, I am filled with apprehension and fear.

The girls are growing and relaxed; life is peaceful and safe.

What will tomorrow bring?

He is home and happy, almost joyful to see us. The months seemed to fly by.

The morning sickness has abated, and I feel wonderfully well this time. But I am starting to show ever so slightly and am terrified he will recognize my "condition."

Maybe it will never happen again. As our life is what I envisioned from the start. He is happy to play with the girls and happy to help me bathe and feed them.

We talk and have friends in to play cards.

Life is normal. Finally.

Today the sun is shining, and it is a beautiful day. Rick is carpooling with some other guys from the base, so I have the car every other week. I have taken the children to visit Mrs. Leibowitz and coming home; the ice was so bad at the driveway, and I slid the car into the ditch. I am right in front of the house, and not knowing really what to do, I leave it there. Maybe Erick next door can pull it out when he gets home from work.

I get the girls out of the car with great difficulty and trudge through the snow to the house.

Will Rick be mad? I know he will be. But more than that, I am pregnant again. And I am terrified to tell him. Actually, I have decided not to tell him.

Clay Fly was stationed with Rick in Biloxi and recently has been transferred here. He and his wife, Nita, have come by several times over the last few weeks. I like her very much, and last night as we sat in the small cozy kitchen waiting for the guys to come in to play cards, I told her I was once again pregnant. She and her husband, Clay, are one of the few friends we have and I desperately needed to tell someone. Clay seems nothing like Rick, he is soft spoken and gentle. I think they come because, like me, they are lonesome for home and she and I like each other. I feel I can trust her, hopefully that is true. Nita rested her hand on mine. "Cara, you really must tell him, why, my Clay would be over the moon."

I am sure, well, I am hoping he will be as happy as I am. The palms of my hands sweat as I think of telling him. Nita is right, he has a right to know. I look out the window and see the car as it sits at a sharp right angle in the ditch…surely, he will understand that I had no control over *that*, only be happy, we are all safe.

I think as long as I have all this difficult news, I will ask if we can get a telephone. I write letters to my parents, his parents, and my grandparents all the time. But it would be wonderful to talk to them.

I see the car stop at the driveway and Rick emerges…swearing and throwing his hat in the snow as he looks at the car.

I run and put the girls in their room. Jillian can crawl out of her crib, so there is no sense in putting her in it. I close the door and tell them to "stay in here."

Closing the door, I look to see Samantha's little face pucker up, the tears start to well, and this little child is wringing her hands. I kneel down before her and say, "It's all right, sweetheart, we've done nothing wrong. Accidents do happen. And the car is not damaged, and we are okay, that is what is important."

I softly close the door and go to face the music.

The back door flies open. "You fuckin' little bitch, look what the fuck you've done now. That is the last time you drive my car." He grabs my shoulders and is shaking me so hard my teeth are literally rattling. "Do you understand? You are never to set foot in that car again! Say it, say you understand!"

"Yes, I understand," I say through clattering teeth. He shoves me with all his force into the refrigerator. My head snaps as the cake plate falls, crashing into a thousand shards of broken glass. One of them sticking straight up in my forearm.

He looks at me. As if pondering what to do next. "Shit," he says with such vehemence as can only be witnessed.

He's out the back door. Slamming it so hard, it flies open again. "I'll be back," he says through bared teeth.

I hear the girls' bedroom door open and see Samantha peeking out with her finger in her mouth and her blanket in her hand.

I pull the shard of glass from my arm, licking the blood as it pools on my skin, and tiptoe to her door.

Kneeling before her, I say, "It's okay, sweetie, its okay, he's gone."

"But he's coming back, Mama, he's coming back."

"No, he probably won't. Don't worry, let me clean up the mess, and I'll fix you girls something to eat."

We watched as he and someone else pulled the car out of the ditch.

He didn't come home that night. Or the next night.

The waiting, *terrifying*.

I called the base from Ruth's, and they said he had asked for some personal leave.

A week later, he appears with a brand new Thunderbird. Black with red interior.

I watch as he gets out of the car. He has on civilian clothes. Those expensive clothes his parents had bought him.

I go to stand at the back door waiting for him to come through it.

The door opens, and he looks at me then down at the floor.

"Where have you been?" I ask him.

"None of your damn business," he says quietly.

"Where did you get that car?" I ask him, unable or unwilling to keep my mouth shut.

"I bought it."

"With what?" I ask, angry now. This is much bigger than seat covers or a television, I think to myself.

"Shut the fuck up," he says, pushing past me to the bedroom. I follow and watch as he pulls the suitcase from the top shelf in the closet. Slinging it on the bed, he starts to pull his clothing from the closet and the dresser drawers.

"What are you doing?" I whimper. Disgusting, even to me.

"I'm gettin' the fuck outta' this hole, that's what I'm doin', somethin' I shoulda done years ago." He is speaking almost calmly, quietly.

"You can't go. What about me? What about our children? You can't do this," I am begging him, clinging now to his arm.

"Oh, you just watch me bitch, oh, I know your dirty little secret, when were you going to tell me, when it was too late? Bitch, fuckin' stupid little bitch."

"I'm sorry, I'm sorry, I'll be better, I'll try harder."

"Oh yeah, you should have thought of that a long time ago. Knocked up again, you make me sick to my stomach. I'll be happy never to see you again."

"Please, please, don't leave us. What will we do? Please," the pleading in my voice portraying a fear I didn't know existed until this moment.

"Get away from me," as he is reaching into the closet for his cowboy boots.

I reach down and with my hand on his back, said, "Please, Rick, no, I am so sorry. Please, no."

The boots rise in the air … I see them coming to land on the side of my head.

From one side of my head to the other, he hits me with the boots.

I lost count of the number of times they plummeted against my freshly healed wounds.

Fighting for consciousness, I back against the wall. A mistake, I knew, as he drove his clenched fist with all his might into my stomach, again, and again… I would feel the unbearable pain engulf me.

"That should take care of that little bastard" were the last words I would hear as I delved deep into darkness.

Yet again, I am awakened by the soft soothing voice of Ruth.

"Samantha came and got me. The children are all right, and I have called his parents and they are on their way. Come on, let's get you cleaned up."

I am lying once more in a pool of my own blood.

"The baby…" I sob, knowing there will be no baby.

"I think you have miscarried, Cara, come, let's see if you need to go to the hospital."

"He's left me, he just left us." The tears turning to uncontrollable sobbing once again.

"What a mess, I have made of my life, my children's lives."

"Hush, *you* didn't do this. Stop it now."

As she half-carries, half-drags me to the bathroom, my eyes are swelling shut and already turning blue. My mouth is swollen and my lip split.

"My word, what in the world did he hit you with?"

"His cowboy boots," I say, feeling all of a sudden like I could laugh. "And his fist."

"My nose looks all right," I look at her, and all she can do is laugh.

"Is he really gone?" I start to sob again.

"I think so, Erick is watching to see he doesn't come back. And he is also putting new locks on the doors and nailing the windows shut."

"Oh, Ruth, I'm so sorry. What would I do without you?"

"Come on, let's take you to the hospital" was her only response.

"No, no, I can't. I don't have any money, and besides, what are they going to do?"

But at her insistence, we do go to the hospital, the base hospital, as I know I have no money.

The baby is dead…I have severe damage… the "brig" I hear the doctors speaking with Ruth, as I drift in and out of blackness.

They performed a D and C and sent me home to "heal." Would that ever happen?

I can feel the cold porcelain on my arms as I sit in a near-fetal position between the tub and the toilet. The glint of the razor blade lying at my bare feet.

The morning light filtering in through the high window of the bathroom.

It hurts to cry, and I am still crying. I have no idea how long I have been here. Only that it occurred to me sometime in the night what a despicable person I was, an embarrassment to my family and my children, that I really had no right to them. I had no right to have these beautiful children in my care.

He was right. I was stupid, inept, and generally worthless.

They would be better off with any one of their grandparents. Mother would take good care of them. She loved Samantha, and she would love Jillian. They were really good little girls. Smart little girls, and Daddy would keep them safe and never hit them; he would protect them. I am so sorry for you, precious little girls.

I am so, so sorry to have been such a bad parent to have let this happen to you.

I squeeze more tightly into my tiny sanctuary between the cold of the porcelain. I hear Samantha at the bathroom door, whimpering, "Mommy, Mommy, come out."

He left me; he left all of us.

It would be better if I got in the tub, less mess. But I can't seem to stand.

Just do it.

Something in my mind is not right. Something I can't seem to control.

Do it! My mind is screaming. I reach for the razor, my hand is trembling so much, my fingers will barely hold it, my body battered and in shock. My arms are so white, the blue veins standing taunt against the white of my skin; it would be so easy.

I hear the tremendous *thud* against the bathroom door as the lock cracks and the door splinters.

Vera is kneeling in front of me, tears of grief plummeting down her cheeks as she reaches out her hands to pull me to her.

"There, there, girl, it's all right, it's all right. Come to me, baby, come to Mama."

She pulls me out of my huddled sanctuary and into her arms as I sob and say, "Oh, Mama, he's left me, he doesn't love me."

"There, there, come on, Cara, we're here now and we're going to take you and these babies home."

"He doesn't love us, he left us. I tried to be good, but I don't know what he wanted."

"Shush, that nice lady Ruth has told us the whole sad story, and I am so sorry, Cara, that I could have such a mean-spirited son. Come. Can you stand? Amos, come help me get her up."

He lifts me up like a small child, and with tears in his eyes, he says in a tight little voice, "It's all right, Cara, I won't ever let him hurt you or those babies again."

"What if he comes back?" Fear grips me.

"He won't come back. I've gone to see his commanding officer, and he has gone AWOL…so if he comes back, he'll be in the brig."

23

I don't remember the packing up of the house or the trip to New York. Only feelings of safety... and grief. *What strange bedfellows.*

My wounds healed yet again. At least the physical ones. I was, once again, able to love and care for my children. But what was I going to do about supporting them? Vera and Amos were wonderful, but we couldn't go on living with them forever. It had already been more than a month.

With nerves becoming somewhat frayed as their household had quadrupled in size.

With smelly diapers and constant chatter and the noise of happy little people.

Too, as I healed physically, I was angry with them. Not identifiably so, but angry nonetheless. Was it something they knew of that made him like that? Did they know and not tell me?

However, they had been far too kind and generous for me to verbalize my fears and frustrations.

Ricks brother Lyle and his wife Dorian arrived in what would turn out to be *the nick of time.*

Wonderful, kind-hearted, Dorian. Aunt Docky, Samantha called her.

"I have an idea," she said one day. "You are beautiful, Cara, tall, skinny. Let's go to the city and get you job as a model. They make lots of money."

Dorian, Vera, and I went shopping, and they bought me a plain little black dress, shoes, and bag. I had my white cashmere coat from Vera and Amos.

Vera loaned me her pearls, and Dorian and I left for New York City early one morning.

We went to Elaine Frank; we went to every modeling agency in the telephone book.

Who is my agent? Do I have any head shots? Who did I work for last? What photographer did I last work with? Did I do lingerie? Did I do runway? Could I see without my glasses?

The questions were endless, and we had no answers. Except that no, I could not see without my glasses.

"Well, we can't use you if you have to wear glasses."

At last, someone at one of the agencies sent us to Clairol. They needed a hair model.

"I can't do that, my hair is awful."

"Oh, they will put hairpieces on you. You just need a pretty face."

"Okay," I stammer. "When, where?"

As he is scribbling the time and the address on a sheet of paper, Dorian says, "How much do they pay?"

"Forty-five an hour, but you probably won't work but a couple of hours. Unless they like you. Or you are very photogenic."

I took the piece of paper from him and calmly left my name, address, and telephone number, should anything else come up. "Fine," he said, "but after this, we take 20 percent."

I could hardly contain myself, and Dorian didn't even try. "Forty-five dollars an hour!"

Four of us had been living on less than a hundred dollars a month.

I could pay Vera and Amos back.

We could go home.

Nervous and filled with anxiety, Dorian went with me to the next two jobs. Yes, two jobs.

The studios were filled with beautiful women. Tall, skinny women. With big eyes and long, thin legs.

I was shy and reserved, but I managed to make friends with Lilith.

She was sympathetic and a bit of a romantic to say the least, but she was exceptionally kind.

"I have just the agent for you, dahling," she would say with her exaggerated speech.

And she delivered. All I had to do was what I was told.

Stand this way, look this way, stand still, don't blink.

They screamed at you; they shouted orders. They threw you clothing and practically ripped it from your body if it wasn't to their liking.

They glued false eyelashes on my eyelids and plastered my face with makeup.

"Get rid of those damned glasses. Can you see without them?"

"Of course I could," I said, praying for literal physical guidance.

"Take that brassiere off," they shouted as someone nearly tore it from my body.

"Can you do lingerie?" someone shouts.

"How much?" I ask, nearly as submissive and frightened of them as I had been of my dear husband.

Lingerie paid eighty-five dollars an hour. How could I say no?

They once more roughly jerk the clothing from my body.

Fans blew my fake hair, as jet-black eyeliner made my already-almond-shaped eyes look even more oriental.

Lilith cautioned me about the "couch, some girls sleep to the top," she exclaims. "It makes life hard, but ya gotta eat."

"What do you mean?" I asked her.

"You know…" She looked at me coyly.

"I won't do that."

"You will." She smiled knowingly. "We all say that, but in the end…"

Modeling was a world of sex, drugs, booze, vomiting, and ex-lax. All for the money.

And Lilith. Lilith was somehow different from the others. She was hard, talked tough, and her language was anything but saintly.

I had paid Vera and Amos back for moving my "stuff" and was paying them rent.

And… I had $1,039.40 in the drawer in the dresser.

The money to get us home. The money to keep us safe if he came back.

When *it* happened.

He asked me to his office, told me he would get me this wonderful job if only I would cooperate.

Certainly, I was more than willing to do whatever it took.

My babies and I were going home, and I needed the work. Looks don't last, and the other girls were constantly cautioning me with this piece of evidence. At the ripe old age of nineteen, I needed to make hay while the sun was still shining.

The *sun* was falling quickly as his hands groped my breasts, his mouth searching for mine trying to kiss me. His hands pulling at my clothing. His thick fat fingers groping my body. The sweat from his face staining the collar of his shirt. The smell of him, sour and repugnant.

I push him away. "No! No! I can't."

"Oh, but you can, and you will, if you want to work."

His stained teeth inches from my face. His hand holding both of mine behind my back.

"What's a little pussy between friends?" he hisses into my ear.

A remembered panic swells in my chest, and I feel my knees weaken, and my palms begin to sweat.

"You let go of me now! You filthy bastard," I say to him through teeth clenched tight.

My anger, a force to be reckoned with.

My hands are free, he steps back. "Have it your way, *queenie*, you'll never work in this town again."

"Screw you," I say on my way out of his office.

Truly the "big" city teaches you lots of things. Nasty things about the world and people.

"Cara, are you all right?" I hear Lilith as she comes into the restroom. My stomach retching from the vomiting.

"I'm okay. I just got fired, I think."

"Yeah, we heard. I told you so." As she pushes open the stall door.

"Can he do that?" I ask, astonished that I even considered he wouldn't have that power.

"Yeah, he can and does."

I am fighting tears, as I say, "I don't know what I'll do now."

"You'll be all right. Read this, it'll help. And here, this is the name of a gal over at Lander. I have an offer to be a rep for them, and I told them about you."

She hands me a paper with a name and address on it and a little green book.

"What is this?" I ask. "Are you leaving too?"

"Yeah, ya know, I'm thirty-five years old. My jobs are getting fewer and farther between. I've tried to commit suicide twice, and well, I thought I could at least make some money working for a cosmetics company."

"And this?" I hold out the little green book.

"Oh, well, it'll help ya get your head together. My shrink gave it to me."

I gather up the few things I have there and put it in my satchel.

"Come on," Lilith says. "I'll walk with you to the train."

She lived in downtown Manhattan with her husband Dutch but walked with me to the train. Each of us promising the other to "keep in touch."

As I sit on the train that afternoon, I open the little green book and am touched by its profound significance and simplicity.

> Chapter I: Life is a game that cannot be played success-
> fully without the knowledge of spiritual law, and the Old
> and New Testaments give the rules. Jesus Christ taught

about giving and receiving. "Whatsoever man soweth that shall he also reap."

"Keep thy heart (or imagination) with all diligence. For out of it are the issues of life" (Proverbs 4:23),

"Ask and it shall be given unto you, seek, and ye shall find, knock, and it will be opened unto you" (Matthew 7:7).

… that any man who does not know the power of the "word" is behind the times. "Death and life are in the power of the tongue" (Proverbs 18:21).

Chapter II: The Law of Prosperity. Jesus Christ gave a wonderful example to his disciples, "Say not ye, there are yet four months and then cometh the harvest. Behold, I say unto you, lift up your eyes and look on the field, for they are ripe already to harvest."

His clear vision pierced the "world of matter," and he saw clearly the fourth dimensional world, things as they truly are, perfect, and complete in divine mind. So man must always hold a vision in his mind and heart of the journey's end; the manifestation of that which he has already received, whether it be perfect health, wealth, love, or self-expression.

Chapter III: By thy words thou shall be justified, and by thy words thou shall be condemned…sickness and unhappiness come from the violation of the law of love.

The metaphysician knows that all disease has a mental correspondence, and in order to heal the body one must first "heal the soul." Man's work is with himself.

Chapter IV: The Law of Nonresistance. Jesus Christ said, "Resist not evil."

Resistance is "hell" for it places man in a state of torment. The robbers of time are the past and future. Jesus

Christ was said to have said, "Behold, now is the accepted time, now is the day of salvation."

Living in the past is a failure method and a violation of spiritual law.

Chapter V: Karma and the Law of Forgiveness. Christianity is founded on the law of forgiveness, for Christ redeemed us.

Order is the first law of heaven.

Under grace or forgiveness and not under law. "But take heart! I have overcome the world" (John 16:33).

Oh my gosh, I am so engrossed in what the book has to say I have nearly missed my stop.

There are only ten short chapters, so maybe I can read them tonight. Such a sense of relief I felt, reading no more than I did.

24

The house seems to "feel" funny. Strange…

Everyone is setting down to dinner, a dinner of cornbread, onions, steak, and pinto beans. This is common fare and, believe me, cannot be altered to include salad or a vegetable. The table set with the bare necessities of eating and a common "rag" used as a napkin that is passed at your request. Thankfully, they eat out frequently and then order salads and other items to sustain them.

Setting down my "things" from work, taking off my coat, I go in the kitchen, the atmosphere as if they already know I have been fired. Vera is feeding Jillian, and Dorian cutting Samantha's meat. The house is still warm and inviting, but something is not right.

"Hi, I'm home…how are my babies doing?" I bend and kiss Vera's forehead.

"Hi, Mama."

"Sit down, girl. Git' somethin' to eat, y'all look tired."

"Yeah, I'll tell you about it after we put the girls to bed."

Would they be mad at me? What was I going to do now? There are few work opportunities in Keeseville, and I so very much want to take my children and go *home*.

Home, to me that means San Diego, but there is no one there. Mother and Daddy have moved again and are in Texas now. I don't want to follow them around all the time. They have been in New Mexico and now Texas. I just can't do that to the girls, remembering the desolation I had felt as we left what I had considered home. I need to decide what to do. I could go see the person Lilith recommended. But I can't live in the city, and I simply can't commute. I would never see the girls. Lord, tell me what to do.

Dinner conversation is laughter and chatter, as Samantha tells me all the things she and Aunt Docky did today. With intermittent squeals of laughter and delight as Jillian pounds on the high chair and Vera and Amos tell them how wonderful they are, the evening progresses as usual. The three of us clean up the kitchen while Amos and Lyle play with the girls.

I am certain Dorian and Vera are exhausted. Taking care of two babies is difficult at best.

I'd trade places with them in a split second.

As I come down the stairs, the atmosphere is static with—what—sadness? Anger? How would they know I got fired?

The four of them are sitting in the living room; the television isn't on. Amos is sitting in his favorite chair in an old pair of pants and his sleeveless ribbed undershirt. All ribbing deleted in its desire to cover his great girth. His legs extends to the matching footstool where his bare feet rest, ankles crossed. A cigarette dangles from his mouth.

Lyle sits on the very edge of the beautiful cocoa-colored sectional. His elbows resting on his knees, his fingers laced, with his chin resting on them.

"Caralee girl, come sit down." Vera pats the sofa next to her.

"What's the matter? Why is it so quiet? Have I done something wrong?" The fact that I just got fired having escaped my mind in the building tension in the room.

Vera puts her arms around my shoulders and looks at me with head lifted to enable her to see me through her bifocals; I see the tears as they well in her eyes.

"Cara, Butch called today. He's comin' for you and the children."

"What!" I nearly shout as I rise from the sofa. "You told him I was here?"

"No, no, Deddy said we didn't know where you were, but he said he knew you were here, and he was comin' to git you. We tol' him no, but he's comin'. We think he is comin'. Cara, come, sit down. You don't look good, girl. Come," she said, patting the sofa.

"Do you really think he's coming? Maybe he was just testing you."

"Naw, he's comin'," Lyle says.

"Oh my God, what am I going to do? What about the girls, where will I go? When…when is he coming? Did you tell Samantha?"

"No, no, we haven't said a word to her."

I feel numb, sick with impending doom. No tears, no hysteria. As if I were having an out-of-body experience again. Lord, help me to know what to do.

"Cara…Caralee…girl."

"I'm…I'm all right, really, Vera, I'm all right. I just have to take the girls and leave.

Do you know where he is? When he'll be here?"

"When I talked t' him, he said he was in Chicago, he coulda' been lyin', though," Lyle says as he runs his hands over his face. So…I figer'…maybe two days."

Lyle is Vera's son by a previous marriage, possibly ten or twelve years older, and there seems to be no love lost between he and Rick.

He is the epitome of tall, dark, and handsome. Black, wavy hair, nut-colored brown skin, and dresses like a gangster. Suits, ties, and silk shirts.

As I sit next to this kind, loving woman, surrounded by all of "his" people, the people who had rescued me, I am angry. So angry at them. A nearly uncontrollable urge comes over me to scream at them that it was their fault that he was such a monster.

"So sorry, Cara, we're so sorry." I hear Vera's voice, and it brings me back to the present.

Dorian is coming in from the kitchen…I don't know when she left.

Lyle is saying, "…And Dorian will drive you."

"What? I'm sorry, I can't seem to think."

"This is all your fault, Ver-ra, you spoilt him rotten, ah told ya this'd happen." Amos is angry. I've never heard him even raise his voice. He's out of his chair and padding barefooted across the floor to the kitchen. Cigarette dangling from his mouth. I hear the freezer open. I know he is getting ice cream.

"Now, Deddy…this isn'a a time to go on 'bout wha''ah shoulda' done."

"Be quiet, Momma…" Lyle leans in close to Vera. "My gawd, le' me tell her what we decided…Dorian is gonna' take y'all to Texas to yur momma's, ya' jes' gotta' call 'em, an find out where they at. Ya know, she kin see her kin, and it'll git ya outta here, 'cuse I know that Butch, an all hell's gonna' break loose."

I sit in stunned silence. Nearly unable to distinguish the meaning of the cacophony of sounds coming from everyone's voices, as they all seem to be speaking at once.

"Deddy, ya' jes' dropped yur' ash," I hear Vera holler at Amos.

"Shut up Ver-ra" was his only retort.

"Dorian…" I look up, and she is standing behind Lyle.

"It's good, girl. It's settled. Y'all have ta leave. We'll pack in the mornin'. Y'all call yur Momma and Daddy, and we'll just scoot on down to Texas. An' I can see my boys."

25

I look in the back seat, and Jillian is asleep on the crib mattress we put across the back of it, and Samantha is sitting cross-legged looking at storybooks.

Dorian is at the wheel of her and Lyle's Chevrolet, as we maneuver through the streets of New York in the wee hours of the morning. We have decided to drive straight through, with one of us sleeping and the other driving.

We left at four this morning. Putting the girls in the back seat still in their pajamas.

Stopping at a gas station to wash them and change their clothing.

Yesterday, I may never remember. Piling things in boxes to have Amos and Vera send to my folks in Texas. Throwing other things in the car. Diapers, clothes for the girls, what little belongings we had. Jars of baby food and thermoses filled with milk. And coffee. Bread and bologna, peanut butter and jelly.

Each time the phone rang, the bustle would stop, and we would all stand frozen until someone would answer it and we could be sure it wasn't *him*.

The cars on the street outside slow, on the small incline to a stop sign, causing nearly as much anxiety.

Jillian started teething today and is fussy, so unlike her. She has been such a good baby, happy and contended with nearly every surrounding, as she invariably finds something to get in to. Last week, she ate all the leaves off Vera's African violets, which gave her immediate diarrhea. Not wanting the runny stuff on her fat little legs as she stood at the coffee table, she proceeded to smear the poop on the coffee table. She recovered fine. I am not certain about her granny.

To Samantha; Dorian, Vera, and I extol the virtues of our new adventure. We were going to drive a very long way and then… we would stay with Gramma and Poppa. Wouldn't that be fun?

Samantha's three-and-a-half-year-old response was one of resignation and confusion. I hugged her and told her, "It would be fun."

Dorian thinks it will take about twenty-four hours to get to Texas.

My parents didn't seem to be concerned as to why I was coming. They asked no questions, so I didn't volunteer any information.

We traverse the large expanse of freeways with an expertise that caused us both to laugh. Dorian is so funny. A pervading and subtle sense of humor. She is excited to see her three sons, whom she has left with their father, to marry Lyle. Something I could never understand.

But Dorian was crazy about the Bohemian good looks of this younger man, Lyle. She was forty-three, and he was thirty-eight, and Rick always said Lyle was "not so bright," but he was a quiet man, so who knew?

After all, it was at his insistence that we were presently "on the lam," as Dorian put it.

She is a wild thing. Drinks, smokes, and wears a ton of makeup, with a base of egg whites—yes, egg whites. She says it smoothes out the wrinkles. It seems to work, as she has very few wrinkles. Her skin is thick-looking and dark, and she has bleached blond hair she does herself, so on any given day, it can be orange or gray, depending on the time she had to do it. She is short and squat and dresses "cheap." That is what Vera says.

"Bless her little heart," Vera would say.

She is one of the nicest people I have ever known with a heart of gold and an unfettered attitude about living.

She sits at the steering wheel now, big curlers in her hair, and she is smoking a corncob pipe. Her black eyes dancing in amusement at my hysteria, as it is the funniest thing I have ever seen.

Ordinarily so interested in all my surroundings, I am unaware, as we pass from New York to Pennsylvania, on through West Virginia. We sleep and drive and sleep and drive. Stopping every couple of hours to potty and get gas.

I tell Dorian I got fired, and in small detail, as Samantha was all ears, I try to explain why.

"Ya' know, girl, that's what they all want, men. 'Cept of course, Lyle. He has trouble gettin' it up, if ya git my drift," as she laughs infectiously. "But hey, I jus' go with other guys."

"Really?" I say. Shocked beyond comprehension. "What does he do, when you do that?"

"Well, girl! I don't tell 'im," laughing again. "So what's ya gonna do now? That Butch, he'll fin' ya, ya kin' be sure now."

"I don't know. I have some money I've saved the last couple of months, but now, it doesn't seem like much. I need a car, a job, a place to work, to say nothing of a place to live."

As the miles flew by beneath the Chevrolet, I told her about the little green book and Lilith.

"So…me, I'd call that friend of yours and go from there." Her pudgy wrists hang over the steering wheel, hands dangling, with chipped red nail polish, showing off nails bitten to the quick.

Missouri and Kansas are flat and dry. The air hot and stifling, windows rolled down as the dust invades the automobile and all occupants within.

It is evening, and we have stopped at a truck stop to eat, as Dorian says they are a safe place to stop.

Jillian has fussed increasingly for the last several hours. And I really don't know what to do. By midnight, she is all-out screaming, as we pull into a gas station for gas.

"Let's jus' put some whiskey on her gums. That'll help," Dorian says.

"Where are we going to get whiskey?"

"Oh, girl, I got whiskey."

So out of the trunk comes a fifth of Jim Beam. And we rub in on her gums.

But to no avail. She is screaming blue murder, and Dorian is trying to calm her as I drive through the flat, dusty land.

It is 3:00 AM and Dorian has given Jillian a little bit of whiskey and sugar in a bottle of water.

Finally, quiet.

Dorian is sleeping, her head leaning against the open window, her mouth hanging open in exhaustion. We have been on the road for twenty-four hours, and we still have nearly six to go as per Dorian's "figurin'."

I can hear the happy little chuckles of a baby, and as I look in the rearview mirror, I watch as she crawls to pull herself up behind me, fat baby hands on the back of the seat.

"Mama…Mama…" happy little chatter as her very own language comes in slurs from my baby's drunken stupor.

She is drooling down my neck and clasping fat little arms and hands around my throat.

"Hi, sweetheart, so you feel better, do you?"

Gurgling and slobbering down my neck, she has now pulled herself to a standing position behind my seat. Squealing with delight. "Patty-caking" on my head and jumping up and down on the mattress.

Now, her hands are across my glasses. "No, no, Jillian, Mommy's driving. I have to see. Sit down."

Squealing and laughing with the innocence only given to children, she now has a firm grip on my white, horn-rimmed glasses.

Good grief, it is funny, but I can't see. I reach over to Dorian to wake her, but too late.

Snap! The glasses break in half at the nosepiece, brittle with age. She falls back on the mattress, as each of her little hands now hold a portion of my much-needed spectacles.

"Dorian, Dorian, wake up," I say as I am patting her on the leg. "Wake up."

We continue careening down the road, the driver now rendered sightless. For what seemed an eternity, given I could not see a thing in the blackness of the early morning hours, thanking God that this country was so flat and the road so boring, taking my foot off the accelerator.

"Dorian, wake up." I am laughing at the ridiculousness of it all, as Dorian rouses from her semiconscious state.

"What…what's the matter?" wiping the drool from the side of her face.

"Our Jillian is drunk and has just broken my glasses, and I can't see."

She looks to the back seat, and Jillian is licking the half of the glasses she holds in her hands. "Mama, Mama," she chants, giggling.

"Good Lord, pull over," she said with thick, sleep-induced laughter, shaking her.

"Where? I really cannot see a thing."

"Slow, girl, slow, jus' pull over here now. Good, good, now jus' stop the car."

Was it because we were so tired or because it was so funny? We didn't care. We sat and laughed until the tears were rolling down our cheeks.

We found some electrical tape in the toolbox in the trunk, and extracting the glasses from Jillian's fingers, we taped my glasses together.

Samantha slept on in blissful ignorance.

26

We arrive in Fort Worth at nine the following morning. My parents are both gone. The house is cool and enormous.

The only thing familiar was some photos on the wall. All new furnishings, a new Imperial in the garage. A swimming pool in the backyard.

I am astonished. And hurt. Didn't they know how desperately I needed help?

We haul all the soiled diapers and our belongings from the car to the garage and a bedroom—whose, I am not certain.

Dorian is both dumbfounded there was no one home, and reticent to leave me.

"I'll be fine. Go, go. Go see your boys," I tell her.

We wander through the expanse of the house, and as I enter the kitchen, Samantha says, "Mama, Mama, Poppa's hat."

As I look, I can see my father's cowboy hat lying on the counter.

Funny the things that bring joy to both the very young and their mothers. So…we were in the right house.

I have no idea where my mother would be. I thought she would be expecting me and be excited to see the girls, if not me.

We locate the bathroom, and I bathe my weary children, fix them lunch, and put them down for a nap. I put a load of diapers in the washing machine. It takes me a little time to figure out how to use an automatic washer, and there was an automatic dryer.

The rest of my life I would clout the invention of these things as the most monumental discoveries of the century.

After all, I was used to Laundromats or lizards or frozen clothing. Wringer washers.

Finding clean clothing, I stand for an indeterminable period of time in the shower. Lots of hot water, washing dust and tears and exhaustion from my weary body. Being sufficiently clean to do so, I crawl into bed with my tiny daughters and sleep.

I awaken to Jillian poking in my ears and eyes. "Up, up, Mama." The extent of her vocabulary very limited indeed. Samantha could talk a blue streak by the time she was a year old while Jillian only poked, pointed, grunted, and growled. With her great blue eyes denoting any and all things she was in need of. Such a funny little girl, I laugh and cuddle her.

"Shush, let's not wake Samantha, okay?"

Still, no one is home. It is three o'clock.

Certainly someone will be home soon, at least for dinner.

Peeling potatoes over a garbage can, I have made a salad and set the table. The girls are playing quietly on the floor when I hear a truck enter the garage.

The back door bursts open, and there is my handsome father, all decked out in a navy blue suit, white shirt and tie, his head down, his shoulders rounded.

"Daddy! Poppa!" Samantha and I shout simultaneously.

Jillian holds a block in her hand, looking up with huge blue eyes at this unknown stranger we are apparently so happy to see.

Before I can get to him to hug him, my mother is in the door.

She looks wonderful, her hair a deep rich auburn, a gold skirt and sweater grace her very trimmed-down figure. Chocolate brown pumps cover her tiny feet.

Not acknowledging our presence at all, she is screaming and shouting as she follows my father through the hallway to the kitchen door.

"How dare you? I'll leave you and take everything you ever had! If you think for one minute you can do this to me, you have another thing coming, mister. I won't put up with this, not ever, do you understand!"

I have scooped Jillian up into my arms, Samantha has scurried to cling to my leg as we retreat as far away as possible from this woman's wrath.

Standing in front of the kitchen sink, I pat my whimpering daughter's head and bounce the shocked baby in my arm.

"Shush, shush, it's all right."

"Don't you shush me." She turns to face me. "Who do you think you are?"

"I'm…not…Mother…I didn't mean…" I said as my limbs are turning to water, as my life flashes before me.

"Shut up!" She scoops up the garbage can and throws it at daddy.

Oh my gosh…potato peelings and lettuce and cucumber peelings hang on his head and drip down over his suit. Little red tomato heads lie lodged in his shirt collar.

With a speed I have never known my mother to execute, she has retreated to the garage. We hear the sound of the garage door going up and the engine of an automobile.

She did not come home that night or the following day.

Apparently it was over a woman at work that had her eye on Daddy.

Was he in fact an innocent bystander, we will never know. However, he then and now attests to his innocence.

The girls and I were there for nearly four days before my mother spoke.

The atmosphere one we were used to.

When she did speak, it was to tell me they were moving yet again. Daddy was being transferred to Vandenberg AFB in California. I could go with them if I wanted to, but I could not stay with them long. Did I understand that?

"Yes, yes…" I understood, and I would appreciate any help they could give me. Could I please make a couple of long-distance telephone calls to arrange for my allotment to be changed? And I needed to talk to a friend about a job.

"Yes, just get the time and charges."

I scrubbed and cleaned and cooked for our room and board. My mother was, in fact, working with my father. She, in time, was happy to see the girls and was more than "good" with them. Always loving and kind and more than interested and encouraging in instructing them as to how to read, write, and count.

Samantha, to her, was a joy, as she played and talked with her for hours.

Jillian frustrated her, as she was happy to just "be." She was not interested in learning how to talk or walk, and she was into everything. Scooting along on her bottom to drawers and pulling plants to the floor. Eating anything that was lying about.

Jillian loved the swimming pool, and it was *hot* outside—the temperature often reaching in excess of one hundred degrees on any given day.

We would all get in the pool, and I could drop Jillian in the water; she would swim like a dolphin, never coming up for air unless we panicked and pulled her up by the back of her diaper. Then she would splutter and spew water and squirm to get back in the water.

The moving van sits outside the house. My things have arrived from Vera and Amos, and they too have been loaded.

Daddy will drive the truck, Mother will drive the Imperial, and Paul and Denise and I and the girls will drive in Paul's car. (Nice—my brother has a car at seventeen, and he has never had a job.)

Their plan is to stop two nights en route. What a relief.

The morning of the third day, the girls refused to get in the car. Samantha, crying and saying she "didn't want to go on any more rides. No, no, no!"

"No more 'bye, bye,' Mama," tears of anguish streaming down their pretty little faces. Jillian, bracing her little feet against the door as we try to bend the firmly planted baby legs and push her in the car.

It was humorously sad as I tried to explain why we had to do this, laughing outwardly, secretly wishing I, too, could demand this all stop.

Jillian began walking shortly after our arrival, and it is plain to even the unobservant, that as a tiny baby, she was merely resting. For she is into everything. She apparently has no fear.

Mother and Daddy bought a new travel trailer and a new house. With, of course, landscaping. The piles of manure were everywhere, and for some reason, this small child decided to eat it. Her tongue and mouth are swollen and she is miserable, as we travel the distance to the base hospital.

She has trench mouth.

"Good grief," my mother says. "Now what will we do? We will all have trench mouth."

We wash all the dishes and silverware in bleach, and ultimately, no one else comes down with the dreaded disease.

Do you know where they got the term trench mouth? During the sixteenth century, few people had plates, and they ate out of trenchers, a piece of wood with the middle scooped out like a bowl. Often, trenchers could be used for quite some time. Trenchers were never washed, and often, worms and mold got into the wood and old bread. After eating off wormy, moldy trenchers, people would get trench mouth.

We did not eat out of trenchers, so I can only assume it was the cow manure in the backyard that caused the dreaded trench mouth.

She just recovered from that and tried to eat the tar stick the men were using to tar the ends of the fence posts. Her eight small teeth are now firmly glued together. With a line of black apparently being the culprit.

My mother is hysterical.

Once more, we go to the base hospital. They simply use nail polish remover to extract the tar from her teeth.

I could have done that, had I known it wouldn't have poisoned her.

She will not wear any clothing, having gotten used to the heat of Texas (that was quick). And literally rips her clothing from her body, screaming, "Off, off."

Mother and Daddy went to San Francisco for the weekend. They brought Jillian back the cutest little red furry boots. She loves them and will wear nothing else on her feet. With winter coming on, I am relived she will wear something.

While shopping at the Goodwill store with the girls one afternoon, Jillian eyed a little white straw hat, a rounded affair with a medium-sized brim trimmed in black velvet, the same black velvet spanning the base of the cap, with miniature plastic flowers adorning it. Jillian wanted the hat more than anything she had ever had, with the exception of her lop-eared bunny, which she drug everywhere, sucking her thumb and rubbing the satiny ears under her nose. And of course, her little red boots.

"Oh, Jillian, that is for a big lady, it won't fit you."

"Yes, yes!" She's ecstatic in her admiration of the hat.

"That's an ol' ladies hat," my nearly-four-year-old, fashion-conscious daughter exclaims to her sister. "You'll look funny."

"Momma, peez, peez'"

"Let's see," I say as I pick up the hat and examine it. After all, we were at the Goodwill, just my luck it would have lice. Wouldn't Mother have a fit?

I place it on the tow-headed pile of curls, and it readily sinks down to cover her ears and most of her cute little face.

"Pitty, pitty," she says, her dimpled little hands clutching at the brim of the hat. Cocking it to the side so she can see.

"Oh, darlin', we can't see your pretty face. Let's see what else they have."

"No, no, Mama, pitty."

"Oh, Jillian…let Mama see how much it is."

She very obligingly hands me the hat. Squatting down in front of her, I look at the hat—ten cents. Oh, for goodness sakes, if ten cents will make her this happy…

She wore the hat home that day, and with the exception of sleep, she wore the hat, the little red boots, and drug her lop-eared bunny. As long as she could wear these things, she would wear anything else we deemed appropriate.

27

On the fateful weekend of Mother and Daddy's trip to San Francisco, I would once again suffer the onslaught of the male of our species.

Mother and Daddy's friends have arrived from Oregon to look for work and will be staying here for approximately a month. They "can't be sure..."

I really don't know them except in reference to my childhood. He is about Daddy's age. Bald, but very nice looking. Tall and has a nice physique.

She, nearly fifteen years younger, and the most unattractive woman I had ever met. With pock-marked skin, waist-length black stringy hair, with legs, arms, hands, and feet that belong on a man. They have a daughter Samantha's age. He has two children my age by a previous marriage.

We have a pleasant evening. I fixed dinner, and we chatted awhile. I bathed the girls, read to them, then returned to the kitchen to do the dishes and clean up. They were having drinks and talking.

"Mom said you can stay in the room I am in tonight, and I and the girls will sleep in their bedroom. Is there anything I can get you? I think I'll go take a bath and go to bed."

"No, no, everything is fine."

Snuggled close to Samantha, both of us deep in blissful sleep as Jillian slumbers peacefully in her crib, I am suddenly roused by the sense of someone handling my breasts. Reaching up with my hand, I place it over the top of a very large hairy hand. My heart is pounding so rapidly, I can feel it in my head. I look to the sleeping angel beside me and see she is sound asleep. I grab the hand and, jerking on it, try to pull it away from my body.

"Shush, you'll wake the little ones," a male voice whispers in my ear. As he pulls me tightly to his body, so tightly I can feel his arousal at my back.

Think, be calm, and think, I silently tell myself.

"Please, Earl, don't do this, what about your family? Please let go of me." The anger and fear rising fast in my body, causing me to sweat and tremble. This man is in my parents' bed, trying to rape me with my children not two feet away. Was he insane? If I scream, it will awaken my children.

It would get me help, as I am fairly certain his wife and daughter are in the next room. But what of my children? I simply can't let them see this.

"Stop this now," I whisper through tightly clenched teeth. Teeth all too recently shattered by another man.

"You want me, I can tell Cara, you are trembling. You are the most beautiful thing I have ever seen, and I am so lonesome."

Isn't it just like a man to interpret trembling and sweat with desire, not fear and anger?

Only moments have passed, moments that to me seem an eternity.

I try to turn toward him, and thinking I am acquiescing, he allows me to do just that.

As I turn in the bed, I push with all my might, shoving full force, plummeting him to lie shocked on the floor at the edge of the bed.

Still my children sleep.

I am out of bed before he can rise from the floor. "Come with me, you bastard," I say again through clenched teeth. Shocked by my own language, and thinking, these men are making me mad.

By the time we get to the kitchen, I already have a glass of water in my hand. My first impulse is to throw it at him. Remembering the beatings, I decide perhaps that would not be a good idea. (Only my father would put up with that.)

He is coming at me as if to embrace me.

"Sit down," I say in my "mother's voice." "Now!"

He sits. I am shocked. "What in the world were you thinking?"

"Cara, I love you, I have loved you since the first time I ever saw you. I am so sorry, that was the wrong thing to do, will you forgive me?" He starts to rise from the chair he is sitting in.

"Sit down and stay there." Again, my mother's voice. "You have a wife and a child in this very house. How dare you do such a nasty thing?"

"I know, I know, I can't tell you how sorry I am, but after all these years, you're all grown up and well, I heard you are separated from your husband, and I well…jeez, I don't know." He is rubbing his face with his hands as he lowers his head to his chest. A very large, hairy chest, I might add.

"Look, understand, I don't know you, and you are probably a nice, decent man, but I will tell both your wife and my father if you ever, ever do this again. Go to bed and don't *ever* come near me again."

"Yes, yes, I will." He went to his assigned room.

I to mine. To lay awake the rest of the night waiting…

The next day, I scrubbed and cleaned and took all the children to the park.

My parents arrived home at ten thirty that night.

I slept.

I, of course, could not know that in twenty years, this man would be diagnosed with scleroderma, a disease that atrophies all tissue and internal organs. Or that he would seek me out at my place of business to tell me he still loved me and how sorry he was to have assaulted me that night so many years ago.

For the most part, life was as it had always been living in my parents' home. There were scintillating conversations, laughter, and teasing. Card and game playing, picnics in the evening, and work. As long as Mother was happy…

Mother was excellent at delegating, and there were boxes upon boxes to unpack and store. There were curtains to hang and meals to fix. Laundry to do and children to care for. These duties primarily delegated to me.

I have an eleven-year-old sister and a seventeen-year-old brother who were "too busy" with their lives to be able to help.

And "Denise really would be no help anyway, housework really isn't her thing," my mother informs me one day as I am knee-deep in laundry and unpacking *her* things.

"But she could unpack her things and help with the dinner dishes, fold clothes, lots of things, Mother, and she certainly isn't going to learn any younger."

We were starting to get on each other's nerves.

A very bad place for me to be.

28

"Are you going to move soon?" my mother asks one morning from her "station" in the recliner.

I'm shocked, as it's only been a month since we have been here. And she seemed to have so much work for me to do. "Well, yes, Mother, when did you want me to move?"

"I thought we could go look for you a place today. You know, with Earl and Lisa here, it's hard."

I am bending over, unpacking a box, so relieved she couldn't see my face. *I had to leave because their friends were here. Boy, could I tell her about her "friend."*

"Okay, Mother, that would be nice. But I need to get a job first."

"Well, I would have thought you would have done something about that by now."

"Mother, I just thought you needed my help, I…I…"

"You what? You just thought you could stay here forever? You should have thought about all of this before you left your husband."

"But, Mother…" I stammer. "He was beating me up. Ask Vera and Amos."

"Oh, posh, like you were modeling in New York. Cara Leah, you will be the death of me." She rises from the chair and sticking a hairpin in her ear to scratch it, she walks to where I am unpacking the box, her turquoise robe flowing from her body, her little terry cloth scuffs shuffling across the carpet. "You are just like Auntie, such a vivid imagination. I'll go get dressed. I've been looking in the paper, and there are a few places we can go look at."

Okay, so we are moving. (I do have nearly all *her moving in* accomplished). Thank you, Lord, for the money from my imaginary modeling job. I have no car and no job and two small children to feed, and *she* is evicting me. Without notice, does Daddy know? That is a hopeless thought. If Mother says I have to move, he would second the motion.

I am *so* tired of wanting to cry, to just sit in the middle of the floor and cry. I breathe deeply and pray for the strength not to cry.

We looked at several places this afternoon and found a darling one-bedroom place only about three miles from them. It is clean and well-maintained. Set in a U-shape, there were maybe fifteen other units, all on the ground floor. There are no yards, but as my mother was quick to point out, the girls would be at a babysitter's the better part of the day, and it wasn't like it was forever.

Easy for her to say. Just what was it she saw for our future? It looked pretty glum to me.

"Are you going to file for divorce?" she asks me on the way home. "You know, no one in the family has ever had a divorce."

"Oh, Mother, two of your brothers have gotten a divorce."

"Well, certainly no women. Well, your father's grandmother, but that isn't *my* family."

"Oh…I don't know, I need the allotment, and the military will take care of the girls and me if we get sick."

"Where is he?"

She had never wanted to talk about it. Any time I brought it up, it was "That is your business—I hope you are prepared for the consequences of your actions. You know you never have thought of anyone other than yourself." So now she wants to know— interesting. Again, I fight tears as I look out the window of the car. Am I selfish? Lord, please don't let me be selfish.

"Amos went to his commanding officer and they said he was AWOL, so I can only assume that is still true, or he could be in the brig."

"So he'll probably come to get you. And this will all be over."

She is pulling the big Imperial into the driveway, and as the words fall from her lips, I feel physically assaulted.

"No, Mother, he beat me half to death, he left me. He isn't coming to get me."

But her words left a grotesque premonition. And Lyle's words come to echo in my heart.

It's been three months since we arrived in sunny California. The skies are clear and blue all day long, the night skies filled with stars.

The girls are well and appear to be happy, after all, chaos is all they have ever known, and it has been a very peaceful, serene two months.

Mother was right; we are much happier by ourselves. I got a job in a very small dress shop, and the owner is a delightful older woman. She and her husband have been most kind to us. I am the only other person working in the store, so we have become quite close.

She is most encouraging and very lenient if I am late or need to leave early to pick up the girls.

The lady across the street from Mother is delighted to babysit, and they are close to Mother and Daddy, so I feel they are safe. I am only making a dollar an hour. Life is still pinching one penny tighter than the last. I bought an old, beat-up car. Daddy went with me to look at it and said he "would keep it goin'."

The three of us pile into the old car at every opportunity and head for the beach. The beach is lovely. Long deep stretches of golden sand, billowy waves spewing white froth as it plunges like thunder against the shore. The sun kissing the changing colors of the water that rests in angry torment against the azure blue of the sky.

It fills my senses with tranquility.

There is a small cove at the end of this very long beach. It is warm, private with soft golden sands, and we go there to laugh and play. Sometimes taking a picnic lunch, sometimes just going for an hour or so in the evening.

It decidedly is not the life I had envisioned…but it will do…
much better than our *history*.

Thank you, Lord, for not giving me the time to think, for I
am heartbroken and so very sorry I don't understand how to be a
good wife, so my children can't have a father…or a mother that is
home for them. To love and care for them, even to yell at them. I
would do anything to have them have a normal life.

In the wee hours of the morning, I would awaken feeling quite
sorry for myself.

The warmth of my children next to me, their sweet smell. The
tousle of red and gold curls and the shimmering white curls mix-
ing together on the pillow.

We long ago decided it was much cozier to all sleep in one bed.

The crib sits in the corner of the room, filled with stuffed animals. Will it be forever empty?

29

It is Saturday evening, and I only have to work every other Saturday, so we have been at the beach most of the day. We turn the corner to the small courtyard of our home, and sitting on the steps is Rick.

"Mama, it's Daddy," Samantha whispers to me from her standing position on the floor of the back seat. Her small voice filled with trepidation.

"I see, baby, it's all right."

As I look in the rearview mirror, I see her slide back in the big seat and put her finger in her mouth. She hasn't done that in months.

I decide it best to get it over with out here. After all, there are people all over.

As I open the door, he comes around to hold it for me.

"So how are y'all, sweetie?" he said in his little girl chuckle. "There's my girls" as he starts to open the rear door.

They are locked in, and I make no attempt at opening the doors.

"How did you find us?"

"Ah, sweetheart, y'all weren't hard t'find at all. Were y'all hidin'?"

"You girls sit in the car a minute while Mommy talks to Daddy," I say, getting out of the car, wrapping the sarong tighter around my waist. Extremely conscious of how thin I am.

"Why are you here? What do you want?"

"I jus' wanna see my girls. That's all, sweetheart. That's all."

"I don't think this is a good idea. So maybe you had better go."

"Ah, Cara, are ya still mad? I am sorry, ya know. I sure as hell think I been punished enough."

"Really, well, I don't think that is possible."

"Look, Cara, sweetie, I wooda come sooner, darlin', but they threw me in the brig. I had a lotta time t' think in there, an I'm rightful sorry for all I done t' y'all. I love ya, Cara. I know that now, and I'll make it up t' y'all, I promise."

"I don't think you can. I think you had better leave."

"Ah, come on, Cara, I came all this way to see my babies, let me just see my babies."

"There they are, see?"

"Ah, Cara, ah know I did ya wrong, but I love y'all an' I promise I'll make it up to all y'all. Momma said you wouldn't see me, but I tol' her I had t' try."

"How are your parents?" I ask.

"Oh, they're good. They're livin' in San Diego again. An' so when I got out, I came back to see if I could find y'all, and I been stayin' with them. They send their love."

"Tell them thank you, and I love them too. Now, we have to go, I have to feed the girls."

"You always were a good mother, Cara. Guess I shoulda appreciated it more. Do ya love me still?"

He is standing so close to me I can smell the English leather he wears. He is handsome, as handsome as any movie star. His curly gold hair tousled perfectly, with still the military cleanness of it. His chiseled features and red-gold skin. Lean and muscled, he stands well over six feet. No wonder my children are so beautiful.

"I don't know, Rick, how could I?"

"I know I don't have the right t' have ya for my wife, but ya still are my wife, Cara, and I love ya." He reaches out to touch me, and I pull back.

"Kin I hold the children and talk t' them, jest a minute, please? I am their deddy. I ain't never hurt 'hem."

"Yes, you have," I said. "Where have you been?"

"I tol' ya I been in the brig."

"Where?" I ask.

"In Texas, why d' ya ask?"

"Because I can hardly understand you." I laugh.

"Oh, yeh, well…what kin I say." Chuckling again. "Y'all know us Texans. Kin I see my girls? Please?" he pleads.

What is going through my mind? Am I nervous, terrified, not really. Surprised. Shocked. Yes, I am shocked. I should have been prepared. I wish I knew what to do. I wish Daddy was here.

"Please, Cara, I promise I jus' wanna hold 'em."

"If they want to, but then you have to go. Do you understand?"

He pauses, but for a brief minute, he then says, "I guess I got no choice, now do I? Whatever you say, Cara, from now on whatever y'all say." Tears glisten in the dark eyelashes that surround the blue of his eyes.

The little green book flashes through my mind. I was thrilled when I unpacked it. There are no accidents, it says, and that God has prepared a way for us under grace.

God, please let me not be making a mistake here.

I reach in and unlock the car's back door. I walk in front of him, and opening the door, I kneel down and say, "Samantha, Daddy wants to hold you a minute and talk to you, do you want to do that?"

She pulls her finger out of her mouth and, looking down at the ground all the while, climbs from the car and goes to stand in front of him.

She stands very still as he bends to pick her up. The tears slide down his face unrelentingly as he holds her and tells her how sorry he is and how he is going to make it up to her. That he will never ever hurt her mommy or her again, and over and over how sorry he is. He is sobbing, as I extract her from his arms. And give him Jillian. Who, being unafraid of anyone, feels unthreatened by this strange sobbing man. So unlike her Poppa.

As I hold Samantha close to me, I feel her sobs as they shake her little girl body. "Shush, shush, sweetheart, it's all right. Shush."

Jillian pushes back from him with her fat little hands placed firmly on his chest, to better survey the situation, under the brim of her bonnet, red boots dangling from stovepipe-fat legs. All that and a little swimming suit.

He can't help but laugh, she is pretty funny. "What's all this?" he asks, referring to her strange attire.

"Oh, well, mostly it is just Jillian. She likes it and won't go anywhere without it."

Hugging her and telling her who he is, as she certainly hasn't a clue. "They're right prutty little girls, jus' like their mama."

"Okay," I say, using my mother's voice. It has been effective in the past. "You have to leave now."

"Kin I take y'all t' dinner? Please, I'd be right honored."

"No! You have to go."

"Okay, okay, I tol' ya, from now on, Cara, it's whateva' y'all say."

He walks to the street and climbs into the black Thunderbird of a long ago time. At least he still has the same car.

We go in the house, and I fix dinner and bathe the girls. "It's early. Do you want to go see what Gramma and Poppa are doing?" I ask.

"Yeah, yeah," a resounding "yeah."

I have to tell someone, and really, I am so nervous I can't sit still.

The door stands open, the screen stands filtering the night-flying insects, as darkness has begun to fall. I hear the tinkling sound of my mother's laughter and the music of Henry Mancini drifts from the house we had so recently called home.

"Knock, knock," I holler as I pull the screen door open.

"Gramma, Poppa," the girls yell in unison as they scamper to my parents, who sit playing gin rummy at the kitchen table.

"Hi, where are the kids?" as I bend to kiss each in turn.

"Oh, they are out with their friends," my mother says as she pats my arm. "What brings you over? Would you like some coffee, tea?"

Samantha and Jillian are squealing in delight as they head for the toy box in the living room.

"I just needed someone to talk to. Rick was waiting for me when I got home from the beach today."

My father continues to look at his cards. Mother lays her card on the pile and shouts with glee, "Gin!"

"I'll be damned," my dad says, grinning from ear to ear. Pushing back the chair, he goes to the refrigerator and opens a beer.

"So I knew he'd come. It's about time you got this thing straightened out," my mother says as she shuffles the cards. "Sit down, do you want to play? We could play something else."

"No, no, I just…maybe I was afraid to stay there, I don't know. I think Samantha still remembers and is afraid of him."

"Are you afraid of him?" my father asks.

"Well, not right now. But I think it is foolish that I'm not."

"So…what did he have to say for himself?" my mother asks, laying down the cards, going to the freezer to dish up ice cream for everyone.

Neither of them have much to say as I repeat the conversation of earlier that evening. Listening intently, with all of us careful to not be overheard by the tiny ears in the living room.

"Are you asking for my advice? Because if I give it, you'd better be prepared," Mother sits imposingly at the kitchen table, waiting for my response.

I sit thinking of a lifetime of Mother's advice, how harsh it often seems to be, and know that if she gives it, she expects you to follow it.

"Did he go back to San Diego?" Daddy asks.

"I don't know. I just told him he had to leave."

"What are you going to do with your life, Caralee? You have made a mess of it thus far, and you have two children to think of. Surely you can grasp the enormity of that responsibility. And mind you, it *is* your responsibility."

"I know that, Mother, but he hurt us bad, physically, that is dangerous."

"And just what do you mean? You say he broke your nose. It doesn't look broken to me, and your teeth have always been like that."

"Oh, Mother…" I stop myself. This isn't going to help me; to argue with her is pointless.

"Daddy…what do you think?"

"Let me finish," my mother interrupts. "Have you thought about how you're going to support those girls? Have you thought about the rest of your life? Marriage is not for everyone, but it is forever. You made your bed, you lie in it. If he wants you back, be grateful and go be a good wife to him. He is, after all, the father of your children, isn't he?"

I want to slap her. Why does every conversation with her end up this way? "Of course he is, Mother. Stop that."

"The kids are what to consider here, and the best thing a man can do for his children is to love their mother. Does he love you, do you think?" Daddy asks, completely ignoring Mother's jab at me.

"I don't know. He says he does, but he never acted like it. And he left me in Michigan all alone with the girls."

"Oh, for goodness sake, this is not *Gone with the Wind*, and you are not Scarlett." She is so distraught that she pushes the ice cream across the table. "A divorce is out of the question. You are not stupid. You have an eighth-grade education, thanks to your dallying. Where are you going to get a decent job? You'll simply have to marry again anyway—better the devil you know that the devil you don't."

Well, I got what I came for. And so rapidly. I don't know what I expected, but this was not it.

I quickly change the subject. "He says Vera and Amos are in San Diego, did you know that?"

Amos had worked for Daddy for a couple of years, and they both still worked for the same aerodynamics company.

"Yeah, I'd heard they transferred him back to San Diego."

"Why didn't we get transferred back to San Diego?" my mother is furious to hear that had been an option, any concerns of mine quickly vanishing from her mind as she continued to reiterate the wonders of San Diego and the limitless impossibilities of the present location.

We adjourn to the living room to play with the girls, the evening ends, and I take the girls home and place them snugly in our bed.

The little green book sits on the nightstand, and I pick it up. I went to sit in the tiny living room to read.

"No man is your enemy, no man is your friend, every man is your teacher through this journey we call life." So that explains my mother. I ponder whether I will I ever speak to my daughters like that.

The weeks come and go, and each weekend, he arrives—with flowers, with clothing for the girls, darling clothes I am certain his mother bought, but perhaps not. He does like to shop.

With each visit to my parents, my mother wants to know if he came again and echoes her previous argument.

The intervening weeks bring reality to rest on my beleaguered shoulders. There seems to be more bills than money, as of course my allotment checks are no more. The rent, the gas, the babysitter, the groceries seem to add up to more than I earn. I take as little out of the little cache I have from modeling, but I now have only nine hundred dollars left. Maybe that will get me through a whole year.

This week, the car broke down, and Daddy said it would cost about two hundred dollars for a new engine. I nearly panic. Do I need a car? I do; this is California, not New York City.

Jillian has a rash that she scratches at endlessly, and she simply must go to the doctor. There is the cost of the medicine, and I have to stay home with her.

The anxiety about money overwhelming me, I peruse the green book.

"Money is God in manifestation, as freedom from want and limitation. But it must always be kept in circulation and put to right uses. Hoarding and saving react with grim vengeance."

Lord, I pray, please guide me in your infinite mercy. Help me to make the right decision.

As I remember, the green book says to pray, giving thanks that you have already received. Thank you, Lord, that you have given me the wisdom to make the right choice.

Rick arrives on a sunny Sunday morning as I am preparing to go to church. "Kin I come in?" he asks hesitantly, as I have yet to let him in the house.

"Sure, I guess, but we are going to church, and…"

"I'll go with y'all."

I can't believe my ears—is this the same man who strangled me for giving twenty-five cents to the church.

"Okay," I say quietly as I bend to buckle Jillian's patented leather Mary Jane's and tying the bow in the back of Samantha's organdy pinafore before rising.

"Did ya' momma make yur dresses?" he said, addressing Samantha.

"Yeah," she says, smiling at him for the first time, spinning around to show off the pretty little dress and pinafore.

"Pitty," Jillian announces as she parades her finery before him.

We all pile in the Thunderbird. It is a very nice car.

"I foun' a house t' rent up on the hill above San Diego, y'all like it. It's got two bedrooms an' a nice big backyard for the children."

I say nothing. I only watch as the scenery passes, silent prayers echoing in my mind, silent fears tucked deep in the recesses of my heart. The thundering echo of my mother's words playing harsh notes of recriminations on my soul.

He takes us out to dinner and leaves shortly after having brought us home, never mentioning the house again.

My father has come to help Rick load the rented trailer with our belongings.

My mother, nowhere in sight. Well, I am going to go tell her good-bye. Lord, I don't understand her.

I am cleaning the cabinets in the kitchen, and Daddy has come to get yet another box. Without turning to look at him, as he bends to pick up the heavy box of dishes, I say, "Daddy, do you think I am doing the right thing?"

"I think you are doing the only thing you can," he rises, and checking to see we are alone, he hugs me and says, "It'll be all right, chicken, you're strong, you can do this."

As I stand and think of the only other *option* I had had over the ensuing months.

A very nice young mailman who came into the store daily asked me out, and at Mabel's insistence, I had gone. We had a nice time. He was a nice man, who made every indication he would like to marry. We had coffee several times a week after that.

He was killed in an automobile accident five weeks ago. I hadn't been in love, I hadn't really entertained the idea of marrying him, not really. But was that too a message? I am so confused.

30

The street is tree-lined, just two blocks off a very busy street. There is a slight curve to the street, lending an illusion of spaciousness to the lots. The house on the far corner one of soft yellow, the yard meticulously groomed.

The house seems enormous to me, having just left approximately three hundred square feet. This was twice as big, with two bedrooms and a bath, living room, and kitchen with a very minuscule dining area at the end of the kitchen. The outside, turquoise stucco, and indeed the yard is big by any standards. And it is fenced. He certainly didn't lie.

Vera and Amos have arrived to help unload and unpack. We will stay with them tonight. I am dreading "tonight," as I cannot fathom how uncomfortable that will be.

Rape, he has never resorted to. So I can only hope that should I be unable to do this, he will respect my wishes. Mother's words, "a good wife," come to mind, and I shove them away. We have never identified what exactly "that" was. With her example one of manipulation, anger and pouting, with the occasional *silent* treatment… I just thought it was not the right way to treat someone.

Vera is hugging me with heartfelt emotion and gratitude. "I'm so happy y'all kin work this out, Cara, I missed ya' an' those children more then I eva' thought possible, an' I think his deddy has had some words with 'im. I'm sur' it'll be all right now, he jes' didn't like bein' in the military. An' Amos an' me, we got a good surprise for y'all."

"Is he working?" Blunt and to the point. I had never asked him.

"Why, girl, he has a right nice job in San Diego, at a store for men's clothin'. An' he can git commissions, ah think he'll do all right by y'all, I do, girl. But don't you go lettin''im hit you, ya understan', girl?"

"Just how do you keep a *man* from hitting you?"

"Why, girl, ya hit back."

That night, he crawled in bed, turned his back to me, and went to sleep.

My Lord, was I never happy? Was this in fact Vera and Amos's idea?

The next morning, Rick went to work, and Vera and I go to the house to unpack. What a wonderful, helpful, caring person she is.

About noon, a truck arrives with two white poster beds, a dresser, and a nightstand. They are beautiful, trimmed in gold, with pink, yellow, and blue flowers hand painted on them.

"For me and my Jillian," Samantha is beside herself with joy, running along behind the delivery men and looking with wonder as they set up each piece.

"Oh, Vera, you shouldn't have done this. Thank you so much, but it is just too much."

"No, no, we wanted those pruty little girls to have it, and Butch said yu' was all sleepin' in one bed."

"I will never be able to thank you enough. They are gorgeous."

I would, over the next few weeks, make pink chintz dust ruffles, and white eyelet coverlets trimmed in pink ribbons for them. Their bedroom looked just as if it came out of a magazine.

"Now, girl, ah think ya otta know, Amos and me, we paid the first and last month's rent. So y'all 'av a good nuf start." She is putting groceries she has purchased in the cabinets.

"Oh, Mama, you can't be doing this. You have helped enough, we will be fine."

If they helped a little less, and my parents had helped some, maybe this would not have happened to begin with. Shame on me, I think. Mother and Daddy have helped. Daddy's helped a lot. Mother…will I ever get so I am able to understand her?

Long lazy days of just being with my children have turned to three weeks. Yesterday, he bought a television. I didn't say a thing. The one we had had in Michigan had broken, and I didn't feel I could replace it.

For three weeks, Rick has been exemplary, no harsh words, no rocking in silence. We have gone for rides and gone out to dinner and taken the girls to his parents and gone to the movies.

He still crawls into bed and turns his back to me.

I lie in bed; this should make me happy. I should be relieved, after all, that is the one thing I was the most worried about. So what in the world is wrong with me?

I am a young, healthy woman, with a man I am married to, lying in the bed next to me. That is what is the matter with me. The soliloquy goes on.

I turn and tap him on the shoulder. "Do you want to make love to me?" I ask, rather shyly.

Or was I embarrassed.

"No" was his only reply.

Could I leave it at that? No, it simply is not in my nature. "Why?" I whisper.

"'Cause I ain't havin' no more fuckin' brats, that's why."

"So we are never going to have sex again? What are we going to do about that?"

"I don' know 'bout y'all, but I'll jus' jerk off in the shower, 'fore I touch y'all agin, then agin I jus' might go sumplace else."

I turn and am now certain this move was not his idea.

Rick mows the lawn and washes the car, we go to the grocery store together, he plays with the girls and reads them bedtime stories.

I can live without sex. He has been nice to me and the girls, I have a home, and that is what I have always wanted. I would like other children. But in time, perhaps, he will feel better about all of this.

He arrives home this evening and is joyous. The table is all set, and I have picked the last of the volunteer snapdragons for the centerpiece. I can hear his voice as he scoops Jillian up into his arms and arrive at the door in time to see him boost Samantha up into another. He has a hanger in his hand with a large cloth bag over it. And it swings in rhythm to his long stride as he approaches the front door. As he sets the girls down in the living room, he bends and kisses me. That's new.

I am grateful. Grateful to be kissed, I shrink from thinking of what that means.

"Looky what ah got," he exclaims gleefully, and he gently lays the bag on the sofa.

"What?" I ask him. "What have you got that makes you so happy?" I am both thrilled and curious.

"Ah bought me a Botany 500," he says as he unzips the cloth bag. "Looky here, y'all, deddy's got a new suit." Holding the suit for all of us to see. "What'd think, purty, huh?"

It is navy blue with a pinstripe and beautiful tailoring. "It is beautiful, but don't those cost a lot of money?"

"Well, yeh, but I'm gonna make money with it, y'all see, yur deddy's gonna git rich with this here suit."

"How are you going to make money with it?" I ask, as I really have no idea. I do realize he was addressing the children and not me. But…

"'Cause folks come in ta that fancy store. They expec' me ta look good. I gotta look good."

"But, Rick, you do look good. You're handsome and well dressed, clean. And you're a good salesman." I truly can attest to that, I think.

We say no more about it. After the girls have been put to bed, I say, "So tell me how much the suit cost you."

"Well, they gave me the discount so t'was really cheaper… so little over a hun'ed twenty-five dallars," he says as he rocks in his rocker.

One hundred twenty-five dollars, nearly three-quarters of what he made a month…my mouth hangs open in shock. "What about the rent? It is due this week, and it is ninety dollars," I ask as he has given me no money but has paid for the groceries, and the movies. I assumed he was going to handle the money, and although that wasn't a pleasant thought, I thought it might be an enlightening one for him.

"Oh, Mama and Deddy paid it," he said as he sat rocking, his eyes glued to the television screen.

"She told me that they paid first and last. So we will have to pay the rent this month."

"Caralee, jus' shut the fuck up. Okay? I wanna watch this show."

Funny, how articulate he can be when he wants. I get up to go to bed.

My name is Cara Leah, pronounced Lee, and he and my mother seem to use my full name not as an endearment, but rather as to further articulate their disapproval of me.

He has not paid the rent, and the landlord has been here twice this week. Each time I tell him that he will have to talk to my husband.

Each time I talk to my husband, he becomes more infuriated. "Rick, we have to pay the rent. What if they evict us?"

The rocker going at a steady pace, he takes the last gulp of his beer. "You pay the goddamn rent."

"Me, with what?"

"Oh, I know yu bin holden' out on me. Mamma tol' me all 'bout all thet money y'all made whilst ya were in New York City."

"Well, and just what do you think I have been living on all this time? It takes money to live, and you left me with none."

"Yur a lyin' bitch." The beer bottle crashes across the old, gray asbestos tile of the living room floor. Surprisingly the bottle doesn't break, the beer pooling on the floor in front of me.

"You do not speak to me like that," I say in my mother's voice, my heart pounding in my throat, and I wonder if he can see my fear. I have been conditioned, and I am afraid.

"Yur my wife, an' I'll talk t'ya any way ah want…got that?" Shouting. His finger poking my forehead.

He turns and the front door slams, as I hear the race of the Thunderbird's engine.

It has not been five weeks since we have moved here. Five weeks. I am having a difficult time processing the whole thing.

I walk to the window to see if he is really gone. He is. I tiptoe to the girls' room and very quietly open their closed door. Stacked in the back of the closet are my great-aunt's dishes. She left them to me when she died, and Grandma sent them to me while I was in Michigan. They are beautiful. An ivory-colored background with a gold rim and small pink, yellow, and blue roses entwined around the edges. There is service for twelve with serving pieces in abundance. I have never had a place to put them. So they stay perpetually packed in these, by now, rather ragged boxes. The money is in the bottom one, and it has not been touched. Thank you, Lord. I understand this is preparing for a disaster, not a happy marriage. But, Lord, you gave me two children to look after, and I'll not give him the money.

Vera and Rick have been after me to get a job. "Why cain't ya' get a job?"

She has always worked and loved it. "It would take so much pressure off of Butch, girl," she says, and he is at me constantly "to git a job, what the fuck do I do all day that I can't git a job?"

I try to tell them that raising children is a job. A job I love, and it would be just as expensive for me to go to work. A babysitter, clothing, gas, how was that going to help?

The rocking chair moves more swiftly these days, and I worry that soon he will explode. The tension is building with each new day. He throws things, he shouts. Or worse, he says nothing.

I have made a grave error in judgment and put my children's and my life at risk. He and I are both rail-thin, our tumultuous relationship causing such anxiety that it would make no difference what we ate, the pounds melt away from sheer nervous exhaustion. Our only common bond, the girls and his wonderful parents.

Halloween comes and goes; he doesn't pay November's rent.

31

Dinner is ready and waiting as he comes in the door from work. I have made mashed potatoes, meat loaf, peas, and a small salad. We really need to go to the grocery store, the Oreos and Cokes nearly gone as well. I go to greet him and call the girls from their room to dinner. The doorbell rings.

"I'll git it," he hollers from the bedroom where he is already changing his clothes.

It is the landlord. He asks Rick to step outside. I could barely make out the words, but the anger of them both is apparent.

Sitting Jillian in her high chair and Samantha at the table, I am dishing up their food. We don't say grace anymore, as he won't allow it. He sits down and I place his plate before him, already piled with food. He smells it—a habit I find disgusting.

As if a bomb went off in his head, he screams, "Yu 'spect' me t'eat this shit?" And picks up the plate and slings it into the wall, food flying all over the small dining room, over the children, and in their hair. He pushes his chair back so sudden and so hard that it flies into the living room. I see, too late, the back of his hand as it is raised in fury, and it lands squarely on my jaw, my glasses flying across the small space. The blow sends me reeling into the wall, the jolt as painful as the back of his hand had been. He grabs me by the arm and pulls me out the back door to the yard. The darkness has fallen, as he starts to hit me again. I am so frightened; I think I might faint. And then I hear Samantha at the back door.

"Stop this now," I shout at him. "Right now. Samantha go, stay by the baby. Do not come out here." My voice as calm as I can make it, slightly trembling, as I softly say, "Go, sweetheart, go stay with your sister." Samantha is crying, as well as Jillian—big great sobs, sobs of fear, and I am certain of memories of times past.

His arms extended, braced against the fence as if to support himself, as he fights for control. His head hanging down between his arms.

I turn and go into the house. Samantha stands next to Jillian's highchair, picking peas from her sister's hair and saying, "Shush, Mama's gonna be all right. It's okay."

I feel my left eye swelling shut, the coppery taste of the blood as it pools in my mouth. With the back of my hand, I reach up and wipe my mouth with my hand.

The back door flies open, and in its wake comes Rick, pushing past me so roughly I again career against the wall, sliding in mashed potatoes as I do so.

"Git the fuck otta my way, you fuckin' stupid bitch." He looks at me as I fall to the floor, and turning back, he kicks me.

I will not cry. I will not cry.

The front door slams, and I hear the Thunderbird as it screeches from the driveway.

I watch as my daughter goes to the kitchen sink to get the dishcloth, and bringing it to me, she squats down and wipes my face. I am so ashamed, once again, this tiny little girl feels she needs to care for me in this manner. What are parents for but to protect their children?

"Mama, we need to go now," Samantha says, her father's blue eyes look up at me in utter fear. "Please, Mama, we need to go."

I take them to the living room, and sitting with them on the couch, I ask her, "Where, sweetheart, where do we need to go?"

"Away, Mama, away." Great sobs of grief coming from my daughter as I rock back and forth on the sofa with them. "Shush, shush, it'll be all right."

"No, Mama, no. We need to go now."

The tears quietly slide down my face, as I acknowledge my child's wisdom and I mourn for her childhood. She has crossed that thin fine line; she is no longer an innocent in this world of adults, she will never know the feeling of utter safety and calm, the peaceful tranquility offered to and taken for granted by other children in the world. She will never be able to give her life and her soul to another human being for fear of abuse.

She is not yet five years old, and she has more wisdom than that of her mother, and my heart aches with the knowledge of the pain I have caused these children I love so very much.

"I think you are right, Samantha, I think we need to go. But then I'll have to go to work, and you and Jillian will have to stay with a babysitter again."

"I don't care, I can babysit the baby, and, Mama, you can't die, Mama. Please don't die, Mama," her sobs coming in great heaving gulps, as they shake her small little body. "Mama's not going to die, sweetheart, I promise I will do something to make us safe. I promise."

"You gonna make him not hurt you anymore?" Her eyes large and frightened in a way that shatters my heart.

"Yes, baby, I promise…" My heart is filled with the anguish of the lie I was telling my daughter, as how was I going to keep him from hurting us. Help me, Lord, to save myself so I can save these children.

I hug her closely to me and look at Jillian in my arms; she is picking peas from Samantha's hair and eating them.

Through tear-filled eyes and grief-stricken hearts, Samantha and I laugh, my lip splitting yet again.

"So you think you can eat?" I ask them.

"Maybe," Samantha says.

Jillian shakes her little head and, clapping her hands, says, "Mummmm."

It is nine o'clock before I have them bathed and in bed.

As I kiss Samantha good night, she pulls my face to hers and whispers, "You promised, Mama."

"I did, I promise."

The prayers come unceasingly as I clean up the kitchen. I am so nervous I cannot sit still. Will he come home? What am I going to do? The cost of moving is far more than I can afford. A job, a babysitter.

Lord, I give thanks that I am in my right place at my right time, and that I am doing as you wish. Lord, I ask that you stay with my children and me in this, our hour of need. Help me to be strong, Lord.

My sewing machine sits at the little wall adjacent to the living room in the corner of the small eating area; I am making dresses for the girls to wear for Thanksgiving.

I take an aspirin and pile ice cubes from the tray on a towel and wrap it tightly and hold it to my eye and to my lip. My teeth seem to be intact. The blow primarily making a gash at the edge of my eye. It should probably have stitches, but I place a bandage tight across it.

I sit down at the sewing machine. Engrossed in threading the needle, I am surprised by the front door opening.

Suddenly, he is standing at the left side of me, his back to the refrigerator.

Without looking up at him, I can sense his anger. He is as angry now as he was when he left, perhaps more so. I thread the needle to the sewing machine. Strangely unafraid.

Still holding the thread, I am abruptly pulled to my feet by my left arm and shoved viciously against the wall.

"Stop that now," I tell him, more angry than I have ever been and resolute, a feeling I have never experienced.

I return to my seat and again thread the needle. "You fuckin' stupid bitch," he says through tightly clenched teeth. "Y'all ar' gonna give me the fuckin' money, d'ya understan' me. D'ya git it… yet…bitch," his voice cold and his tone measured.

Both his hands clamp painfully around each of my arms as he, once again, picks me up and shoves me against the wall, this time, with a force that jars my head.

"I told you, Rick, you are not to do this to me. Stop...it... now." I am shocked by the sound of my own voice, for it holds the same intensity as his, the coldness of his voice matched now by my own.

I sit back down in the chair and proceed to thread the needle yet again.

His frustration is mounting, and I can sense that this is *it*. There will be no other time.

He reaches down, and grasping me even tighter than before, he brutally shoves me into the wall. My head bounces off the plaster walls as if I were a ball. Literal stars spark in my head and my only thought... I promised Samantha he would not kill me.

Pulling myself again to a standing position, I sit again at the sewing machine.

He is speaking to me again, I can feel the anger, but for some reason, I can't hear him. Am I deaf? I wonder if that last blow made me deaf. I look up at him, and I watch as the words form on his lips.

"I *am* gonna kill you, you fuckin' lazy bitch. Yu' jus' like yur Mamma, yu ain't never gonna change, I'm gonna do y'all a favor. Do ya understand? This is yur last night, do ya understand?"

Everything is happening in slow motion, as I watch the words form on his lips.

I see the scissors as they lie gleaming on the side of the sewing machine: shiny, silver scissors, approximately eight inches in length.

I am as calm as I have ever been, my lip hurts, my eye is swollen nearly shut, and apparently, I am now deaf.

But...I...am...done. *Lord, I know you are with me.* Those are my only thoughts as I slowly pick up the scissors. My hand is closed around the handles, and I have a firm grip, the blades pointing up at an angle—these are no longer the scissors of a fine seamstress, but the weapon I intend to kill this man with.

His back still to the refrigerator, I stand very slowly, and with fierce resolve and with ineffable calm, I take but one step to stand within inches of him. I place the point of the scissors just under his breastbone, and I very quietly say, "You leave this house now, right now, do not stop for one thing. Do you understand… because if you ever…ever hurt me or those girls again, I will kill you… Go…right…now, because if you don't…I will push with all my strength, and I will literally cut you to pieces." The blades of the scissors now imbedded in the cotton of his shirt and pushing hard against his sternum. "It…is…over… It…is…done. Get… out…now." The words coming with such bitter resolve, I cannot believe they come from the person I know to be "me." I cling tightly to that person who is now me, holding the scissors with such authority, as it is my only hope of survival, every instinct within me knows that to be an indisputable fact. I, too, have now crossed that thin, fine line. The thread that was our lives has been pulled taut too often, it has snapped.

His face is ghostly white, the red-gold stubble of his beard standing out against a face barely discernable from the white of the refrigerator he leans against, his arms are raised in submission. He is frightened; I can see it in his eyes and smell the fear on him, that rank odor of chicken soup, cooked too long, as it permeates the small space we inhabit. I am shocked by the ease at which all this fear has ceased within my battered soul as I stand ready to literally kill this man who is the father of my children.

I feel no shame. I feel no guilt, only unabashed relief.

He slides to the doorway as he backs away from me.

"That is the right thing to do," I tell him, still, deadly, quiet in my speech. "For you see, you have stolen my children's childhood from them, and I will never forgive you for that, and I will hunt you down and kill you…I want you to remember that. So back up slowly, and I will see that your parents get your things. Back up very slowly, open the door, and go, because I am going to cut your monstrous heart right out of your chest if you ever come near us again."

He continues to back to the door, his face ashen, his arms shaking as they hang at his sides.

"Now reach back and open the door," I say, my anger so volatile the room pulsates with the intensity of it. The scissors are still securely in my hand, they are not trembling, I am not frightened. Because I will kill him. And I won't feel bad.

The door opens, and as I hear the car drive away, I feel Samantha's hand reach up and touch mine. I look, and she is standing in her white flannel nightgown, pink ribbons at her neck and wrists, the curls of her red-gold hair damp and sticking to the sides of her face. The sweat standing on her tiny face. Her little hand cold as she pulls me to the sofa.

I find I am sobbing, the tears stinging my once-more battered face.

Crawling in my lap, she puts her head against my chest and whispers softly, "Shush, shush, Mamma, it's all right now."

The words I had so often spoken to her now come softly from her lips. Her small body trembling in rhythm with my own.

"Lord, forgive them, for they no not know what they do." The words echo in my head and the anger subsides, to be replaced by peace and a feeling of worthiness.

I hold my little daughter close to me. Her soft, warm body a haven in the storm of my soul.

32

He did come back, sometimes with a gun. But he knew, as I did, that *I would kill him*, as he had taken something from my children I could never replace. It was lost forever. Nothing I could do would ever replace the childhood innocence that he had taken from Samantha. Hopefully, Jillian was so little that in time the memories would only be a "bad dream." For Samantha, they would forever be etched in her memories. Memories of pain and anger, of fear, and dread, of unreciprocated love. She would never trust, and she was so little, she perhaps would not remember why.

At those times, when the monster returned, the man next door would gallantly leap the backyard fence and be in the living room door to face this predator of my family.

Outlandish as it may seem, life went on; we all piled into the old car the next afternoon, and we went to the beach. We had ice cream cones and drove through the streets of La Jolla.

There was a day care center, something I had never heard of. An elementary school across from the day care and in this lazy exclusive village was a drugstore with a sign in it that said "Help Wanted."

These were signs to me, signs that everything was going to be all right. I stopped at a phone booth, called the landlord, and told him that I had the rent for the last two months. He was delighted and most kind. I also called the telephone company and asked them to install a telephone in our home. I had never had a telephone before, the expense perhaps an enormous extravagance in this instance; however, I thought it to be necessary for our safety. It was to be installed the following week.

I was really quite excited.

I feel young for the first time in my life—light, as if an enormous weight had been lifted from my shoulders. Confidence rose in waves of near euphoria.

Pulling up in front of the house, I thought, this is ours, the girls' and mine. We can be happy here. But looking at the house, as if for the first time, I find the shrubbery in need of trimming. The grass needed mowing, the flower beds needed weeding, and the garage was such a mess, I could not get my old car in it.

The girls are playing in the front yard, and I am hauling the lawnmower out of the garage. They haven't been out of my sight but for perhaps five minutes, and I can see Samantha sitting on the front porch and Jillian is coming around the corner of the house.

Running on her fat, eighteen-month-old legs. "Mama, Mama," she is squealing, the white, short little curls bouncing on her little head, her eyes sparkling in glee.

Coming close behind her is a very large, very homely man. Tall, lean, muscular, with great dark horn-rimmed glasses and bucked teeth. In the distance, a lawn mower sits. The man that lives next door, it registers suddenly.

He looks angry.

I bend and scoop Jillian up in my arms. She bends her fat little neck and hides her face in my neck.

"Are you her mother?" he asks.

"I am." I look at him quizzically. "Why? What's the matter?"

"Come with me," he says. I can't tell: Is he mad, or has something happened?

Putting Jillian down, I ask, "Where? What's the matter?"

We walk to the end of the house, and he points to a very large, steaming *turd*. Yes, a turd.

Approximately five inches long, golden brown, and steaming. Obviously still fresh.

I look up at the large looming figure of this man and say, "What, what do you want me to do about that?"

"She did it," he says, pointing to Jillian. They have both followed us to the site of the defecation.

"Oh, I…I…don't think so."

"I saw her. I saw her just pull down her bathing suit and shit in my yard."

I am laughing nearly uncontrollably now. And he does not think that it is funny. But how could it not be funny?

"I am so sorry," I say, trying hard to stifle the laughter that is nearly hysterical by now. "Let me go get something to clean it up. I find this hard to believe. Are you sure it wasn't a dog?"

"I saw her do it," he says. Less angry now.

"I am *so* sorry. Please, accept my apologies."

"Oh, it's all right. It did make me mad. I'm just not used to kids, that's all. We don't have any. We have tried, but my wife… she can't have any, and, I…well… I don't know why I'm telling you this. 'Cept, I hear what goes on here and I wonder if you and they, those kids, are all right."

"He left last night. He won't be coming back, at least hopefully. I'm sorry, I don't mean to tell you my problems."

"It's okay, I really have been concerned, if ya need anything, let me know. Do you have a phone? I'll give you our number. Are ya afraid of being over there alone?" He is rattling off questions and information with a rapidity I could barely keep up with.

"Oh, thanks, that's so nice of you. I called today and they're going to put it in next week. I probably shouldn't have spent the money, but I thought we needed a phone."

"Yeah, I think you're right. Hey, I'll mow your yard, it'll just take a few minutes and I'm doin' mine anyway."

"Oh, really I can do it. But right now I need to take care of the girls. And…I know it sounds strange. But no, I am not afraid, and I don't mind being alone, I never have. I rather enjoy the sound of my own thoughts."

He laughed and said, "Yeah, me too. A lota people I know would rather shoot themselves than be alone."

I turn, pick up Jillian, and with Samantha by the hand, we start to walk away.

"Hey, what's your name?" He stands with his hands once more on the handles of the lawn mower.

"Cara, and this is Jillian and this is Samantha. What's your name?"

"Jeff, I'm Jeff, and really, call me, anytime."

———————

Cleaning up the girls for dinner, it was most apparent that, in fact, my darling daughter had acted very badly and pooped in the nice man's yard. Such a child. When asked why she would do that, her response was "I ha't'potty, Mama."

"But, Jillian, you must go potty in the bathroom, in the house."

"Yeah, only dogs go outside," Samantha says indignantly.

"I no doggie," Jillian strongly interjected.

"Well then, don't poop outside," Samantha says in her best mother voice.

That evening, as I prepared for bed, I peer out the window, expecting what, I don't know. The lawn is meticulously mowed and edged, the bushes trimmed. Jeff would protect me over the ensuing months, as truly as if he were a knight.

The following evening, I dressed up the girls and made the much-dreaded trip to see Vera and Amos and try to explain what had happened, as well as what I had told him.

I did not intend to tell them what I did. I was still not sure that I had really done that. But I wanted them to know they were always welcome to see the girls and to come and visit at any time.

Going into the bathroom to brush my hair, I look in the mirror, I had forgotten that I had a black eye and a split lip, the bruising now mottled in colors of black, purple and green, across the full side of my face. The pain of brushing my hair as bad as that of my face.

The guy next door must have been shocked to say the least, I think, as I decide it is much too painful to put lipstick on.

The visit was surprisingly pleasant, and all she said was that she was "so sorry" and that they would be happy to babysit or give us anything needed. Did I need any money?

"No, I thought I could get a job, and we'll be fine."

We adjourn to the kitchen to get ice cream for Amos and the girls. I find her in the corner of the kitchen by the sink. Sobbing quietly as she tries to scoop up ice cream. I place my arm around her waist and rest my head on her shoulder. "Mama, I am so sorry."

"D'ya know where he's at?" she asks through sad eyes, shining with tears. "I'm heartfelt ashamed o'im, but, Cara, he's ma' son, an' I love 'im."

"You haven't seen him?" I ask, shocked.

"No, girl, 'e ain't bin here."

She would say this to me over the ensuing years, more often than either of us could recount, as he would marry, and repeating the same mistakes, disappear for years at a time, leaving her to think he would always come to me. It is what she wished for.

33

In the ensuing weeks, I was hired at the dentists' office as a dental assistant, enrolled the girls in the day care center, and put in a call to Lilith in New York.

She sounded wonderful, and after hearing the story, she was very happy to hear I was in one piece.

All she could say was "Stupid, stupid. Read the green book." She would contact her "people" and get back to me next week.

The following week, she called just as I was arriving home; there were no openings at the present time, but they would keep me in mind.

I was disappointed, however, I did have a job, and I would wait.

Lilith promised to keep in touch. "I'll call you, I know it costs a fortune for you to call me."

"Oh, thank you, thank you."

The pay at the dentists' office was just enough to make the rent and the child care payment. I could not stay there. The only good thing was that I wore a white nurse's uniform every day, and since I had no clothes, that was a very good thing.

———

He writes children's books, and as I peer in his mouth, I see long, narrow, large, yellow teeth. The stench of his breath is overwhelming. Rotting teeth smell of blood and decay that is warm and pungent.

I have been at this job for about two months now, and it is simply disgusting.

Better to have men pawing me than this nauseating "profession." A dental assistant is worse than anything I have done.

People vomit as you stick trays of nasty goop in their mouths to make impressions. And they often bite you. The pay is the worst yet.

The drugstore has the "Help Wanted" sign out again. I am going on my lunch hour to see what the hours and the pay are. I hate working, and the green book says that when I find what I am supposed to do, it will be like play. "*Perfect self-expression will never be labor, but of such absorbing interest that it will seem almost like play. The student knows, also, as man comes into the world financed by God, the supply needed for his perfect self-expression will be at hand.*"

The drugstore was fun; the pay was only twenty-five cents an hour more, but twenty-five cents added up at forty hours a week.

The people were nice, and I worked in cosmetics nearly all the time. And that was fun.

They had beautiful accessories for the boudoir and the bath. Gilded mirrors, trays for holding perfumes, exquisite crystal perfume bottles. Things I had never seen before. I could have anything at 50 percent off. Lord, what a temptation. Perfumes, cosmetics. Creams to keep you young. Soaps to clear your skin and lotions to keep it soft. Lots of the companies left full-size "samples" for the salesgirls, so I could wear "Joy" if I wished.

Lilith called this morning as we were getting ready to go to church.

"Well, dahling, thought I'd never get you."

"Oh, Lilith, I am so glad to hear from you. How have you been?"

We chat for a short time, and finally, she says, "*So*, dahling, do you think you can handle four big ones a month, travel and expenses?"

"You're kidding! What is it? Do you think I can do it?" I say, I am so excited; that is twice as much as I was making.

"Yeah, I think you can do it. If you're interested, I'll tell my people and I'll call you tomorrow night at seven your time."

"What's the 'travel' about?" I inquire. "And clothes. I really don't have any clothes to wear, should I buy some?"

"Do you have something black you can wear for an interview if I can get one for you?"

"No, but I could make one by, say, Friday. Would that be okay?"

She laughs, and with her husky voice, she says, "I always forget you are Little Miss. Suzie Homemaker."

"Now as to the travel…from what I understand, you would have the southern California territory, ya know, from San Francisco down the coast."

"Oh my gosh! How would I get there? My car barely gets me to and from work. By the way, John Wayne pushed it for me the other day, and I sold a package of cigarettes to Rock Hudson. Oh my gawd, Lilith, he is the most gorgeous man I have ever seen."

She laughed and laughed, but she was duly impressed, as we considered the merits of these majestic males.

Finally the travel. I would be given a car, or I could fly…

I couldn't even suppress my glee long enough to let her finish. "You mean I can keep the car, here at home with me? Use it all the time?"

"Sure." She's laughing again. "So you want me to see what I can do?"

"Do you think I can do this? What about the girls?"

"Look, kiddo, you're working anyway and away from them, right, so you'll be working and making more money. That should help, huh? So…I'll make the call. The rest is up to you."

"Okay, I'll let you know, say a prayer for me."

"Ya got it, kiddo. Are you reading the green book?"

"I am," I say.

"Luv ya." She is gone.

Right on time, Lilith's call came. And I was to go Monday morning to I. Magnin in La Jolla and speak with a Mrs. Blaine there.

After a very lengthy interview, it was decided that indeed I would be hired. That I would start in two weeks, giving me the time I requested to give notice at the drugstore.

The job was not one of infinite glamour. I was traveling from store to store, packing and unpacking boxes and extolling the virtues of each new product. Instructing the salesgirls as to the use of it and how best to market and display it. With the end of each day bringing with it, mounds of information on new products, and what I needed to know to market them. When I wasn't at work I was preparing for work. They have provided me with every conceivable product to use and become familiar with. Who would have thought that beauty was such a big thing in this country?

I arrive at the day care center each day in the nick of time to collect my children, only to repeat the same thing the following day.

It has been four weeks today since I have started my new job, and they want me to go to San Francisco on Wednesday. They are very pleased with my work. I feel panic, as I call Vera and ask if she can watch the girls. I will be gone two days.

"Oh, girl, Amos 'n me'd be happy to watch those babies." She is delighted, as they have not seen them in nearly two weeks. I have been to busy too go over there or to have them here.

The drive up the coast is pleasant, and I find I am not afraid once I am on the road. I took the girls over last night, and they seemed fine with me leaving.

"I know you have t' work, Mamma," Samantha says, with brave blue eyes looking up at me.

I arrive at Amos and Vera's late at night, packing sleeping children in the car with all their belongings. You could move for all the things you need to care for children for a mere span of two days.

Samantha sits quiet and withdrawn in the seat next to me. She is sucking her finger. In the back seat of the car, Jillian lies sleeping.

"Samantha, are you all right?" I ask. Is she upset with me because I was gone? We really have never been apart.

"Daddy came and took us," she says, eyes brimming with tears.

"Did he hurt you?" The fear, and anger at Vera and Amos, rise in spasms in my chest.

"No…but we didn't want to go with him, Mama, and Granny said yes, 'cause he was our daddy. I don't want you to go again, Mama, and Jillian doesn't either. Don't go again, Mama, okay?"

"Okay, I won't go again. You mustn't worry any more, okay? I can get a new job. We won't do this again."

Lord, what to do now.

The next morning, I turned in my resignation, giving two weeks' notice and requesting that I not have to go out of town during those two weeks. I told Mrs. Blaine a bit of "my story," and she said that should something come up within the confines of the store, she would let me know.

I had had no contact with the friends of my school days, as I was immersed in the quest for survival, but I had made a few friends at the drugstore, as well and the body shop that was located directly behind it. Most of the men back there were always flirting with me and making innuendos of things that might be, but the handsomest and funniest of them all was Russ. He was as beautiful as Rock Hudson, not as tall but much more masculine, with green eyes that sparkled like the sun on the ocean waters, hair thick and tasseled with a touch of gray, and a smile that stopped my heart. Alas, he was married…still I would at times stop by to see them, and we would go have coffee.

Telling Russ of my dilemma, he kiddingly said, "You could go to work at the Quad Room—they have go-go dancers, and you'd be good at that."

Knowing where it was, as it had been there for years, I laughed and said, "Sure, how much does that pay?"

"A hundred bucks a night, an' you dance every hour for fifteen minutes, for four hours, an' ya can keep your tips."

"Really?" I say, astonished at the amount of money that could be gleaned from exposing your body and dancing.

"Ya otta think about it," he said as his beautiful green eyes dance with amusement.

— ◦◦◦◦◦◦◦◦◦ —

The Quad Room is dark and smoky as I await my turn. The glass that holds the whiskey, thrown over ice, drips in my shaking hand. The music thrums in my head, and my body is cold and clammy, clad only in a bikini bathing suit with fringe, the patent leather of my high heels gleaming from the Vaseline I have used to polish them.

I now understand how women become prostitutes. My remorse for the dreams I had had, deep and abiding. My need to survive, a tangible one.

In three nights, over a period of two weeks, I have earned more money than I had in all the weeks I had worked. Losing at least ten pounds each night. The "work" was so strenuous.

Did I feel sullied and profane? I did not. I did what I had to do; it was not who I was, nor would it make me someone different.

And no matter how many times I called, and where I went, there were no jobs available. "We'll call you," was the standard answer.

It has been one of the longest three weeks of my life, as I go to tell the manager at the Quad Room I can no longer work.

I. Magnin has called, and I start on Monday. Hallelujah, Lord. It is sixty dollars a week, plus commissions.

I have had three letters from Mother over the last five months, and although I have written her conscientiously, I have never told her what has happened. I did give her my telephone number.

Much to my chagrin, she has never called to see how we were or to ask after the children.

34

From the runways of New York to the quiet village streets of La Jolla.

Nestled at the coves of the beautiful Pacific Ocean, it is serene. With its balmy summer days peppered with the fragrance of the salty air, as it wafts thru the village streets on a gentle breeze. Tall majestic date palms line the boulevard, with gentle mounds of oleander and agapanthus dotting the spacious islands of the street.

The storefronts, tall and elegant in pale pastel shades of stucco.

My children are ensconced in the ultimate day care, and Samantha is enrolled in the school just across the street. Where, she says, she must sit on a green rug and zip her lips.

"Are you talking when you shouldn't be?" I ask her.

She shrugs her shoulders and says immediately, "But I have a lot to say."

Albeit, they hate it. Jillian screams all day, and they have asked me not to come anymore at noon. They just get her quiet, and in I walk, and it starts all over.

Samantha assures me that they are not mean to her, and I have really no recourse. I have to work as there has never been any child support. Perhaps I should file for divorce? That too, would cost money, and what would it change?

Do I live here? Afraid not.

The little house up on the mesa is fine, and moving is something I detest. We have had enough disruption in our lives to last a lifetime.

I bought a 1956 Oldsmobile for ninety dollars, and it is big enough to live in, the old car finally having "given up the ghost."

But I have a good job, with commission on the girls' sales as well as mine—very important, as my salary is spent on housing and child care, so groceries, utilities, and gas will have to come out of the commission.

The store is the most beautiful building I have ever seen. The floors are pink marble, and there are chandeliers even in the restrooms, which has gold fixtures, even the toilet flush handle.

Movie stars abound and are generally very nice.

There is a nice little coffee shop down the street, and we all gather there early in the morning for coffee before work. The counter is long, green marble with a solid wall of mirror in the front to the counter, with the kitchen in between the two. They make the best cinnamon toast. The bread is toasted then dipped in melted butter then dipped in sugar and cinnamon, my one real extravagance once a week.

Sometimes, this really gorgeous man from the shop down the street buys it for me.

He has black, curly hair with slight graying at the temples, the most beautiful green twinkly eyes I have ever seen, soft-looking lips, deep laugh lines around his eyes and mouth. With a perpetual five o'clock shadow. Beautiful white teeth, a chiseled jaw, and a perfect nose. So handsome. And he is funny. I think he's really flirting with me.

At I. Magnin we must wear navy, black, or brown dresses, with matching shoes, so a wardrobe isn't a problem.

Rock Hudson came in today, and he patted my hand and winked at me. I thought I would swoon right there and then.

I hate that I am not home with the girls. My wonderful grandmother told me today (I know I shouldn't spend the money, but I called her) "not to worry, being a mother is more than being home all the time. The queen of England doesn't *care* for her children. Yours will be fine. If I were there with you, I would care for them while you work."

I always feel so much better after I talk to her; it is worth every cent it costs to call long distance. And sometimes she calls me. She always writes me letters, with recipes and little things about her life. She is the Grand Matron of the Eastern Stars and so is making a new formal to wear. And Grandpa is going to play Pontius Pilate in the Christmas play. Imagine Grandpa in a white toga. Actually, he probably resembles Pontius Pilate. With his rotund, bowlegged body and his fringe of white hair encircling his large bald head like a halo. His soft smooth jowly face. With the brightest big, round, brilliant blue eyes.

Jillian has those eyes.

I was terrified of him as a child; he would bite me and pinch me. And laugh a big belly laugh when I would cry and try to get away.

He was a drinker and a gambler and ornery as the devil.

So visions of him in a toga are much more interesting than him shrouded in the white hood of a Ku Klux Klan robe.

Everyone else has a client. So I answer the phone. Not one of my normal duties, but I happen to be standing at the desk.

The counters are all decorated for Christmas, and the music drifts through the store, with its elegant patrons all dressed in the latest designer fashions.

The perfumes line the shelves, the elegant bottles reflected in the mirrored backing.

Worth, Givenchy, Dior, and of course, Estee Lauder. As that is who I represent.

"Cosmetics, this is Mrs. Williams, how may I help you," I say into the phone.

"This is Mrs. Allibertt, and I need a rose lipstick number 42."

"Oh, yes, let me have Jane call you," I say, knowing that she is a client of Jane's, and commissions are at risk during the holiday season.

"No, I don't want Jane. She said she didn't have one."

"Oh, I think we do have that in stock. If you will just hold on a minute, I will check for you."

"I will give you one thousand dollars if you can give me that lipstick."

"I could use one thousand dollars," I say, laughing. I was only joking, but I have to say, I decided then and there I was taking it if she offered again. She was from the East Coast, a very wealthy family, and even if it was wrong, offered again, I would take it.

"Well, I'll give you that much if you can give me that lipstick."

My hands are moist as I open the drawers containing the lipsticks.

I am certain I saw that lipstick when I was ordering last night.

Should I take the money? Can I take the money? Will they fire me if I do?

Hell, that's five times what I make in a month, and very little to her.

If she brings it, I am taking it.

At 9:00 AM on Friday, the store manager's voice comes over the PA system.

"Mrs. Williams, please come to my office at once."

My heart is beating rapidly. Am I going to be fired? Can they fire me?

Lord, what will I do.

Rubbing my hands together, with everyone watching me, I ascend the stairs to the manager's office, counting each step as I go, sure that this will be my last time, as I go over everything I have done wrong over the last month.

There was that palm reader in the store last week. She was reading everyone's palm. The manager came down and told her to leave.

But she wouldn't even read my palm. She touched my hand, backed away, and said, "Oh, dear, oh, I just can't." I was upset for days. What could be so bad that she wouldn't want to read my palm?

In the years to come, I would have readings with palm readers: George Daisly, a prominent psychic in Santa Barbara that could speak with the dead, and Karma Welsh, a prominent astrologer.

Well, here I am. I knock at the door.

"Come in," she says.

The manager of this sumptuous establishment, she is tall and dark, with the chiseled features of a man.

An elegant black dress hugs her voluptuous body, the scarf around her neck a soft red silk.

"Cara, Mrs. Allibertt is here to see you."

My knees are weak as I walk over to the elderly Mrs. Allibertt.

This is it. She has reported me. I have taken a bribe for merchandise, and she has reported me.

"How are you, Mrs. Allibertt? I am so glad to see you. Did you get the lipstick I sent you?"

"Yes, dear, I did, and I wanted the store manager to know that you were most efficient, and that I insist upon giving you a *tip*, as it were."

I look to the manager, who is leaning back in her chair behind her mahogany desk.

"Its all right, Cara, you can take the tip, but this is never to happen again. Do you understand?"

"Yes, of course," I say as I lower my eyes.

Mrs. Allibertt rises from her chair and advances toward me. She has a lovely lavender suit on and a purple hat.

She extends her wrinkled hand, and in it she is holding a check.

"Oh, I don't know, Mrs. Allibertt, I really don't think I can accept this."

"Yes, dear, you can." She puts the check in my hand.

I look down at it. It is made out to me, and it is for one thousand dollars. My knees are weak, my hands are shaking.

I sit down on the sofa. Looking up at this elderly, genteel woman. I am so grateful I don't know what to say. "I don't know what to say, except thank you. This is so much money for me. Just, well, thank you."

"Merry Christmas, dear," she says as she leaves the office.

"Would you like to take the day off, Cara?"

"Oh yes, thank you. Thank you."

I took Jillian out of day care, Samantha out of school, and we went to the most expensive children's shop in La Jolla.

"Buy anything you want," I tell a five-year-old and a two-year-old.

Samantha wanted two white cardigans. "I need two, Mommy," she said.

I had food and child care for six months, and the three of us went to Rosarito Beach, Mexico, for my days off—peace, with enough money to feed and care for my children.

35

"I just can't," I tell her into the telephone.

"But it will be good for you," she states, obviously not going to listen to my excuses.

"I am tired. I just got home from work."

"You need to get out, meet some people, and have some fun."

I looked down at my nails. The red nail polish is chipped and peeling. My hands look awful, and I've always been so proud of how pretty my hands are. And my hair hasn't been done for a week.

"No, really Myrna. I really can't go."

"How long has it been since you've been out?" she asks.

Strange, after three years in San Diego, Mom and Daddy have convinced me to move back up here. I have moved more times in the last eight years than my parents, and that is certainly saying a lot. Remembering how hard it was for me as a child, I have now taken an oath, at least to myself, that this is it, until the girls have graduated high school at least. There is a small college here, churches, it is close to Los Angeles, and San Francisco. Even should Mother and Daddy move, this is it for me. So even though it is their idea, I have given it some thought.

"Cara…" the voice on the other end of the line takes me out from my musings.

"So the girls are gone, and you need to come and go out with us. What are you going to do?" She is unyielding in her pursuit of my entertainment.

"I just bought a hundred dollars worth of material," I tell her. "And I'm going to make the girls and me some new clothes."

"No, no, no," Myrna says again. "We'll be over for you in twenty minutes. Come on, kid, it will do you good."

I think about Myrna; she has been exceptionally kind to me since I started working at Wellenes. She's probably twice my age. But single, and very smart. She goes out a lot, I think. Probably really does have a good time.

She is Portuguese, very attractive, her face square, with typical high, flat cheekbones. A very feminine roman nose, full sensuous lips, and when she speaks, she has an ever so slight lisp. Her eyes, intelligent and mischievous, small and nearly black, with perfectly arched eyebrows, framing her face. Her hair, nearly as black as midnight, with a slight hint of gray.

She has been very generous to me since I moved here. She has come to the house several times in the evenings, bringing a bottle, as I still do not drink and telling me of her escapades, which are many and hilarious, men being the object of her passion.

I can sew tomorrow. But I have never been a good party person. Never good at drinking.

"I don't know," I say again, instinctively knowing I am losing the battle.

"Yes! You're coming with us," she says, laughing, her voice a husky, sultry sound.

"Okay," certain now that she would surely take offense if I refused. "But I'll meet you there." I can just have one drink and come home, I think.

"Good, meet us at Shane's. Do you know where that is"?

"Yes," I tell her.

I put the phone down and go to the bathroom. I touch up my makeup. My eyes are made up heavily, as is the fashion, and I have on false eyelashes, my glasses having been replaced by contacts with Mrs. Alliberts generous *gift*. My hair a burnt sienna color and piled high on my head, with little tendrils falling around my face. The large gold hoop earrings I love nestled in my pierced ears. It'll have to do, I think to myself.

I'm tall and thin with a model's body and have on a navy knit dress fitted at the bodice, long, slim, set-in sleeves, and a large pleat under the bodice that gives it a tent look to about mid-calf. My shoes are navy blue pumps.

Really, for someone so young, I look quite elegant. Classy, except my nails. I just won't think about them, as I glance once more at the chipped polish.

I pile the great mounds of fabric on my bed, take a last look around the small but ample duplex and think, I'll get to all this later. I have the whole three-day weekend.

Mother and Daddy have taken the girls to Yosemite, and so I have nothing but time, and a little fun would be nice. The house is clean, and so I can sew all the rest of the days.

I take one last look at myself and dab perfume on all the appropriate spots. This will be fun, but only for an hour or so.

As I go to the garage, I think, I hope the car starts. It is a car I bought from my brother, and the darn thing is so undependable. But it is the best I can do. Money is something that is so scarce I can't always buy groceries, let alone gas for the car, and often walk to work.

If it doesn't start, I won't go, Lord, that will be my sign. I've been alone with my beautiful little daughters now for nearly five years. Dating has been a nightmare for the most part. I hate it. I am always afraid, uncomfortable. If I could just trust that I could handle whatever came up, I would be all right. But I seem to have made so many mistakes already for someone so young. What is it I am supposed to learn?

I sit in the car at the nightclub where I've agreed to meet Myrna. I don't think I can go in by myself. My heart is racing. I hate bars and nightclubs, the way people look at you when you come in, especially the men. That leering look they give you.

Well, here goes.

I see Myrna sitting at the bar. There are two other women with her. The band is at the far left side of the room, with a gleaming, polished wood dance floor. Couples dancing to "String of Pearls," gliding past the dining tables with white linen, crystal, and silver waiting for dinner guests. The music is wonderful, and I just want to dance. Mother would love this. Knowing instinctively she would not like that I was here. But then she continued to find fault with whatever I did. At work, they refer to this place as "menopause lane," but I think I like it.

I've never sat at the bar before. That's for real drinkers.

"Come on over, kid," she says, patting the bar stool.

"These are my sisters, May and Linda."

They are about the same age as Myrna, and both of them quite attractive. Especially Linda, who is a Latin beauty to say the least. Her features small and patrician, her skin, a flawless golden honey. Linda and Myrna are both single and have children. May is married, but she says her husband doesn't care if she goes out.

They are small women, nicely dressed in suits and heels. Gold jewelry bedeck their wrists and make a tinkling sound as their speech becomes more animated, and their hands flit in punctuation. Beautiful thick dark hair, olive skin that is flawless. Beautiful full lips, nice smiles, as May and Myrna are laughing loudly. Linda, too, is laughing, but it is a soft tinkling sound. They are telling an extremely crude joke, and I am embarrassed. Their laughter increases substantially at the discovery of my embarrassment. They are loud and, to some degree, I think, coarse. But happy and having a good time. They seem to know lots of people, but then, they were born and raised in this small, rural town in California.

I have a drink, a white Russian, and am feeling more comfortable. The music is wonderful, and I am really glad I came out. It is good to get out. A nice-looking older man comes over and asks me to dance. I start to say yes, and Myrna says, "No. We were just leaving."

"Where are we going?" I say, more than a little shocked.

"I thought we would go see Tony," she says.

Tony, I think, *who is Tony?* Oh, I remember, she talks about Tony all the time at work. Her son, what is he, about fourteen? He lives with her I know, I guess I didn't pay much attention.

I turn on the bar stool. "Where is Tony? How come we are going to see him? Really, I probably better go."

"No," she says. "One more drink, and we're going to go see Tony." Linda and May are laughing and winking at Myrna.

Now I'm really confused. I laugh, thinking I like these women, and they certainly seem to know what to do and are not afraid at all. *Worldly*, my mother would say.

"Okay, one more drink, and we'll go see Tony. But why?" I ask.

"You'll see," they say laughingly. We chat about work and men, laughing and having a good time.

We leave the nightclub, and May says she will drive. We will all go in her car.

"Oh no," I tell them. "I really didn't want to be out long."

"No, no, no, you come with us," they say in unison. Nothing will do but to go with them. We all pile in May's car, and off we go to the slums of town.

"Where are we going?" I say.

"You'll see," they say, giggling like young girls with a secret.

We pull up in front of a derelict building, in a stretch of town I know to be called Whiskey Row. Oh, I'm thinking, this is not good. My heart is racing again, for about the third time tonight.

"There's his car," Myrna said. I look, and it is a brand-new car. Maroon, lots of chrome, fancy.

"Whose car?" I asked.

"Tony's," Myrna says.

"What's he doing here?" I asked.

They all looked at each other, and laughing, they said, "Go on in."

"No!" I tell them. "I'm not going in there."

"Yes," they say. "Go on in there."

"No! No!" I say. "I am not going in there."

"Yes, just go in and ask for Tony Tesstorrio."

"What? I can't even say that name. Why should I do that? I don't want to go in there."

"Come on," Myrna says, pushing me out of the car. "I'll go with you."

I'm out on the sidewalk, and thinking, what a dump, why would a fourteen-year-old boy be allowed in a place like this? Maybe she isn't as nice as I thought she was. How do I get myself into these things? Myrna's right behind me. "Go on, go in," she says. "Ask for him."

"What's his name again?" I ask.

"Tony, Tony Tesstorrio," she says.

I walk to the door, hesitate, but I push it open. The music is blaring. Country. Patsy Cline is belting out "Crazy." The room is dark and smoky; there is a long bar to the right of me as I walk in, bar stools with high chair backs, covered in that rare animal Naugahyde, a mottled orange color, with generous amounts of duct tape. There is a man on every stool. You can hear the stools swivel as they turn to assess me. If I thought the nightclub was full of leering men, well, this gave new meaning to the word. You can smell the liquor and the beer, that thick sweet yeasty odor.

And the all-male aroma of sweat. It's loud, with men laughing, talking, and some shouting. The back bar is mirrored, with shelf upon shelf of liquor bottles and a bartender standing behind the bar drying glasses with a white towel. The towel, out of place in such a dark, seemingly dirty place. To my left is a raised area with a pool table and some small round tables and captain's chairs.

I can't make myself take another step. I've never been in a place like this before. I can't think. Myrna taps me on the shoulder. "Just holler his name," she shouts above the din. I take a step forward. There are men all around; I see no other women.

"Look at that beauty," one man says as he undresses me with his eyes. There are wolf whistles, knee slapping. I've never been so frozen, so unable to respond. I step back and turn to leave. Myrna sees the look of sheer panic on my face and says, "It's all right, ask for him."

I turn back to the sea of faces, and the bartender says, "The name's Grady, looks like you could use some help."

"Yes, I'm looking for Tony Estoria," I hear myself reply.

"You mean Tony Tesstorrio," he said. "Tony, someone here to see you."

The sea of men parted. I looked at the far end of the dark, smoky room, and there stands the most beautiful man I have ever laid eyes on. His legs are spread in a stance of deliberate arrogance. He is wearing Levi's, cowboy boots, and a black sleeveless shirt that is cut like a jacket at the waist. The jacket open nearly to his navel. His arms are thick and muscular, and he is holding a pool cue, large end braced on the floor, both his hands tightened around the smaller end, straight out in front of him. He has a mane of jet-black hair that is slightly tousled around his forehead, and his eyes are the softest, deepest brown I have ever seen. High cheek bones and a strong jawline frame his beautiful masculine features. His nose, a perfect Romanesque. His skin, the soft warm glow of honey. His body, lean and muscular with wide strong shoulders. His legs, long and firm in the tight-fitting Levi's.

The room turns quiet, the soft sexy voice of Patsy Cline singing "Crazy for Loving You," everyone seems to disappear in the moment.

He says, "You lookin' for me?"

"Yes," I say, "I am." Knowing, at that moment, that I had been looking for him all my life.

He drops the pool cue and takes long arrogant strides to stand before me. He's inches from my face now. I can't catch my breath. I can feel his presence all through my body. To the very core of my being. My very sexuality is aroused, aroused like I have never felt in my life, my knees are weak, and my breath comes in halting gulps.

"And where has a beautiful lady like you been all my life?" he asks. His voice deep, soft, husky with desire. I can smell the maleness of him. Clean, musky. He is so close, I can only think of him. I am vaguely aware that everyone in the room has stopped what they were doing and are watching us. But I don't care. I only care about him. Only want to be with him.

"Waiting for you," I respond. "Just waiting for you."

"I don't think you belong in a place like this," he says. "Would you like to go get a cup of coffee?"

"But I don't even know you," I say. "I came with your mother and…"

I turn and look, and she is gone.

————~~∽∿⌒◯⋌◯⌒∿∽~~————

He gazes at my tall, lean, naked body, his eyes candid in their deepest desire. His gaze as if I were the most exquisite jewel ever created. For the first time in my life, I am unashamed of my body, comfortable to be exposed. Exposed physically and psychologically.

Seldom do we see ourselves through someone else's eyes. Someone blinded by love. Seeing no imperfection, only the perfection that God alone can design.

Love is perhaps our finest hour, when it is unconditional. Total acceptance of who, and what, that other person is. Unbiased by our own wants and needs. Perfecting itself on another human soul.

The depth of our feelings seem to have no limit. He stands before me, naked, in all his glory. He reaches out and cups my face in his hands. He takes a step closer to me and lifts my face ever so slightly, placing the most gentle of kisses on my forehead. "You are what I've waited all my life for," he whispers. He kisses each eyelid, my cheeks, and finally, my mouth. Our lips gently parted. The softest, most intimate kiss I have ever experienced. My heart is pounding so hard, I can't catch my breath.

We look into each other's eyes, and our souls are locked for all eternity. Bridging the gap of time. Completing who we are. Who we wished to be.

Life began for me that moment, the moment I saw him standing in the bar with the ever-present toothpick in his mouth, the slight come-hither look in his eyes. The way he would gently drop his cheek next to mine, and ever so lithely caress my cheek with his. Sliding his lips around to kiss my cheek.

We made love for hours. I would awaken to the water running in the bath. He would then carry me in his arms to the bathroom. And filling the tub with bubbles, slide his hard, muscled, sensuous body in behind me. The soap on his strong hands gently caressing every inch of my body, sliding through and into unimaginably erotic spots. The passion mounting with each touch. Each sensuous touch. Our skins, slippery with the sweat of our lovemaking, our tongues probing the deepest parts of our bodies. Tasting, probing, uniting our bodies and mind as one. Knowing this was as life was meant to be. One person, one love, needing no other.

We shared our innermost feelings, feelings of pain, sorrow, and joy.

He told me of his love of God, of his love of the Catholic Church. He told me of his pain, of his loss. Of his loneliness. He told me of his fears, of his feelings of inadequacy at being Latin in a world white.

And I told him my fears. My fear of being alone, the hardships I had endured. The beatings and the desperation of being without food for my children.

I told him my hopes of having more children and a man to love me and my children, to take care of me. I told him how I hated to go to work and leave my children.

We promised each other that we would protect and love each other for all the days of our lives.

He was smart and quick-witted; we finished each other's sentences.

The world existed for just the two of us.

We ate, we slept, and we made love, and the nights turned into days, and our future was perfected.

36

Fabric lies strewn in disheveled piles across the carpeted floor. I am making school clothing for the girls. Samantha and I sit crosslegged on the floor, ready to cut out the patterns. She is very excited.

Jillian will start kindergarten this fall—the time has flown by. We bought this house. For a while, I was afraid to move anything, furniture, even small knickknacks. Afraid that Mother wouldn't like it. I just could not believe we actually owned a house, that it indeed was ours. Tony, in truth, was the one to look for the house and to purchase it; I could not take the time off work, and since he works graveyard shift, he was available and excited. I was just happy to think we would have a home of our own. With the exception that it not be in a "bad" neighborhood.

"Not a problem" was his response. "Just get me an appointment."

Excitement welled in me as I called the real estate agent and told him, "Do not show my husband anything in the northwest section of town.'"

The house is small and plain. With a small patch of lawn in the front, but a large backyard that is fenced. There are three bedrooms and two bathrooms, with a very nice-sized living room and fireplace, the small kitchenette sits off the living room with a bar that we eat at.

It is located in the most *northwesterly* section of town. The fields of the Azevedo ranch nestle to the edge of the river, with strawberry fields to the west. I no longer care *where* it is. It is wonderful. We have a home.

Tony has grandiose plans, and he has bought a horse as well. He was raised with the Azevedo boys, so they are happy to let him keep the horse there. Goliath. Yes, Goliath, a monstrous Morgan that stands eighteen hands high at the withers. And hardheaded at that. More than likely, he has been gelded too late.

There is a knock at the front door, and since I am sitting right beneath it, I reach up to open the door. There, on the stoop of the front door stands a very large, dark man of Mexican heritage. In one hand, he holds the hand of a very small, perhaps six-year-old male child. Tear streaked face, clothing askew. In the other hand, he is holding my small daughter's hand in his, her big blue eyes flashing. Her white-blonde Dutch bob flying wild with grass and leaves amongst the strands of white gold.

"Hiram, how are you?" I say from my sitting position on the floor.

"I am not good! Your little girl here, she molested my Juan."

"What?" I say as I extricate myself from my very informal position and reach to pull my daughter from his grip into the safety of our home.

"She molested my Juan!"

"Oh, Hiram, I don't know what in the world you are talking about. He is both older and larger than she is."

"She make him take his clothes off so she can look at…at… you know," he says, highly agitated. Angry, embarrassed.

"Jillian, did you do that?" I look at my angelic-looking daughter.

"No, Mama," she said, looking straight at me with those enormous, clear blue eyes.

"She's lying!" Hiram is hysterical, acting as if his child has been attacked.

"Did she hurt you, Juan?" I ask.

His tear-stained face looks down at the floor as he shakes his head no.

| 258 |

"I want her punished!" Hiram is adamant in his demands. "They were naked!"

I am having difficultly not laughing at this man. Who is *so* upset over the exploits delved into by most curious, intelligent children, but…he is right…

"She is a nasty little girl."

"Oh, stop, Hiram, she is not nasty. I will take care of this, and I am so very sorry this has happened."

"I do not want her playing with my *mieho*. No more!"

"Okay, thank you, Hiram, for bringing her home." I pull Jillian into the house and close the door on this most irate of fathers.

"Jillian, did you make Juan undress?"

"No, Mama, I didn't do that."

Samantha sits on the floor, snickering and pointing at what is clear for all of us to see.

"Jillian, how come your clothes are wrong side out, and your top is on backward?"

She looks down at the floor and up at me again. "I didn't do it, Mama, I didn't do it."

"Jillian, you must not do such things, and you must not lie to me."

"I'm not lyin', Mama."

"I think perhaps you are, so I think you better get your little chair, and you can sit in the corner and think about why you are lying to me."

It has been about five minutes since she has been sitting in the corner, and I have reminded her to not sing or talk several times already. When, suddenly, she turns to me and says, "You know, the real me is standing over there with you. You can only make this *me* sit here."

"Well, my darling little daughter. That will have to be good enough for me. That *that you* sit in the corner."

"Okay," she says with resolve.

I found it difficult not to look for "the one" standing defiantly "by me."

It has been a difficult week at work, to say the least. The state surveyors have been here for their annual inspection for the last four days. I am exhausted, long hours, I am so nervous all the time they are here. Afraid I have overlooked something critical.

"Mrs. Tesstorrio, your neighbor is on line 2," the voice of my secretary comes over the intercom.

"Oh, good Lord, Gerrie, thank you so much, I'll be right there."

I pull up in the driveway, just as the fire department and the police have arrived. It takes me five minutes to get home, so that was a very quick response.

The front door stands open, as does the back door. Samantha stands in the front yard, her hands on her hips, and she is looking as mad as I have ever seen her.

"Boy, Mother, *she* has done it now."

"I know, I know, let me take care of this." I walk the fifteen feet to the open front door. The first thing I see against the background of the olive green-carpeted floor is an enormous pile of horse manure. As I advance more rapidly into the house, I see not one pile, but several. Good grief! "Jillian!" I holler. The fireman, coming closely on my heels.

"Where is the gas meter?" he is hollering.

"Through the back door and to the left," I answer him. "But wait, I need to find my daughter."

"Is that your daughter, ma'am'?" he says, looking at the glass windows that are at the side of the living room.

Outside the living room window stands my blonde tomboy daughter, the reins of the massive Goliath in her hands, the horse docilely standing at her shoulder.

Opening the window, I say, not altogether calmly, "Jillian, what in the world did you bring Goliath in the house for?"

"Because he came here and was knocking at the door with his foot, I opened the door, and he came in. I didn't know what to do, so I was going to put him in the backyard, and when we were going to the backyard, he was pooping on the carpet, 'cause

Samantha was yelling to get him out of the house, and then he got scared and reared up and broke that big gray thing in the backyard. And then the window in the back door broke. I'm sorry, Mother, but I didn't do anything wrong."

"Okay, okay, just stay here on this side of the yard, so he doesn't get more scared. Where is your dad?"

She shrugs her shoulders. "I dunno."

"Ma'am' ma'am, I'm with the gas company…"

"Yes, out that door," I say, pointing to the vicinity of the back door.

"Jeez what's this…" as he picks his foot out of the large pile of horse…"shit!"

"Yes, that is what it is. And don't ask, you would never believe it," disgust echoing in my voice. "Samantha, where is Daddy?"

"He's sleeping," she says as she stands in the front doorway. "I think he is retarded."

"Really," I go down the hallway and open the bedroom door. Lord, what an odor. Booze. He isn't sleeping; he is passed out. Men!

"Mother…the policeman wants to talk to you." Samantha is standing at the bedroom door, her arms folded across her chest, a look of sheer repugnance on her ten-year-old face.

I turn and say, "Tell him I'm coming."

I slowly walk out of the room and turn again to look at my husband. The corral has needed repair for nearly a month now; every day he says he will fix it. Does he do it? No. Damn it.

The police report was very detailed to say the least; there was a fine for having a farm animal in the city limits, strange as the city limits are just twenty-five feet away.

As I stand in the living room, the flies are starting to form around the piles of…

As I glance at the front door, I see the indentations in the door from the hoof marks.

"Mother, can I come in now?" Jillian is asking through the open window.

"The meter is repaired, ma'am." The man from the gas company steps lightly around the piles throughout the house. "Just sign here."

"And here," the police officer says.

The fireman stands, axe in hand, "Ma'am, we have checked all the gas lines, and everything is a go. Just sign here."

Chaos at every corner of the room. I hear Samantha's voice. "Mother, how are we going to get *that horse* otta here?" *That horse* an indication of her thoughts concerning the animal in question.

"Thank you, thank you. Yes, I will, thank you." I thank all the officials for their help and assure them it will never happen again. And "Yes, I do understand the severity of it." Closing the front door, I look at Samantha and say, "I'm going to go change my clothes, and then I am going with Jillian to take Goliath back. Will you be all right?"

"Yeah. But, Mother, what about the poop? It's all over, and it stinks."

"Honey, we have to get Goliath out of the yard, and then I'll clean up the carpet."

"Jillian, bring Goliath back through the house. And we will take him and ask the Azevedos if we can put him in another corral."

Back through the house comes this lumbering, unusually docile, large animal with my not-yet eight-year-old daughter. Why she is not afraid of this animal, I will never understand, but she seems not to know any fear at all.

37

I like it here. It is homey and comfortable, and I like all the old people.

It is much closer to home, and the hours are better. My husband wants me to work, *only* during the week and *only* nine to four. He didn't hear me say how much I wished to stay home with my children either. Everyone hears what they wish. I would have to work without him, and he loves all of us. He handles the money, all of it, I simply hand over my paychecks. He goes off hunting for the weekend, leaving me with fifty dollars, an astronomical amount, telling me to "Lock the doors, and stay in the house." Lord, such a man.

It *is* better. I get to be home with the girls in the morning, and they only have a couple of hours in the afternoon with a babysitter.

Who would ever think I would know how to type and keep books?

I went to the unemployment office as soon as my dear Antonio started complaining. They said they would look and see what they could find.

Imagine, all the people out of work and they would find me a job, when I already had one.

The manager here is very nice. Her name is Selma Stafford; she is maybe forty and very nice looking with a wonderful wardrobe of beautiful, elegant clothing, so I can dress up. She says she prefers that. She is rarely here, so I just do everything. At least in the office.

The building is large, and all on the ground floor. In the shape of a cross, I like that. Sometimes I go and feed the patients, and sometimes I read to them or play bingo. But generally, I answer the telephone, gather up invoices, and send them to Los Angeles, where the headquarters is located. I go to the bank, run any errands necessary, admit and discharge patients, bill them, and take their money.

The fee to care for the patients is thirteen dollars a day. A great deal of money, but if you can't care for them at home, it is a godsend.

It is called a convalescent hospital, but they are, for the most part, old people too sick to care for themselves.

Some of them are "crazy," to say the least. A tiny little lady named Ruth had a bowel movement in the mop bucket today. I thought Larry, the janitor, was going to die. He is very nice, though, and very kind with the patients. He is not quite five foot tall, very black, and very bald with shiny gold teeth.

Some of the people think they are home, and some don't know where they are and call me by their daughter's or wife's name.

The come in and sit in the office and sing and talk. Some just sit, often leaving large wet spots on the chair as they leave.

There are ninety-nine beds and nearly as many employees. Registered nurses, licensed vocational nurses, and nurses aides, janitors, housekeepers, cooks, dishwashers, and people who do medical records. And they are all wonderful. Happy to be there, happy to help.

I love it, and I make ten cents more an hour, so Tony is very happy. And with the new house, we can certainly use it.

It has been nearly four months since I started this job. I love it. Tony can stop by and see me, and I can stop in at home when I am doing errands.

Tony has to work the graveyard shift for two years. Lord, it is awful. We have a big breakfast in the morning, just so he can see the girls. Then he sleeps from about two until ten at night. He has tried sleeping in the morning hours, but he seems unable to accomplish that.

The cooks at work have asked me to type the menus and add some things to them. It has been a wonderful experience. As I add an item, I provide the recipe, for one hundred people, imagine. The number of potatoes peeled during the course of the day is unbelievable. To try and help them, I have looked up the nutritional value, calories, et cetera, and given them a rough idea of a good serving size.

As you can tell, here, I have some extra time on my hands.

The people from LA have called numerous times this week and want to know where Selma is. All I can tell them is she isn't here.

Well, lo and behold, Mr. Gray, from Los Angeles, came today and fired her and told me I was the new manager and to hire someone to help me.

Things have gone extraordinarily well. At least from what I can tell. The employees seem happy; they all show up for work but for the occasional illness. The patients are well cared for, and their families are happy with their care.

I have received bulletins from the state to expect an inspection of the facility, as they are thinking of making them subject to licensing requirements.

For what? I wonder.

This man from San Francisco has called numerous times over the last few weeks, wanting the rent. I merely refer him to the Los Angeles office, as I deposit all the money and send them all the invoices and all the billings.

However, the man from San Francisco says he has not been able to reach Mr. Gray in Los Angeles.

As I add all the billing invoices and subtract them from the income, I am appalled they have not paid the rent. There is certainly sufficient money to do so.

Thank goodness that is not my problem.

It is Thursday afternoon, and as I am coming from the kitchen, I see two strange men in beautifully tailored business suits. One tall and large, with a ruddy complexion. The other short and rotund, with a white fringe of hair encircling his bald head.

They are just now pulling open the large plate glass door of the entrance, and so I go to greet them.

Maybe these are the inspectors.

"Hello, I am Cara Tesstorrio, can I help you?" I say to the men. I, nearly towering over them in my three-inch heels, my hair piled high on my head.

The taller, younger man, extending his hand in greeting, says with a very French accent, "How do you do, Cara? My name is Frank Gillibert, and this is Hank Steiner. I think I've spoken with you on the telephone… We are from San Francisco."

The younger of the two older gentlemen hands me two business cards, and as I glance at them ever so briefly, I notice the spelling on Mr. Gillibert's card. So it is "ghela bear."

"Oh, oh, yes, well, what can I do for you?" Stepping aside to allow them to enter, I said, "Can I get you coffee?"

"No, actually, we came to close you down."

"Close us down, what in the world…? I don't understand. You can't do that, all the people here are sick, and some of them have no other home than this. You can't do that."

"Oh, but we can, and we will. There has been no rent paid on this building for over four months, and we have no choice."

"Well, that is not 'their' problem, and these people are sick. And all the employees, you can't do this." I move to the center of the expansive of hallway, barring their entrance with at least my manner.

"We are going to close this place, and now," says Mr. Gillibert.

"I am afraid I have to ask you to leave. You will not be closing it today."

"Fine," Mr. Gillibert announces. "But we'll be back tomorrow. Will you be here?" He seems to think all of this is very interesting, a slight smile on his face. Or is that a smirk?

"I will, and I will tell you the same thing."

"We'll see you in the morning then, Miss....or is it, Mrs. Tesstorrio?"

"Mrs., and yes, I will see you in the morning."

I called Los Angeles all day. All I got was the recording saying that the number is no longer in service. Lord, what to do? Well, one thing I wasn't doing was telling Tony. He would only worry that I didn't have a job. But tomorrow, I would wear a suit, the one I just finished, with a white blouse and black pumps.

All night long, I could only think of what would happen to all those people.

As quickly as possible I fed everyone breakfast, got the girls off to school, and was at work bright and early. I certainly didn't intend for them to come and me not be there to protect these people.

Arrive they did, a little less intimidating today. Mr. Steiner very pleasant and soft-spoken. Mr. Gillibert, effervescent, yet somehow stern in his attitude toward me.

"Do you have an office?" he asks me, briefcase in hand. They were wearing different suits, and they too were expensive, I was certain.

"Well, sort of, it's small, but I like it. Would you like some coffee?"

"That would be very nice. Thank you," Mr. Steiner says.

"How about fresh cinnamon rolls?" I look at them, as beguiling as I know how to be.

"Really, they bake them here?" Mr. Gillibert is obviously impressed.

"They do every Friday morning. Won't you sit down?" I point to two small chairs across from my small desk.

We are all seated comfortably as the wonderful cinnamon rolls and coffee are brought to the office by Patsy, my secretary, receptionist, and girl Friday. What would I do without her?

Cloth napkins are given them as I bought them for the families when I interview them for a room. I thought it was a nice thing to do.

"So…Mrs. Tesstorrio, may we call you Cara?" Mr. Steiner begins.

"Yes, of course."

"Well, we discussed this last evening at great length, and well, we—"

"Get to the point, Hank," Mr. Gillibert interjects. "We think you can run this hospital, and we're here to offer you a job. What do you say to that?"

"We mean, that *is* what you have been doing, right?" Mr. Steiner says kindly.

"You would have full responsibility for the operation of this place here." Mr. Gillibert says "We really have no interest in it. We are a real-estate syndicate, all of our other properties are in San Francisco, and frankly, the damn thing is a nuisance." He is really quite animated, and his English is somewhat broken, as Mr. Gillibert waves his hands and arms as his speech rises and falls.

"Well"—he looks at me—"what do you say? Come on. We have to get back to San Francisco."

"Frank, for God's sake, let the girl think," Mr. Steiner said, insistently gentle with this great, animated man.

"How old are you anyway?" Again, Mr. Gillibert.

"I…I…I'm nearly twenty-four," I stammer, all this just too much, my mind going a mile a minute.

"Jesus Christ."

"Frank, for goodness sakes," Mr. Steiner admonishes this volatile person yet again. I wonder who is in charge.

"Well," Mr. Gillibert says, "what'll it be?"

"Now! You want an answer now?" I ask him.

"Yes, yes, we do. Can't you answer that?"

"Well…I think I better talk to my husband first. You, know this is a big decision."

"Fine, fine. When can you talk to him?" Mr. Steiner speedily intercepts Mr. Gillibert's rejection of such a thing.

"He…he is home now, he works graveyard shift. I…I guess I could go home and talk to him now."

"Fine, we'll just go in that big living room out there and play gin rummy until you get back."

"Really? Okay, okay."

———⌇⌇∽∾⌇⌇∾∾⌇⌇———

"Tony! Tony! Where are you? Guess what?"

"What the hell, are you all right?" He came out of the kitchen, the worn green bathrobe I had made him hanging untied across his beautiful golden body. He was licking his fingers, a biscuit in his hand.

I ran to him and hugged him and got the most delicious of kisses, deep, warm, inviting. Ah, he thinks I've come home for that. *That* would be nice.

"No, no," I say, giggling, pushing him away. "There are some men waiting for me at the hospital. I can't, later I promise, I'll come back after they leave."

"Really, okay. When…when are ya comin', Red?"

"Couple hours. Wait for me."

"I always wait for you, sweetheart."

"You do, don't you… But listen…"

I tell him the story of their arrival yesterday and what has transpired today.

He sits, his mouth agape. Disbelieving.

"Really!" I say, so excited I can't speak fast enough. "So I'm going to tell them I want a thousand dollars a month, and maybe a bonus if I make a profit…"

"A thousand dollars a month. You won't get away with that, and they'll fire ya." He is up and pacing.

"No, no, they won't. They said it was a nuisance to them, and well, Selma made eight hundred, and I already do a better job than she did. So what do you think? Is it all right with you?"

"Cara, ya can't get fired," he says softly, sitting down again.

"I won't. I promise, if it looks like they won't do it, I'll tell them to name the price. Okay?" I know he worries about money.

For the first time in my life, we have enough to eat and absolutely no bills, with the exception of the house. We have a home that is ours.

He looks worried.

"Really, Tony, I promise."

"Crazy woman…go…go do your high finance thing." He kisses me long and hard, leaving a promise of things to come. He swats me on the rear, and again, "Go, go."

Forty-five minutes later, I find them exactly as I had left them. Playing gin rummy at a dining room table.

As they see me pull up in my cute little turquoise car ("I bought it for you because it matches your eyes," Tony had said, as he had brought it to my work a year ago") they put away their cards and meet me at the door.

Following me to my office, they come in, and closing the door behind them, say, "So what's the word from your husband?"

"Tony says I can do it for one thousand dollars a month, and 25 percent of the profits to go toward the purchase of the business. The purchase being twenty-five thousand dollars." My hands are folded on the desk, and I am looking at them as if I knew what I was doing. Where in the world did that come from?

"Fine, we'll get back to San Francisco and have the paperwork drawn up. You'll have to come up and meet with us there," Mr. Gillibert says, not in the least ruffled.

"I can't afford to come to San Francisco." The only thing I could think of to say.

"So the business will pay for it."

I went home to my husband's waiting arms and related most of the story, and he was thrilled when I told him of the "eight hundred dollar a month" triumph. No need to tell him the rest right now; he would only worry.

And as far as I was concerned, I was only buying me a job. If I owned it, it wasn't likely I would lose it anytime soon.

San Francisco it was—much to Tony's dismay and disapproval. I begged him to come with me as I was both frightened and excited.

But to no avail, he had "never missed a day of work," and he "wasn't going to start now."

They made airline reservations for me and picked me up in a Mercedes filled with dog hair; they wined me and dined me and put me up in the Claridge Hotel. Ancient and filled with old-city ambience. A new world had opened for me. A world filled with excitement and the possibility of dreams and hopes fulfilled, dreams and hopes I didn't know I had. Life had once more turned for me.

Mr. Gillibert stormed and screamed; Mr. Steiner shushed him, saying, "But, Frank, we don't need a business to run…"

The attorneys cajoled and sidestepped the screaming Mr. Gillibert.

It was done.

—⁓⁓⁓⁓—

Over the next three years, I would own the business, and Mr. Gillibert would be my most staunch supporter in all I endeavored to do. And staunch supporters I would indeed require.

True to their word, the state and federal government instituted regulation after regulation. With the mighty Medicare system instituted, as well as Medi-Cal, or in other states, Medicaid. Welfare had a new name—and new boundaries.

During this enactment of rules and regulations, it was decided that because the elderly and chronically ill were more vulnerable to the nuances of privately held health care institutions, it would be necessary for the operators of those institutions to be highly educated, with an emphasis on health care that would, in their estimation, provide for a higher level of care and concern.

I had an eighth-grade education.

Tony said, "Quit. Get another job."

Never having told him the truth, how could I tell him now? Now that everything hung in the balance, I could hire someone, but they were few and far between, and besides, I felt I did a better job…then of course, again there was that lie, or lie by omission to my husband. Oh, Lord, what had I done?

Not only was I faced with the realities of running a business, I had never done payroll, paid the bills, saw to insurances on such a large scale, only my own naiveté kept me going. I anticipated none of what was to come.

Regulations stated that I must have policies and procedures for each and every function within the facility, and they were to been done in "legalese." I would have to write them.

With no health care experience, without previous guidelines, only criticism exuded from the mounds of papers when "inspected" by what seemed to me the FBI.

One of the most daunting arguments I would have over that first year was as to the nutritional value of peas. Imagine.

Unfortunately, argue with them I did—to my despair and frustration. After all, they were the "law."

I talked on the telephone, I wrote letters, I finally told my tale of woe to Mr. Gillibert, who, I am, certain pulled strings.

Finally, it was decided, by those in power. Considering, I did in fact own the business in question and had been running it successfully for over two years, that I could be licensed, if in fact I could challenge the board in all respects to a master's degree with an emphasis on health care administration. Mind you, acute care facilities had no such requirements. This was what they called the "grandfather act."

First, there was the high school diploma, then the English, math, science, and psychology for the bachelor's degree. Then there were the bookkeeping skills. The management skills, the medical and pharmaceutical skills, that I as a health care manager I must be informed and cognizant of. It was endless and daunting. The only thing that kept me going was the fact that I knew I would have to work anyway. That I did in fact own this business and was totally responsible for all who resided therein, employees as well as patients.

More important than all of that, I loved it. I was good at it. It fulfilled me. If I could balance it all, I would have *everything*.

The days for testing came. They were to be held in Los Angeles; I was so nervous I couldn't drive.

Tony drove me, and while he slept in the car, I would take tests, day after day, until they were completed.

The tests were timed. The room cold, windowless, the walls green, as I would sit at the desk, test papers in front of me. The room, deadly quiet. The room occupied by perhaps half a dozen other people who were obviously in a similar position.

I was the youngest, and the only woman.

At least once each test, I would have to take precious time from the testing, go to the restroom, and vomit. My nerves shattered. Lord, just let me pass this test.

Seventy-one was passing. Please let me get at least seventy-one.

I would be one of the first licensed administrators in the state of California. I did it.

In seven years, I bought the building. In the years to come, there would be owners/operators not up to the task of meeting all the requirements mandated by the government. I would purchase one facility after another. But I was happiest working at the first one. I loved it.

38

I assiduously peruse the fashion magazines for the very latest in evening gowns. Every year, Tony's work has a formal Christmas party, and I wait all year for the event. It is the only time he will wear a tuxedo, and the only time I can once again be a "model." (Did that really happen? The years have flown by, and it seems as if a dream, but contrary to what my mother thinks, a dream, it was not.)

I have found I can copy almost any fashion I see in the magazines. This one has to have boning, and I have not done that before. It will make it all the more exciting. I have the same sewing machine I sewed Samantha's first dress on, with its hundreds of hours of use.

Samantha loves to sew even at nearly fourteen, Jillian could not care less. She would be happy to wear the same thing day after day. (Remember her little red boots and the "hat"? She wore those until she couldn't get her feet in them, and the hat until it *did* fit.)

The fabric is emerald green taffeta, with an embroidered leaf design in the same color that transverses the entire fabric. The design a very fitted bodice, strapless, shirring along each back piece that leaves the front soft and flowing to twelve inches above the floor, where a deep ruffle of the same fabric pulled up to form a voluminous bustle in the back at the waist. The insert of the bustle is yards of black rose-patterned lace forming five tiers of bustle. It took me eighty-one hours. It is stunning.

I'm going to wear my auburn hair up in a simple French roll. My greatest desire is to sweep him off his feet.

Our life together has been wonderful and challenging. We can bring each other to ecstasy, and equally, to anger. With mine being verbal and his leaving him quiet and aloof. His Latin heritage accustomed to the volatile expression of emotions, he allows me my frenzy.

We can spend months finishing each other's sentences and weeks not understanding each other at all.

He took quickly to the role of fatherhood, his first wife having left him and taken their two children.

He never speaks of them.

Having been raised primarily by his grandmother, he is a traditionalist at heart as am I…but a strict disciplinarian, and I find that very difficult, which has been an ongoing problem.

We are both philosophical people, both deeply spiritual. But we have found the expression of those things in profoundly different ways.

Antonio is arrogant and insecure in many ways, an enigma to me to be sure. He is macho, and inexplicably, I find that very attractive.

He projects a desire for none of the trappings of a "better" life. Tony is, in his word, "content." I, on the other hand, need security, which seems to be found in having enough money. At the very inception of our marriage, he insisted I work, until we had $1,500 in the bank, and my debts paid.

I begged, I pleaded, but to no avail. They were, after all, my debts. I received no child support, and he came to me debt-free. He never voiced those words, but I knew them to be true. I felt obligated to do as he requested. My secret plan was that I would work until I became pregnant, then I would get to stay home and raise my children.

Months turned to years, as I lost two more children to miscarriage, and the doctors said "there would be no more."

As I lay in my hospital bed filled with the emptiness of my womb, the unbidden tears slide down my cheeks.

"Cara, please, don't cry, we have two beautiful girls, that's all anyone could want. Here I brought you a present." Tony never gives me presents, or almost never. The tiny box, silver with a soft silver ribbon.

"Here, open it," he says, very proud of himself, and somewhat shy at the giving of a gift.

It is a diamond watch. Small and delicate, beautiful. I was touched beyond words, but it did nothing to quell the loss and the pain of a dream gone forever.

Knowing now the permanence of our situation and his continued insistence that I work, I became ambitious. If in fact, I was going have to work, I would make money.

Our biggest challenge—his many "friends." They drank, they partied. I, of course was always invited. I am not a party person. More than once a week was all I was willing to be complacent about.

Even in light of our differences, in my heart I felt cherished, loved, and safe. I felt my children loved and protected.

As I dress this evening, I glance about the bedroom, an enigmatic affair to be sure.

There against the window wall sits a large, four-poster bed that we purchased at a garage sale for fifty dollars. A bandolier filled with bullets and supporting a holster filled with a .357 magnum hangs lethally from the right-hand poster of the headboard. The right wall, painted a stark white, lays siege to rifles of great and small calibers. The carpet is avocado green, and the bedspread is dyed to match. There is a tall chest of drawers of nondescript color standing awash of all things masculine. German Lugers lay in implicit order of importance, some in signed rosewood boxes, some placed lovingly in rag upon oiled rag. We have all been drilled in the use and maintenance of all things related to guns, and I feel certain are among the only women of this century to be a "crack shot." This being an obsession with my husband. Strange to me, as there seems no violence in his nature.

The other side of the room depicts total femininity. Slippers with marabou, peignoirs of gossamer fabric, a dresser with perfumes, fans, and hair accessories.

My reflection, as I look in the mirror above my dresser, is tantalizingly provocative. The dress is lyrical as it alludes to the curves of my body, the flow an insinuation of softness, the fabric an illusion of grandeur. Unique and intriguing.

I tie the black velvet ribbon around my neck, adding black earrings that dangle nearly to my alabaster shoulders, tug at the tendrils of curls at the nape of my neck and around my face. Done. It is as I had envisioned.

As I walk into the living room, I am rewarded by his look of unbridled desire, his pride in me, being his.

Ah, it was everything I had hoped for.

As we arrive at the party, stopping at the foyer, I look up at my handsome husband. His bronze Latin face, the silver strands of hair glint in the glow of the chandelier. I love his thick mane of black hair, but I must say these little silver hairs add a charm beyond measure.

The music drifts to us, and friends and acquaintances chat as we dance, drink, and eat.

There is a blonde woman, whom I have never met, that continues to look at us.

She seems to be everywhere we are. My intuition is heralding a great sense of grief.

I watch as he goes to the bar to get me a drink, as I converse of light and airy things with those standing about me.

The blonde woman intercepts him, her hand white against the black of his tuxedo, as she touches him softly on the arm.

She is shorter than I, thin, with poor posture. The royal blue chiffon hangs in soft drapes over her rounded shoulders. She is without adornment of any description. Her nose, beaklike, her face round and plain. She looks into his eyes and down at her feet.

He cocks his head to one side as if to listen to her. He whispers something to her, and she turns and leaves.

My heart is in my throat, with the blood from it pounding in my head. I hear the rustle of my dress, and feel at once tawdry, garish, in the presence of her mousy simplicity. Was this to be my Melanie of *Gone with the Wind?*

Why didn't you wear something simple and elegant? I chastise myself for the flamboyance of the dress, the drama surrounding my emotions. *You don't know, you don't know.* Be calm, be still.

I feel his lips brush my cheek as he hands me the glass. "Who is that woman?" I calmly say to him.

"Who?" he says as if he really had no idea what I was talking about.

"The woman that you were speaking to by the bar."

"Oh, oh, that's Inger, she's new here. From Germany."

"I'd like to meet her."

"Why, why would you like to meet her?"

"Because she seems to find you so attractive," I say beguilingly to my princely-looking husband.

"Okay, first chance I get."

The party goes on, we are nearing the end of the evening, and alas, who should appear but Inger.

"Tony, come, introduce me to your friend."

"In a minute."

"No, now is a good time," as I take his hand in mine and lead him to stand next to her.

Her speech is heavily accented, the heavy German of her native tongue giving a thick, guttural quality to her speech. She is shy and does not look at me, only at the floor.

We sit in the car in the parking lot. "Have you slept with her?" waiting breathlessly for him to answer. In my heart already knowing the answer...

"No...I...Cara...I..."

"Tony, I already know."

"How do you know?" he is quiet, and that ghastly green color he gets when upset. He won't look at me.

"Tony, you know how I know. I know, because of all the things *I know*, I know because I know you, I know because I can *feel it*. I know because I saw the way she looked at you, the way you evaded her."

"All right, goddamn it, all right… I fucked up. It was…it was…you know, she doesn't speak English very well. Her old man left her with two little boys, all alone in a strange country. I just wanted to help her. She was so…you know…alone."

I was once that girl.

Is that how he really felt about me? Was there really nothing to it but a rescue mission?

I sobbed with grief and sadness; I yelled with rage. I collapsed against his broad chest that night and sobbed in his arms, then pushed away and pounded on that same, strong chest and begged him to say he really didn't do it.

He listened and cajoled. He said "it was over," that he hadn't seen her in a while "except at work." He promised never to see her again. He cradled me in his arms, and we wept.

Our marriage was tarnished. Was it beyond repair? Should I have not said anything? I don't know. People do what they feel they must. I could not live a lie, not with him, of all people. Could I live without him?

Never.

The days fly by as Christmas is fast approaching, and life goes on. There are cookies to bake. The house to decorate. Pajamas to be sewn in the waning of the moonlit nights.

The house is warm and inviting, smelling of greenery, cinnamon, and cloves, as the girls stuff cloves in oranges to give for presents, and we make ornaments of flour and water, painting them with food coloring.

The red felt stockings with beads, small angels, Christmas trees, drums, as well as a small, intricate train sewn carefully on them hang on the mantel piece above the fireplace. Stockings my mother has made for each of the family, with the exception of Tony and I...I made those. Her omission, by design I am certain; she hates his ethnicity, his Catholicism. "A Mexican and a heathen? What more will you disgrace our family with?" Shades of my grandfather I fear, neglecting to see that we are happy, well cared for, loved. We have lived here for over seven years. They live less than a mile away, but she and Daddy have only once come here to visit us.

The girls' excitement is palatable and infectious as we sit on the living room floor wrapping presents and talking of their excitement, for tomorrow is Christmas Eve.

Samantha is bursting with excitement over the very large, brightly-wrapped package that sits beneath the tree.

"It's for you, Mother, it's from Daddy. I wrapped it. It's beautiful, don't you think?"

"It is beautiful, you really did a good job. What is it?"

She laughs. "I wouldn't tell you, but I don't know anyway. It is in a big plain box, and he just asked me to wrap it."

"Shall we shake it?" I ask her, a gleam in my eye.

"Daddy said, 'Don't let your mother touch it.'"

"Okay," I assure her, "I will not go near it." The surprise always more alluring to me than the knowing, I do not venture to it.

Christmas morning comes softly, in the early morning hours of darkness, Jillian shaking us intermittently to get up. "Santa has been here. And there are tons of presents. Come on, get up."

We rise slowly from our slumber, her exuberance demanding to be satisfied; at nearly eleven, she is still very much a little girl. Her small, slender hands with her long fingers, the pale, nearly white, of her sleep-tousled hair hangs in a shimmer of radiance about her oval-shaped face. The large, round, royal blue of her eyes, surrounded by thick, dark lashes, as they dance in excitement and anticipation.

"Come on, get up!" she exclaims, laughing, as her daddy pulls her up into the bed with us.

"No...we aren't opening presents today, you opened all the presents last night," he says. In mock earnest.

"Daddy, we have to, it's Christmas. Besides that is pajamas 'n slippers, we always get them."

"Ya think, my little loon?" as he holds her tightly and nuzzles her neck.

"Yes, yes," she said, giggling and leaping from the bed.

Tony goes to wake our sleeping Samantha, and I go to make cocoa and heat breakfast rolls.

It is not yet dawn as Christmas music drifts from the stereo, and the smell of coffee and warm bread fills the little house.

Finally, my package is handed to me. All three of them wait in anticipation of the surprise in such an enormous box.

Tony sits in his chair in his green robe, with as much expectation as if the gift were for him. It *is* better to give than to receive.

I untie the ribbons and tear into the paper, and behold there is a smaller box, wrapped and beribboned as well, and within it another, and then another.

The girls are jumping up and down at the trick, and I am secretly hoping that it will not end up to be a joke gift. Everything we own is paid for, as he is insistent upon that, and we have money in the bank. Surely he would buy me a real present.

I have unwrapped seven boxes, each smaller than the last.

This box is a small silver box with a soft silver ribbon.

I look up at him; he his grinning from ear to ear. "Open it," he says.

Inside is the most beautiful diamond ring I have ever seen, more than a carat in size, a solitaire.

"I...I... Oh, Tony, I love it, thank you, thank you." As the tears stream down my face, I slide the ring on my finger, resting it in place over my wedding band. "It is perfect."

39

Antonio Tesstorri stands within the realm of a world he had never imagined himself to be and was not certain how or when this had transpired. It had been fifteen years ago that she had walked into that bar, and other than brief hunting trips and her business trips, they had never been apart. Had never wished to be apart. His world was now one of an opulence he would have never imagined, a world of financial security and love, a family that was *his*. She was responsible for that—Cara; he glanced in the mirror at her reflection.

A feeling of overwhelming doom imbued him, he shook his head as if that would erase the feeling.

The gold vein of the white marble countertop sparkled in the lamp light, the gold of the Greek Key design that embellished the white porcelain of the sink reflects in the mirror before him, echoing his well-muscled body. Naked, in all its youthful glory. Glistening like some bodybuilder just well oiled. His maleness stands at half mast, spent after the torrents of their lovemaking. He had always been so proud of his sexual prowess. So proud of this enormous appendage of his. But this is a different thing. The sex between them, more intense with each passing union.

I don't know about this, he thinks as he runs his hands through his thick mane of black hair. *I don't know if this is so good.*

"What's the matter, are you okay?"

The voice, her soft husky voice comes from the bed where she lay. Scarcely distinguishable from the white of the sheets.

Her skin like creamy, white satin. Glistening from their lovemaking. My God, I love the touch of her, the smell of her. The long lengths of her arms and legs, as they wrap around my body. The hollow of her neck as her head arches with her back to meet me. The low moaning in her as she begs for release. He closed his eyes for an instant, and lowered his head in memory of the moments just past.

"Tony, are you all right?"

"Yeah, yeah, I'm all right, it's just, I don't know, I…"

"You don't know what, what don't you know?" An almost maternal fear resides in her voice.

She rises from the bed and comes to stand next to him. Her arms encircle his waist, the muscles of his stomach hard and rippling as she caresses the firmness that is him, laying her head on his shoulder, she softly says, "What, sweetheart, tell me."

They stand together, and he pauses a moment to look at their reflection. Two beautiful bodies. His firm, stocky and brown. Hers long, lean, revealing no definition of muscle, as if molded out of some soft firm substance, even her neck is long and elegant. And her hands, the fingers, long and tapered.

He places his hand on her arm to pull her to him. The difference in the color of their bodies he finds astounding, even after all this time.

"I don't know, Cara, it's this lust…this lust I feel for you. It just doesn't seem right, I mean you're my wife, it just seems wrong. But how can it be wrong? I…I guess I am a little confused. I don't know…it feels like I am losing myself. I mean… Like I'm willing to…to give *all* I am to you… I mean…I *want* to give you who I am…just so I can have *all* you are. You know…I can't be without you, not ever, do you understand, it makes me feel weak…and so powerful all at the same time. I don't know…"

He holds her closer still, the slickness of their bodies seems to form a bond that binds them even more closely. He nuzzles her neck as she kisses the soft hollow spot at the base of his thick neck. Licking the salt from his skin, kissing, nuzzling.

"Come, come back to bed with me, hold me," she whispers softly to his chest. The answer is in the rise of his manhood as he pulls her across the carpeted floor to the bed. Sitting her firmly on the side of the bed, he says "Wait, wait…it's just that…I have never…you know, I've slept with a lot of women…I mean…you know, I've had a lot of females."

He squats before her, his hand resting on her thighs, as he stammers, searching for an explanation to this upsetting conundrum of events or feelings. She sits, waiting quietly, patiently with expectation, and some trepidation.

He rises now, pacing the soft blue carpeted floor, his arousal obviously forgotten, he continues to stammer, and pushing his hands through his hair, once more stands before her.

"I always thought is was simple, screw them, tell 'em you'd call, and leave. It was…it was that simple. But now, still, even after all these years, Cara, I feel like I am losing my soul, losing who I am to you—you make me feel like falling on my knees and bowing my head before you…and yet I want to take you and push you to your knees and hold your head to my cock to prove I can, to prove I am still a man. That you'd let me do that. That you would be powerless to stop me."

He is on his knees before her. The tears glisten in his soft brown eyes, the lashes wet, black with them. "Do you understand how I can feel that way? Wanting to hold you gently and protect you from everything and everyone, yet still wanting to crush you in my arms until there is no breath in you? To hold your breasts so tight there are bruises on that white skin of yours? Do you understand that…I don't think I do."

Cara's throat is tight with emotion, the tears threateningly close as she reaches out to hold his face in her hands. "I think I know, yes, I do think I know." She whispers softly, fighting for control of the emotions that threatened to overtake them both. "I feel the same way with each kiss, with each caress. It's our souls, Tony, our souls we have given to one another. There are times I just want to be a part of you, not separate, but a real part of you, and then it happens, it happens when you make love to me. Not just our bodies meld, but our minds, our very existence dependent upon each of us. As if without you I would no longer be…I simply would cease to exist…and there are times I want to prove my existence apart from that.

The tears are flowing freely now, as I kiss his face, holding his upturned palm in my hand, his thick, strong hand, these hands that have given me such joy, such peace. I bend my head and kiss the extended palm, tears dripping to be held softly in the palm of his hand.

"There are times like now that I what to protect and care for you, as a mother would, hold you close to me, rocking you gently until the fear subsides…I am not sure, I have never felt this way either, but I think it is simple. I think we are in love. Hasn't it been like that from the first time we saw each other?"

"Oh, God, Cara, I don't know if I can stand it."

"Oh, I think we have no choice."

His strong arms reach to pick me up, to slide me to his side of the bed, effortlessly he pulls me to the croak of his arm. I run my fingernail lightly around his dark, taut nipples, and I gaze at his chest, thick, strong, lying inches above my body.

"What is it?" he whispers, his lips, lush and full.

"I just want to remember what you look like, to remember what you feel like, to remember what you taste like."

"Oh, sweetheart, you're not goin' anywhere, you are mine, you belong to me, you will always belong to me."

I laugh and pinch his nipple.

"Ouch, you know I'm gonna punish you for that."

"Go ahead, punish away," as I feign screaming and fright.

He, after all, was right, I would always belong to him. He would always belong to me.

Our souls were eternally united. Was that possible…a chill went down my spine as I prayed it was.

AUTHOR'S NOTE

Every day in the United States, more than three women are murdered by their husbands or boyfriends. At present *every 9 seconds* in the United States alone, a woman is assaulted or beaten. Most often the abuser is a member of her own family.

Around the world, at least one in every three women has been beaten, coerced into sex, or otherwise abused during her lifetime. Based on reports from ten countries, approximately 75 percent of those women who had been physically abused by their partners had never contacted the police, shelters, or nongovernmental organizations for help.

Domestic violence is the leading cause of injury to women, more than car accidents, muggings, and rapes combined.

Studies suggest that up to *ten million children* witness some form of domestic violence annually. Men who as children witnessed their parents' domestic violence were twice as likely to abuse their own wives, than sons of nonviolent parents. Daughters of those fathers will more than likely marry abusive men and submit to that very same abuse. Creating yet another generation of abusers.

The cost of intimate-partner violence in the United States alone exceeds *$5.8 billion per year; $4.1 billion* are for the direct medical and health-care services, while productivity losses account for nearly *$1.8 billion.*

Know that each and every hour, *seventy-five* woman have been raped. Know that *seventy* children have *died* this last week, and every other week of every year, *at the hands of a parent*, another *four million* were physically abused this year.

That before your next breakfast, another *twelve women* will be killed by *intimate* enemies.

In nearly all cases, the violence that preceded the final violence was a secret kept by several persons. Right now, as you read these words, at least one woman in America is being beaten by her husband…and now another…as it happens every few seconds.

The structure of a family leaves that there is always one person who holds that power, either for food, money, or shelter. *And most desirably* love, comfort, and security.

Women who find themselves in an abusive relationship stay because of their children. Ironically, that is the very same reason they leave that relationship—to protect their children.

Read more of Cara's journey in...*__what doesn't kill you...__*